I0527783

Only a Shadow

by

Iona Morrison

A Blue Cove Mystery

This is a work of fiction. Names, characters, places, and incidents are either the product of the author's imagination or are used fictitiously, and any resemblance to actual persons living or dead, business establishments, events, or locales, is entirely coincidental.

Only a Shadow

COPYRIGHT © 2017 by Iona Morrison

All rights reserved. No part of this book may be used or reproduced in any manner whatsoever without written permission of the author or The Wild Rose Press, Inc. except in the case of brief quotations embodied in critical articles or reviews.
Contact Information: info@thewildrosepress.com

Cover Art by *Debbie Taylor*

The Wild Rose Press, Inc.
PO Box 708
Adams Basin, NY 14410-0708
Visit us at www.thewildrosepress.com

Publishing History
First Fantasy Rose Edition, 2017
Print ISBN 978-1-5092-1712-0
Digital ISBN 978-1-5092-1713-7

A Blue Cove Mystery
Published in the United States of America

Her eyes focused

on a small structure in the midst of the trees. Its outline emerged through the spooky mist as she ran closer. What she saw stopped her in her tracks. Sinister in appearance, gothic in nature, its small spires and gargoyles stood watch and seemed to be staring at her. Creepy, and the fog didn't help. The gate creaked as she opened it to go inside. The building was smaller than it looked from a distance. Was it a small chapel? It didn't feel like any church she had ever been in. Maybe it was someone's tomb. She shivered. A strange odor met her when she opened the door. Incense, perhaps. The light from her headlamp told an eerie story as it danced on the walls. It settled on a strange stone slab in the center of the aisle, which had something smeared all over it. Oh, this was worse than she had thought. She slumped to the floor. She had stumbled into something awful and didn't want to be trapped here. Where were the dog and the person who had fired the shots? "Get hold of yourself, Jessie," she whispered. A quick check of her phone told her she still had no service. *Run, get out of here*, her mind screamed. Matt would want to see the place, and she had no idea how to tell him where it was located. Back outside, she took a deep breath, gasping for air. She couldn't believe this place was actually here in the middle of the woods. She checked her phone again. *Please let this work.* She held it up to snap a picture, then slipped out the gate and ran. The spots from the flash blinded her for a moment as she ran through the thick vapor.

Praise for Iona Morrison

"Thank you for hours of pure pleasure. I enjoyed my read immensely. I found myself excited just to get to the next chapter."

~*Judy Klemas*

~*~

"Great characters, suspenseful, and making you want more."

~*Ann*

~*~

"I just finished *THE GAME CHANGER* and it was the best yet. Wow, I can't believe the author can keep all this straight in her head and tie it all together. It was a great read…"

~*Mary Beth Brugler*

~*~

"Love the development of the story between Jessie and Matt. Can't wait for the next book! These are fast, exciting reads."

~*Linda H.*

~*~

"All through this book I kept rooting for Jessie and Matt to catch the murderers. This was a riveting read and I had a hard time putting it down!"

~*Sheila H.*

~*~

"The opening to *DANCE WITH A DEVIL* was fast and furious! My eyes could hardly read fast enough."

~*Christi Summers*

Dedication

Dedicated to the memory of my mother, Ethel Hurst,
who encouraged me to reach for my dreams.

Chapter 1

The woman hurried in the door, pulling it closed with a bang. "I'm sorry, I didn't mean to shut it so hard," she stammered. Her hand reached up to stop the ringing bell. Gasping for air, she swayed and leaned against the nearest chair.

"Are you all right?" Jessie rushed toward her.

The woman nodded. "I need to catch my breath." She faltered, holding onto the chair for support.

"May I help you?" Jessie asked, standing close enough to catch the woman. Concerned by the colorless face glancing back at her, she wasn't sure what to expect next.

"I'm only looking, thank you." The woman lifted a book from the shelf; it trembled in her shaking hand. She turned the cover over, touched it with reverence, and clutched it to her chest. A car driving by backfired. The book suddenly hit the ground. The woman jumped, nudging Jessie aside as she darted behind the bookshelf. From there, she peered out the window. The fear on her face sent a sudden chill down Jessie's back.

"I'm sorry about your book. I didn't mean to drop it," the woman muttered. "I'd be happy to pay for it." She wrapped her arms around her thick waistline, her lips set in a thin line.

Jessie took note of the woman's long sleeves on a warmer than usual day, the dark shadows under her eyes, and the hopelessness that seemed to radiate from her. Her baggy clothes couldn't disguise the fact that she was pregnant. "It's fine." Jessie waved it off. "You know what?" Jessie recalled how she had touched the book. "You can have it." She smiled at the woman. "Are you looking for anything in particular?"

"Yes," she said, "another exit out of here." A bleak look crossed her unhappy face. She stole another quick glance out the window, bent down to pick up the book, and slipped it into her bag. "Thank you." Her lips curved into a tentative smile. She ran her hand through her tangled brown hair trying to straighten it.

"You're welcome." Jessie's decision was quick. "I have a door at the back of my store. Here, let me show you the way out." Jessie pulled some cash out of her purse as she walked past the counter and stuck it in her pocket.

The woman grabbed Jessie's hand. "Please..." She paused, looking around in desperation. "If a man comes in asking about me, can you tell him you haven't seen me? I need time to get away."

Jessie nodded, stunned by the cries for help filling her head when the woman touched her. "Are you okay?" The image of bruises on white skin flickered in her mind and vanished. "Do you want me to call the police?" she asked, but the woman shook her head.

"No police! Please, don't call them," she pleaded.

"I won't call, but take this." Jessie pressed the money into her hand. "You look like you're hungry." The woman's hand flinched.

"Thank you." Her reply was barely audible. "I need to get out of here. He'll hurt me if he finds me." She looked away from Jessie. "He'll make your life miserable too if he finds out you helped me." She slipped out the door and hobbled quickly away.

Her limping run was painful to watch. Jessie stood in the open door until the woman was out of sight. Locking the back door, she grabbed the new bookmarks to put in the basket on the counter. Armed with a feather duster, Jessie straightened the store before the next customer came in, but the desolate look in the girl's eyes intruded into her thoughts.

The woman was younger than Jessie had first thought. When her shirt collar had fallen open, the marks Jessie saw around her neck were real. Someone had abused her.

The bell above the door rang, and Jessie's body tensed instantly. Without even seeing who it was, she knew *he* had just walked in. She turned and observed the man as he took a book off the shelf. He glanced at the front cover and then flipped it over as he looked around the store. Not quite six feet tall, his brown hair was tidy, dark shades covered his eyes, but nothing could hide the anger exuding from him.

"May I help you?" She walked toward him.

"Yes, ma'am, I sure hope you can." He lifted his glasses and rested them on the top of his head. "Did you happen to see a lovely woman come in here earlier? She's my wife. I told her she could shop while I took care of some business in town." He slipped the book back onto the shelf and slid his hand into the front pocket of his jeans.

Jessie looked directly into his hazel eyes. "No, I haven't seen anyone," she lied. "As you can see I'm having a slow morning." She smiled at him and gestured at the nearly empty store. "It's been like this since I opened."

A dark look passed over his face. "I was hoping my wife would be here. At home, she always has her nose in a book. If you should see her, tell her Roger was here looking for her. She knows where to find me." His mild tone belied his veiled anger.

She nodded. "I will. What's her name? I need to know who to give the message to in the event a woman comes in later." She picked up a piece of paper and a pen.

He glanced at Jessie, his gaze betraying his suspicion. A smile slowly crossed his face, but it never quite quenched the anger in his eyes. "Lily. She's a pretty one like you. Be sure to tell her I'm looking for her." His sneakers squeaked across the floor as he made his way to the door. Roger called back over his shoulder. "Tell her I have something special waiting for her when she gets home."

Jessie shivered, feeling the undercurrent of violence in his words. She watched him get into a motorhome in front of the church.

It looked nice enough. What had she expected, an old painted bus? Jessie shook her head. She felt instantly sorry for Lily. Was Lily even her real name? It didn't seem to fit her somehow. Jessie stood at the window until he drove off. She rubbed her arms. Roger gave her the creeps. He appeared normal; some might even consider him good looking, but nothing about him appealed to her. Jessie could sense the anger beneath his charming veneer.

She was still standing in the same spot when Reba pulled her car into the open parking space in front of the store. Jessie returned her wave and held the door open for her.

"Hello, Jessie dear. I find myself in need of a few books. I do believe I'm becoming addicted to this new author. I hope she keeps them coming." Reba patted her neat hair. "How's your morning been? If my feelings are working right, it's been an interesting one for you."

"Of course, you're right as usual. Everything is working fine inside your sweet little head." Jessie walked with her over to the shelf where the books by Reba's favorite author were on display.

"After you pick out what you want, I'll sit with you for a few minutes and tell you what happened this morning."

"Sounds perfect, dear." Reba picked out several new books after carefully reading the covers. Finally, she made her way to the table in the center of the store and sat down beside Jessie.

"Did you find what you wanted?" Jessie sat back in her chair and crossed her ankles.

"I did. She has written quite a few books; they should keep me in reading material for a while." Reba pushed the books toward her.

Jessie picked up the first one to get a better look at the cover. "I know how many books I can go through when I'm in the mood to read." She checked the other titles as well. "These are all good stories. You'll enjoy them."

"Let's get down to business, shall we?" Reba got comfortable in her chair.

Jessie nodded and told her about the young woman and the man who had come into the store looking for her. "The thing is I saw in my mind the bruises that were on her body. Something wasn't kosher."

"No, I know it wasn't. I knew when I got up this morning something was amiss." Reba glanced at the doors that opened into Java Joe's Coffee Shop, and she softened her voice. "I don't think he's from around here. They don't live in town anyway. If he doesn't find her, he'll stay around, which concerns me."

Jessie glanced out the window and noticed the motorhome driving slowly by her store. "When she grabbed my hand, I was overwhelmed with her sadness. It was easy for me to tell him she hadn't been in my shop. I lied and would gladly lie again to protect her," Jessie said fiercely.

"Did he believe you?" Reba patted Jessie's hand and smiled, but her frown lines deepened. "From what you said, his anger could make him act in an irrational manner if you crossed him. If he doesn't believe you, he'll blame you. Keep your eyes open for him and be sure to tell your nice Mr. Parker about him."

"I will. Don't worry." Her lips pressed together.

"Good, he'll know what to do."

"The strangest thing of all was when I took her hand. I heard the cries of many women. It wasn't just *her* screaming in my mind." Jessie paused. "There were too many to count."

"Ah," Reba said, nodding. "The not-so-silent screams for help, my dear. She is but the tip of the iceberg; you will have more coming. Abuse is something that happens in the best of homes. What we think is hidden from society's prying eyes has a way of coming out into the open." Reba sat forward in her chair and spoke softly. "He can't believe she finally got up the nerve to leave him. I hate to consider what will happen if he finds her." Reba shook her head, her lips pursed.

"She is probably long gone by now." Jessie shifted in her chair.

"Oh, Jessie, I wish. She'll come back to you because she has nowhere else to go, and he'll be watching. It's about control for him, and he's angry that she has defied him."

"Are you telling me I've stepped into the center of something again?" Jessie closed her eyes for a moment.

Reba nodded at her. "Trouble has found you again, dear. There is more to this story than meets the eyes, as they say."

"That's just great." Jessie sighed, rubbing her forehead.

"You know me, dear, always the bearer of good news." She patted Jessie's hand again. "Don't let this get to you. It will all work out, you'll see. There will be some rough patches for you, but all will end well. Something good will come from it, too."

"I sure hope so. All I can say is, there had better not be any bullets, bombs, or ghosts this time. I'm over it." Jessie's chin edged up.

"My advice is to take it one day at a time." She smiled as she stood. "I'll pay for these now." Reba picked up her books. "I see a tour bus has pulled in across the street, and you're about to be inundated with customers."

Jessie rang up Reba's books and walked her to the door. Reba was right about being busy. The next chance she had to sit down again came hours later, and her feet were sore. She took one shoe off and rubbed her aching foot. The bell above the door rang, and she smiled at Matt as he walked in.

"Can I take over for you?" He sat in the chair beside her, lifted her foot, placed it on his lap, and massaged it. She leaned her head against the back of the chair, her eyes drifting shut. He lifted her other foot, removed her shoe, and massaged it, too.

"Oh my, this feels wonderful." She opened her eyes to find him smiling at her. The familiar heat started at the base of her neck. "What are you doing here at this time of day?"

"I was on my way back to the station and wanted to check in on my best girl." He stopped rubbing her foot. "Do you want to go to dinner and maybe catch a movie later on?"

"Hmm, that sounds nice, almost as nice as this felt. My feet thank you." She smiled at him, glad that he had stopped by.

"How's your day been?" His eyes roamed over her face and paused at her lips.

"I'm glad you asked. I was going to call you. Something happened this morning, and you need to know about it." Matt sat forward in his chair as she told him about Lily and Roger. "I'm not sure if those are even their real names." She paused when his hand brushed her cheek lightly, removing the errant curl springing loose from her ponytail. She exhaled. "Then Reba stopped by and added a few more details to my concerns. Another case has found me."

"You bring them out of the woodwork, for sure. Let me know if you see either Roger or his wife again." Matt let go of her foot.

"I've seen him drive by several times in his motorhome. Reba seemed to think that Lily would come back and find me because she has nowhere else to go. She said he would be watching," She grabbed her shoe from the table and placed it on the floor next to the other one.

"Damn, Jess, how is it that with all the stores in this town, she wanders into yours?" He shook his head and exhaled. "Reba's probably right."

"Come on, Matt, you should know how this works by now. They come looking for me. I must wear a sign that says, "Available to help." I saw the bruises on her body as it flashed through my mind. Her shirt collar opened, and I saw them for real on her neck. This man is abusing his wife—if she's even his wife. Maybe he kidnapped her. I don't know, but I do know she was afraid, and I can't say that I blame her." A sudden chill went down her back. "I only spent a few minutes with him, but the anger bubbling beneath his thin facade was intense. I'm here again through no fault of my own. I'm a little sick of saying the same thing. It is my new normal, period." She raised both hands in surrender with a half-smile.

"You're pretty when you get riled up." Matt leaned close to her.

"This is serious." Her pulse leaped when he was inches away from her face.

"I know, sweetheart." He leaned closer, a mischievous glint in his eye.

"They keep coming to me. Maybe it's because they know I'm a soft touch, and I'll help." She sighed. "Knowing you the way I do, you're in it, too."

He lifted her chin. "You've got that right." He kissed her. "If you're there, then so am I. Do you have anything else you need to tell me?"

She shook her head. "Other than I heard her cries

for help even though she never uttered a word, I believe that about covers everything." She moved back and slipped her shoes on. "What's next?"

He kissed her again. "You're something, Jess." He chucked her chin. "We wait to see what happens, if anything. When it comes to you, though, something major always happens, and we'll be back in the thick of it. I was getting used to the quiet we've had over the last few weeks." He frowned, but his eyes smiled at her. "It was short-lived."

"Nothing might happen." She kept her tone light. "The whole thing could go quietly away, but in case it doesn't, do you know of a women's shelter that could take her in?"

"We have one here, but we would need to get her out of the area as soon as possible. If Roger is as bad as you think he is, he'll find a way to get at her. Domestic violence is dangerous. Any police officer will tell you they hate working those cases. Many officers have lost their lives in domestic violence calls. They're hard to prosecute, and even with a restraining order in place, the women are often killed."

"There has to be something we can do. I mean we can't let this jerk continue to hurt his wife."

"We won't!" His mouth tightened. "If she comes back around and we find out someone is abusing her, then we'll do something." Matt stood up. "Hell, I've seen men mess their wife or girlfriend up bad, but the women are too afraid to press charges. The man ends up going free. I'm saying all this to tell you to be careful, sweetheart. If Roger comes near you or this store again, call me right away."

"I will. What time are we on for tonight?" She

tilted her head to see his face.

"I'll stop by, and we can take your car. Shall we say a little after five?"

"Sounds perfect to me." She walked with him to the door.

"See you soon, sweetheart." He gave her a quick kiss and went to his car.

Jessie waved as he drove away. She enjoyed his company and experienced a brief pang of sadness. How long would it take before he got tired of the crazy baggage that came with her? He said he was here for the long haul; she hoped he could take it. He was a tough guy, but how tough could one hot police chief be?

Chapter 2

Remembering Matt's tender words to her last night every time he kissed her filled her with longing. Her face warmed even though a chill edged the morning air. She pulled her scarf tighter around her neck as she walked from the parking lot to the church. He could make her forget every good intention she ever had not to marry for a while. Last night she was the one asking him to stay longer. She touched her hot cheek. Blushes. How she hated them.

"Hello," she called out and waved at Audrey, who was opening up the store. Audrey was a perfect fit. Jessie had trained her to work at the church, too. They now split the mornings between the church and the store. The church needed a receptionist more hours each week than she could work, and Audrey needed to make more money. It was win-win all the way around.

She walked down the familiar hall to the office. Her life had been a piece of cake until she had come to work here. She put the key in the office door and unlocked it. Would she trade living here for a nice peaceful life? Probably not. She tossed her purse on the desk and took off her coat. Except for the bullets and bad guys, maybe. Yes, she would be glad to live without *them*. She made the coffee first so it would be ready when the pastors arrived.

The two men laughing as they walked down the

hall brought a smile to her face. Another day was off and running, and the phone was already ringing. "First Community Church, may I help you?" She waved at John and Kevin as they walked past her desk. The phone clicked on the other end. "I guess not." She glared at the silent phone and hung it up.

The phone rang again; she answered with her usual greeting, again, and silence met her. "May I help you?" Jessie repeated her voice louder and slightly irritated this time.

"I'm sorry, I'm trying to build up the nerve to talk to someone; please don't hang up." Jessie could barely hear her soft voice.

"I won't." Her irritation vanished instantly, replaced by concern. "Would you like to talk to one of the pastors?"

"Yes, I mean, no." There was a pause, silence, and then a rush of words. "I can't do it now. I hear—" The dial tone buzzed, and Jessie found herself holding a silent phone once again. How strange. She placed the phone back on its cradle and waited to see if the woman would call again.

Melinda charged into the office, her face pale. "Call the police, Blondie. Tell them I found something, and they need to get here real quick." Melinda paced between her desk and the office door.

Jessie didn't ask what she had found; she called. The look on Melinda's face told her it wasn't good. "Hi, Joe, this is Jessie. Melinda is in my office, and she found something. Could you send an officer over to the church?"

"Sure. I'll send a car right over."

"Thanks, Joe."

"Do you know what we're looking at? Is it an emergency?"

"She didn't say what it was, but she is clearly upset, and yes, I would say it's an emergency. It takes a lot to rattle Melinda." Jessie listened to him put out the call over the radio.

"They'll be right there."

"Okay, Joe, we'll be waiting." She hung up.

"Are they sending someone?" Jessie nodded. Melinda plopped down in the chair and then promptly stood back up again. "It's not good. I'd better go watch for them." Melinda walked out of the office before Jessie had time to say anything to her.

Maybe she should follow her. It had to be bad. Before she did so, Jessie told Pastor John what Melinda had said. He stood up from his desk immediately, and they went together to find her.

She was at the side door waiting in the parking lot, frantically pacing and muttering under her breath.

"Melinda, what's this all about?" Pastor John's voice startled her.

"I was taking the trash out to the dumpster. When I opened the lid, I found—" She broke down and sobbed incoherently. Melinda swiped at the tears running down her cheeks. "Don't look in there." She managed to get the words out.

Pastor John disappeared into the building and came out carrying a chair and a box of tissues. "Sit down, you can tell us when you're ready." The police car rolled into the parking lot, Kip and Gary got out, and John motioned them over.

"Jessie, Joe said you needed an officer." Kip looked from her to Pastor John and the sobbing

Melinda. "What's up?"

"Melinda is the one who wanted me to call." Jessie placed her hands on Melinda's shoulders.

"Melinda?" Kip waited patiently, but Melinda seemed unable to stop crying.

"Whatever is bothering her, she found it in the dumpster when she went to empty the trash." Jessie pointed to the bin. The full trash bags were still sitting on the ground beside the dumpster.

"All of you stay here; we'll check it out." Kip opened the lid. He took a step back, shaking his head. Then he made a call.

He came back over. "Did you see anyone around the area this morning?" Kip looked at each of them, one at a time. Jessie shook her head, and John did the same.

"The parking lot was empty when I arrived for work," Jessie said. Shudders racked Melinda's body. It had to be bad. A body? A person? A chill run through her. Not the woman from yesterday, oh please, no…

"What are we looking at, Officer?" Pastor John's eyes narrowed.

"Right now I'm not sure. A possible homicide." Kip turned at the sound of another car pulling into the parking lot. "Don't go anywhere; we need to get your statements."

"Kip, is it a woman?" Jessie held her breath.

"The victim is female." Kip turned and walked over to Matt who was pulling into the church's lot.

****

Matt sighed with relief when he drove into the church parking lot and saw Jessie standing there next to the pastor. The report of a problem at the church had concerned him, especially after her news yesterday. Kip was stepping forward to meet him. He rolled down the window as he came to a stop.

"Chief." Kip nodded at him. "We have a female victim in the dumpster. From preliminary observations, she has several bruises on her face and defensive wounds on her hands."

"Who found her?" Matt asked him. *Oh, hell, not Jessie…*

"Melinda. She's having a hard time." Kip pointed to where she sat.

"I understand." Matt nodded. "We'll take it easy when we question her. Let's have a look. Don't disturb anything until Marcy takes pictures." Matt looked into the dumpster. Damn! He turned quickly to glance at Jessie, her face was pale. Was this her battered woman? A mewling sound came from the garbage, and something moved the trash slightly. A kitten? Whatever it was, it seemed to be buried beneath the woman's body. He climbed inside, careful not to disturb the position of the body. The odd sound came again, and the hair started to rise on the back of his neck. Then he spotted the tiny foot moving. "We need an ambulance right away," he shouted. Kip called it in. The baby, still attached to the woman by the umbilical cord, was alive. Matt took a deep breath and moved the mother's leg. "I need a sterile knife or something to sterilize mine," he yelled.

"I have some rubbing alcohol in my car." Marcy pounded away and returned moments later with a plastic bottle.

"It'll have to do." Matt took out his pocketknife, poured the alcohol on it, and cut the cord, tying it off with one of his shoelaces which he had first soaked in the alcohol. "Do you have a blanket in your car, perchance?" he asked Marcy.

She ran to her car once more. "Here, Chief," she panted when she returned. "This should work, and it's brand new." She handed him a large, blue bath towel.

He wrapped the baby tight, handing the small bundle to Kip. Matt climbed out of the dumpster brushing himself off. "Jess, come here. I need you," he called. The baby was probably cold, and she was barely moving. "Marcy, take your pictures, and then we'll go through the trash. The whole bin." He turned as Jessie ran up and transferred the small bundle into her arms. "It's a girl."

Jessie stared down into the face of a newborn infant, looking horrified. "Who could throw this precious little girl in the trash?" Jessie held the baby close, tears glimmering in her eyes.

He walked over to Melinda as the stunned Jessie cradled the baby. "Are you doing all right?" He squatted to see her face.

"I've been better. I didn't know there was a baby in there." Melinda raised her tear-stained face to him. "Will she be all right?"

"I don't know. I sure hope so."

"I didn't know she was there." Melinda watched them working in the dumpster.

"The baby was hidden beneath the mother. I'm sure the mother was enough of a shock. I only looked because I heard something." He patted Melinda's hand and then stood up. "Pastor, why don't you take her inside, and I'll be in to talk to her in a few minutes."

"Good idea. Come along, let's do as the chief said and leave the officers to their work." John followed

Melinda into the church. The ambulance pulled in as they were leaving.

Jessie walked over and handed the small bundle to the medics who went to work on the infant right away. Matt came up behind her. "I called the police," she said numbly, "but I didn't know what was going on because Melinda didn't tell me anything. She was in shock."

"I'm not surprised." He shook his head. "A dead body in the dumpster would be a shock for anybody to find. I'll talk to her, but I doubt she can tell me much."

"What are we looking at, Matt?" She watched Marcy snapping pictures.

"She's a young woman. I'll want you to go to the morgue tomorrow to see if she's the same woman who came into your store."

She nodded at him, her expression agonized. "Poor woman. Was she murdered or did she die giving birth to the baby?"

"The coroner will determine how she died, but I believe she may have had some help."

"Why this dumpster, of all the places in town? She is a lucky little one that the dumpster hadn't been emptied yet today."

"Damn lucky." Matt watched the ambulance leave. "I need to get back to work." He noticed the tears in her eyes. "Are you going to be all right?" He caught a tear on her face with his finger. His hand rested on her cheek.

She nodded. "It's sad, that's all, a sad ending, and a sad beginning." Jessie leaned against his chest, another tear slipping down her cheek.

"We found the baby, so I believe she's going to make it, and some loving family will adopt her."

"A perfect way to think about her; I'll believe that way, too," she said softly. Matt watched the gentle sway of her hips as she walked toward the church. He went back to work.

"Chief, I'm done here. When the coroner wants to remove the body, he can. I'll stick around in case you need some more pictures." Marcy walked over and sat down in the chair John had left out.

"Kip, you can start. You know the protocol. Proceed with care and bag the evidence. Don't overlook anything. Gary, search the parking lot and all around the dumpster. If you see anything, have Marcy snap it. Lewis will move the body as soon as he arrives." Matt called Collins to get a hold put on the trash pickup at the church.

The next person he needed to talk to was the coroner. Matt had questions. The answers would determine how he proceeded with the investigation. He walked toward Dave's van when it pulled into the parking lot. Matt was sure it was a homicide, but he wanted confirmation.

"Hi, Dave." They shook hands.

"Not the most pleasant way to start a morning." Dave eyed the officers checking around the dumpster. He helped pull the stretcher out of the van and grabbed his bag.

"When you determine the time and cause of death, let me know, would you?" Matt walked with him to the dumpster. His assistant wheeled the stretcher with the body bag behind them.

"Sure enough. I hate it when the body is in the trash." Dave climbed into the dumpster.

Matt rubbed his temple. "What are we looking at?"

"The body temperature and rigor tell me she died a few of hours ago at the most. I'll work on the exact time, cause, and identification at the morgue and get back to you as soon as I have more information."

"I appreciate it, Dave. The woman had a baby at some point. We found the infant alive in there, and she's on the way to the hospital."

"It's a damn sad business." Dave shook his head. "The mother might have died giving birth. The more likely scenario is someone beat her nearly to death, first. Her body has bruises and multiple contusions. I'll know more when I get into it." They carefully removed her body from the dumpster and loaded the stretcher into his van. "Bag up some of the trash underneath the body and send it to the lab. I can learn a lot from the fluids."

"Will do."

When Matt walked into the office, Jessie had a notepad in front of her. She looked at him, smiled, and went back to what she was doing. He could almost see the wheels turning in her head. She was thinking about the case. Before he had even had a chance to talk to Melinda, she was working on an angle. Quite the partner, that one, even if she wasn't official. He shook his head and walked down the hall to Pastor John's office.

****

Jessie's day at the church was finished. Pastor John had sent Melinda home after Matt talked with her. Matt had left when Melinda did. Kip and the others were still at work in the dumpster when she crossed the street to her store.

"What is going on over there?" Audrey asked in

hushed tones since there were customers in the store.

"Melinda found a body in the dumpster when she took the trash out this morning. I'm not sure what details they'll release to the press yet, but Matt found a newborn baby there, too, when the baby whimpered."

"Thank God they hadn't emptied the dumpster yet. It's trash day." Audrey glanced out the window at the church. "Is the baby going to be okay?"

"We hope so. The hospital is caring for her." Jessie's face softened. "Oh, Audrey, she was so tiny and precious. Matt heard her weak cry and saw her tiny foot when he got into the dumpster. I have a feeling she's going to make it; she's made it this far." A tear slipped down Jessie's cheek.

Audrey shook her head. "What is the world coming to when a woman has a baby in a dumpster? It must have been awful for Melinda."

"Melinda is resilient, but I know it had to be shocking for her to find the body."

"How do you erase something like that from your mind?" Audrey shook her head.

"She'll need help. Pastor John talked to her and then sent her home to rest." Jessie saw Kip carry bags of evidence to his car. She walked back to the counter and busied herself, hoping to put it all out of her mind. *As if that would work! Who was it? Lily?* She had a sinking feeling she was going to recognize her in the morning.

"Since you're back, I'm going to leave. I have some shopping to get done today before I go home." Audrey grabbed her purse from underneath the counter.

"Happy shopping," Jessie, said absentmindedly. She waved at Audrey as she walked out the door.

****

Matt stared at the sketchy file on his desk. He needed to fill in some blanks. He couldn't believe the baby had cried at the exact right moment. They would have found her eventually when they moved the mother, but by then it might have been too late. Time is of the essence when a baby is first born. He couldn't erase the memory of the young mother's battered face from his mind. Had her husband or boyfriend done it? How could you injure the woman carrying your child? His hand raked through his hair. Matt had seen his fair share of domestic violence cases over the years, but he still didn't get it. His instinct was to protect Jessie. He couldn't imagine beating her. He shook his head. Men could be real jerks.

Matt's phone rang. "Chief, Lewis is on line one."

"Thanks, Joe. I'll take it now." He pushed line one. "Hey, Dave, what do you have for me?"

"No identity yet, it may take a while. Our Jane Doe was alive but severely injured when the baby was born. She had a ruptured spleen from the beating and was already hemorrhaging internally. It looks as if the placenta separated too soon and that did it. She probably bled to death very quickly. I'm still amazed she could last through the labor and actually manage to wipe the kid off before she died. I couldn't tell you how she got in the dumpster unless someone threw her in. There was no way she could have made it in on her own. She had a badly broken left knee, a broken right ankle, and a fractured pelvis from some well-placed kicks. Whoever did this deserves little mercy as far as I'm concerned." Matt heard Dave swear under his breath. "Sorry, I'm angry right now. A man most likely inflicted her injuries. The person or persons had to be strong." Dave paused. "How anyone could beat a pregnant woman is beyond me."

"My thoughts were traveling down the same path before you called. I would like to put this guy in prison for a long time." Matt turned his chair to look out the window. "I don't get it, but I've seen it often enough."

"Yeah, me too, but this was especially brutal. Some man had a vendetta against our victim, I guess. I'll get back to you when the toxicology comes back and if I get an ID."

"Thanks, Dave. I'll bring Jessie by the morgue tomorrow to look at her. She may be the woman who came into her store yesterday."

"Okay by me, but you'd better prepare Jessie." He sighed grimly. "I'm not sure if she'll be able to tell anything by how her face looks now. It might be worth a shot, though. I'll make her as presentable as I can. Besides, I wanted to show you some unusual markings I found on her body."

"For the victim's sake, we need to try. Thanks again, and we'll talk soon." Matt hung up the phone.

It was bad. If Lewis said it was bad, then it was bad. Matt drummed his fingers on the arm of the chair. He grabbed the file and his jacket and headed out of the station. He hated the whole idea of this case.

****

A fearful young woman had walked into her store yesterday; her husband had driven by her store several times afterward in a motorhome, and now this happened. Were they all somehow connected? She might find out tomorrow. Jessie phoned a couple of customers to let them know their book orders had arrived. She straightened the book table, dusted a few of the shelves, and went through the bills that needed her attention. A quick glance at the clock told her she had only ten minutes until closing time. The afternoon had been a quiet one, and she was happy it had been. It gave her plenty of time to reflect. Not that she had come to any conclusion, but it was hard to make small talk with customers when you had something else on your mind.

The clock said there were eight more minutes to go before she could close. She wanted to close now. While she argued with herself, the bell sounded at the door. Jessie turned to look and froze. The bell was ringing, but no one was there. Jessie ran to the door and locked it. She reached up and stilled the ringing bell. A young woman stood outside the door staring at her. The dark shadows under her eyes and the sadness on her face held Jessie in place. She was younger than the woman who had come into her store yesterday. Her hair was lighter in color, too. Chills raced down Jessie's spine in multiple waves. The woman she was looking at wasn't alive.

Chapter 3

Was she to be a gathering place for unsettled spirits? She shook head and looked again. The young woman was no longer standing there. Who was she? She was definitely dead. Jessie was becoming accustomed to the bizarre, and she knew she hadn't imagined it. She lifted a hand and rubbed her eyes. The bell had rung without the door opening. Blast that stupid bell. It had been a strange day. Her mind could be playing tricks on her, but she knew it wasn't.

Turning off the store's main lights, she sat in the leather chair. What would happen to the sweet baby girl whose life had begun in the dumpster? She would never know her mother. Tears filled Jessie's eyes. Stupid waterworks. She grabbed a tissue. If she was going to work with Matt on cases, she'd have to toughen up, or she'd be crying all the time.

When she'd called the hospital earlier, the nurse had told her the little one was stable. Good news. She wiped the tears from her cheek. Could the mother be the woman she had seen standing outside her door? Maybe if she knew the baby was okay, she would be able to rest in peace.

Her phone startled her. How long had she'd been sitting there? She glanced at her watch. "Hi, Matt, what's up?"

"Are you home yet?"

"No, I haven't left. I was too busy thinking and forgot the time, I guess." She glanced out the window and saw his car out front.

"I know. I can see you in there." He waved at her when she looked his way.

"Then why did you ask?" She planted a fist on her hip and glared out the window.

"I wanted to. Do you want to eat dinner with me?" He leaned against the car and winked at her.

"Sure. I'll get my stuff and be right out." She slipped her coat on, pulled her keys out of her purse, and slung her bag over her shoulder.

He was standing at the door when she opened it. "I'll lock it." He opened his hand for the keys. "I thought maybe we would walk to Angelo's if that's okay with you."

"Fine with me, maybe the cold air will clear my head." She slipped the keys in her purse when he handed them back to her. He was the perfect person to distract her from this crazy day.

"Thinking a tad too much, are we?" He smiled at her as he grabbed her hand.

"I'd have to answer an emphatic yes to your question. I can't seem to help myself." She glanced at him out of the corner of her eye. "You were, too."

"Yes." His expression was serious. "It's been a tough day. I checked on the baby, though, and she's stable. She's doing well, all things considered."

"I know. I called the hospital, too. I was happy to hear that the baby is doing well." It would be so awful if…she shook her head to chase away the bad thoughts. The baby was doing fine. Matt held the door open so she could walk in ahead of him. The host seated them at a table by the window.

Once the waiter had taken their order, Matt grabbed her hand turning it over in his. "What are you thinking about?"

"I wonder who she is, of course." Jessie glanced out the window. "Naturally another question is who would want to hurt her?" She glanced back at him and caught her ghostly visitor's movement as she passed the window. "Uh-oh. Why?"

"I have those same questions, but what else?" He was watching her. "Is there something interesting out that window, or have I lost my appeal?"

"Yes, to your first question and a definite no to the second one." She turned to face him, smiling in spite of the little chill the ghostly stroller had given her.

"What are you finding that interests you out that window? I don't see anything." He reached across and lifted her chin.

"A woman just walked by, not a living woman, but one of a ghostly variety. She showed up at my shop earlier today." She gave him a crooked smile. "Maybe she's fond of me or something." Jessie rubbed her arms and pulled her jacket up around her shoulders.

His brows rose. "Let's hear it, Jess."

She loved that he didn't question what she perceived and told him about the ringing bell and seeing the woman outside of her door. "It makes me wonder if she is the mother of the baby and needs to know her baby is okay—although I'm not sure if the ghost or the woman who came into my store are even the same people." Jessie shook her head. "She obviously did what she could to protect her child."

"It's never simple with you, is it?" He studied her

face. "What do you suppose it all means?"

Jessie shrugged her shoulders. "I don't know. Somehow, they're all connected. The woman who came into my store yesterday, a strange call I had at the church today, and the poor woman in the dumpster. They have to be connected, if only by the nature of the crime." Jessie stopped talking when the server arrived, placed their salads in front of them, and refilled their iced tea.

"What call? You never mentioned a phone call," Matt asked the minute they were alone again.

"It must have slipped my mind." She described the strange call at the church. "I got the distinct impression that she had to hang up because someone was coming. She was afraid to get caught."

"Putting it all together, what are you thinking? I know your mind is at work, and you're deep in this case already." He took a bite of his salad.

"Of course, my mind is working. I don't have much of a theory as of yet other than the fact that the woman who walked into my store yesterday was afraid. She was pregnant, but I don't know yet if she's the woman Melinda found in the dumpster or not." Jessie frowned, and forked up a piece of lettuce, then stared at it. "The man, Roger, who said she was his wife, had a mean streak in him. The anger radiated from him no matter how much he tried to be charming. He could hardly contain his rage." She put her fork down, her appetite suddenly gone. "The caller today was afraid, and the ghost doesn't look like the woman who came into the store yesterday. I have more questions than answers."

"Tomorrow I'll take you to the morgue, and maybe

one of those questions will be answered." He watched her as she sipped her tea. "If you had to venture a guess, what do you think we're up against?"

"Fearful, bruised women usually mean that a man somewhere is abusing them." She took a deep breath, pushing down the anger that wanted to rise. "It could be a father, a husband, a boyfriend, or even a brother. I wrote a piece on it when I was in New York. It's not pretty, and it happens too often, sometimes in reverse. Women also abuse men." She took a slice of the garlic bread from the basket and put it on her plate. "Beating a pregnant woman puts the unborn child at risk, and often, child abuse is involved." *What an ugly world it can be.* She shook her head and tore the piece of bread carefully in half.

"I wonder if it is more than similar crimes, but they are linked in some way." He drummed his fingers on the table.

"I don't know." She covered his hand with hers to stop him. "I imagine we'll find out soon enough." She pushed the thought of tomorrow out of her mind.

"You're right. We'll know soon enough. Let's eat, and you can tell me about something good that happened to you today."

She smiled at him, her eyes turning misty. "Nothing can compare to holding that precious baby girl in my arms this morning." She was so *innocent*. "Life out of that awful tragedy, it's a miracle."

"I know." His tone was sober. "I felt the same way when I found her. It could have ended so differently. I'm glad I was there and heard her soft cries. It almost felt as if it had been orchestrated."

She looked up and met his eyes. "Maybe it was."

****

Jessie thought about it long after dinner was over, and they had gone their separate ways. Whether it was providence, fate, or a miracle, one precious baby girl would live on and have a chance to grow up. The mother's trauma alone could have killed the baby. She chose to see it as a miracle named Matt. She smiled. Life certainly was more exciting since she had become his partner and he had started his campaign to charm her.

What was going on? Were all three incidents connected? Who was the ghost and why could she see her? Jessie turned on her computer. She opened up the file in her archives on domestic violence. The more she read, the more upset she became.

Every nine seconds a woman is beaten in this country.

How awful!

Domestic violence is the leading cause of injury to women, more than car accidents, muggings, and rapes combined.

She could only imagine how many children witnessed this and what it did to them.

Statistics prove that boys who have seen their dads abuse their mother often abuse their wives and girlfriends.

Her eyes scanned the page until she came to one sentence that stood out.

In this country, three women die every day from abuse suffered at the hands of a husband or boyfriend.

How sad was that? Today, another statistic for the record books had taken place right here in Blue Cove. She paused to answer her ringing phone.

"Jessie, Jessie, it's me, Sally. How are you doing, girl?" Sally sounded out of breath.

"I've been waiting for you to call. When are you coming for a visit?"

"I'll be there Monday sometime."

Jessie smiled. "It will be good to see you again. Do I need to pick you up?"

"No, I'm renting a car." Sally paused, taking a deep breath. "I can't talk right now, but I wanted to let you know, so you'd be watching for me. I'll see you soon." The phone clicked off.

Jessie looked at the phone. How strange! Her call so abruptly ending was…eerily similar to the calls she'd had at the church. Coincidence? She shook her head. Sally would never hang up like that. She was nigh unto impossible to stop talking once she got started. What the heck was going on? Jessie picked up her phone. Another strange element to add to the events of the past few days.

"Hi, it's me. I wanted to let you know Sally will be here sometime on Monday."

"Great, it will be good to see her again." Katie squealed. "Did I tell you that Liam and Connor found the perfect location for their pub and put in an offer today?"

"No, where?"

"The only bar in Seaside Village closed last week, and it's a perfect place for what they want. It's an excellent location. Liam was excited because everything inside goes with it. They're hoping to hear back today. With a little work they can make it into Donovan and Moore's Pub—or should I say dream?" Katie laughed. "You should have heard the two of them, just like they were in high school all over again. Filled with excitement after the big game…only this is their business adventure."

"I know the feeling and so do you. It's great!" Jessie sat in her favorite chair. "Do they know where they'll live?"

"They'll rent my other cottage for a while. I don't care as long as I get the rent money out of my brother. If all goes well, both of them will be here to stay in a couple of weeks. Of course, when they move out, I'll probably have to redo the entire cottage." She sighed heavily. "They aren't the neatest pair."

Liam living right next to her? Whew, what would Matt think about this news? "Maybe they've changed. Who knows? I can't imagine the two of them being neat, but then again it could happen."

"Not even a little possible. I've seen his apartment in the city. You know how he was, Jessie."

"I remember Liam's room was a mess, growing up. Your mom was always on his case about it." Jessie laughed. "It will be fun to have everyone here. I wonder if your parents will be next."

"You never know. If I found a husband and gave them grandkids, they'd be on the next plane." Katie snickered. "That's all my mom talks about when I call. No wonder I feel the pressure to get married."

"Not to be entered into lightly, if all the divorce statistics are correct." Jessie shook her head. "Take your time; the right man will come along."

"I know," Katie said sarcastically. "It's my mother who doesn't get it. I'm tired of making excuses. She never asks Liam when *he's* getting married."

"It's different for a son than a daughter. Of course,

I'm not speaking from experience as an only child, but it seems the way of it to me."

"Oh, it's different all right." Katie sighed.

"I'm glad Liam and Connor are moving here." Jessie meant it.

"Me, too. Liam came way too close to losing his life, and Connor needs to get his back on track. I hope they can handle the slower pace of Blue Cove," Katie said.

"I have yet to experience this slower pace you're speaking of." Jessie laughed. "It certainly has been interesting, though."

"What's going on now? I heard the police were at the church today."

Jessie told her what she knew at this point. "I called the hospital, and the baby is stable. Katie, she is precious."

"How sad…I feel so sorry for the mother and the baby. Jeez, how awful. I wonder if she saw signs of his anger before she married him."

"From everything I've read about it and learned in my investigations, there are always signs. We should know them."

"I need to know. I'm so crazy about men I jump first and think later. I'm not sure I would see it before it was too late. If you see those signs in some guy I date, tell me, okay?"

"I will, but you have to promise you won't get mad."

"Pinky swear." Jessie imagined Katie lifting her little finger the way they had when they were kids.

"I'll talk to you later. I need to scoot. I have some guests returning for the evening. I want to make sure they're taken care of."

"Good night, friend." Jessie plugged her phone into the charger.

Chapter 4

Jessie prepared herself to go to the morgue with Matt. It had kept her tossing and turning most of the night. Who knew what she would see and whether any of it fit together? It could all be a coincidence. She would find out soon enough, she guessed. As it stood, she had seen enough sadness and murder since she moved here to last a lifetime. It would be nice to turn it all off, for once. She stared at her reflection in the bathroom mirror as she brushed her hair. Reba had told her once she had been trying to find a way for years and hadn't discovered the means to do it yet. She was probably stuck with this crazy stuff in her head. She wasn't sure what to call it besides weird.

Jessie drank her coffee and rushed down a bowl of cereal. Matt would be here soon. Her phone rang, and she went in search of it. "Hello, this is Jessie," she answered when she found it next to her purse.

"I'm on my way. Are you going to be okay doing this?"

"It depends on what you mean by okay. Will I survive? Probably, yes. Will it be hard? That's another question entirely." She took a deep breath. "I admit that I'm not looking forward to it, but I'm also curious as to who the mother is."

"I get it, and I appreciate you doing this, sweetheart." He coughed. "If you don't want to, I'm good with it."

"I'll be fine." She heard him cough again. "Are you feeling all right?"

"I have a little scratchy throat, but I'm fine. I'm almost there; I drove past the Inn. I'll talk to you in a few."

Jessie slipped on her coat and went out the door as he pulled into the parking space beside her car. "Good morning," she said to him as he opened the door.

"Hi, sweetheart." He waited for her to slide into the passenger seat.

"You sound hoarse. Are you sure you're up to this?" She looked at his watery eyes.

"I'll be fine; we need to get this done."

She reached across and touched his forehead. "Matt, you have a fever. You should be home in bed."

"I'll head there as soon as we're done at the morgue and I get you back to your car."

He was so darn protective…and stubborn! "You could have had Dylan or one of the others escort me."

"Jess, this isn't going to be easy for you. Lewis told me it was bad and to prepare you." He reached for her hand with a lopsided smile. "I didn't want you to lose it in anyone's arms but mine."

"Promise me you'll go home and rest when we're done." She fastened her seat belt.

"Yes, ma'am," he said, as he drove past the Inn and turned on the road toward the morgue.

"I'll bring you supper tonight, so you won't have to cook. A pot of chicken noodle soup is just what the doctor ordered. Delivered with love, of course."

Matt had been right. One look at the body on the table and her knees buckled. Thankfully, he was there to catch her. A cloth covered the body from the neck down, but her face was bad enough. Why? She couldn't make sense of it.

"Does she look like the woman that came into your store?" Matt handed her a tissue.

She shook her head as she fought to get control of her emotions. "It's not her," she spoke softly, so only Matt could hear. "She is the one I saw standing outside of my store. There are some similarities between them, but it's not Lily."

Matt stroked her back. "Are you sure?"

"Yes." She glanced up at him. "It is possible that they're related, though. They look sort of alike." She shook her head. Another ghost. Unbelievable. This was getting absurd.

"So, as far as you know, the woman you saw in your store is alive and hiding out somewhere?"

"Yes." She gulped back the sob building in her throat.

"Matt, don't forget I need to talk to you before you leave." Dave stepped forward to intercept them as they walked out of the morgue area.

Matt escorted her into the reception area. "Sit here. I'll be right back; it shouldn't take long."

She nodded and watched him walk back through the doors.

****

"I wanted to show you something, but I didn't want Miss Reynolds to see it." Dave pulled back the sheet and pointed to a series of cuts in her abdomen and chest. "From these symbols, it looks like we have something religious or some kind of ritual abuse."

"Not something you see every day." Matt stared at

the cross and several other less obviously Christian symbols that had been carved into her flesh.

"What kind of sick customer are we looking at who would do this to a pregnant woman?" Dave shook his head.

"Could you send me some pictures of the markings? I need to check around to see if anyone who deals with ritual murders has seen any of these before." Matt wanted Tom to see the markings.

"I'll make sure I include the photos in the report."

"Thanks, Dave." He turned around to leave. "Nothing should surprise me anymore, but it still does."

"I know what you mean." Dave covered the body and pushed the drawer back into the refrigerated chamber.

Matt saw Jessie look up with a tentative smile when he walked out. "Are you okay, sweetheart?"

"I will be as soon as I can get the waterworks to shut off." She managed a weak smile as he handed her another tissue. "How about you? Was everything okay in there?"

"I'll tell you about it later."

"Are you sure you're feeling all right?"

He forced a smile. "I'll live."

"As I told you earlier, I'll bring you some chicken soup tonight. It always helps when I don't feel well." She leaned closer to him. "And I'll bring me, too, to hold your hand."

"I'd be happy to have the soup and your company for dinner." He smiled for real this time. "A good night's rest wouldn't hurt either." He stood and reached for her hand. "Let's go. Dave will call when he has more info on our victim."

She took his extended hand. "I'll be at your house no later than six."

Chapter 5

The motorhome went by her store. It pulled into the church parking lot, and the door opened. Roger crossed the street and came her way. At least, there were customers in her store. She wouldn't be alone with him.

"May I help you?" she asked him when he walked in the store.

He smiled and nodded. "I thought I would buy a book for my wife. Do you have a favorite you'd recommend?"

She walked over to a shelf and pointed to several books. "Women seem to like this author. You might find one she would enjoy among these books. They are the store's best sellers." Jessie started to walk away.

"Okay, and by the way, thank you for giving my wife the message the other day."

She stopped. Was Roger testing her? "I never gave her the message; she didn't come in that day. I'm sorry."

"I guess one of the other merchants must have told her. Here, I'll take this one. I'm sure she'll love it. Ring it up, and I'll get out of your hair." He grabbed the first book off the shelf without looking at it.

"I know she will. This woman is a good author." Jessie took his money and placed the book in a bag. She watched him cross the street and rubbed her arms to ward off the sudden chill that came over her. Wound as tight as a top, he could spin out of control at any moment. She shivered. She had passed his test, whatever it was about, or he would still be in here. He must not have found her yet. *Keep running from him, Lily.*

****

Jessie made it to Matt's on time. She carried in a fresh loaf of crusty bread and a crockpot full of chicken noodle soup. She studied his face when he opened the door. His glassy eyes and flushed face told her that he wasn't feeling well.

"Hi, sweetheart." He gave her a wan smile. "I would give you a kiss, but I don't want to pass this on to you."

She kissed his cheek as she walked past him. "I hope you're hungry. I didn't have time to make this myself today, so Katie made it for me. I'm sure you'll be happy with it, though." She put the box she was carrying down in the kitchen. "It smells heavenly, anyway." She touched her hand to his forehead. "Did you rest today?"

"I tried, but with an active murder investigation, I have to fit it in when I can. I'm sorry. I should've helped with the box. I'm really not with it." He grinned at her.

"If I were mean"—she smiled at him—"I could lecture you. As someone I know always does to me. I would tell you about the importance of taking care of yourself." She patted his shoulder. "Instead, I'll take pity on you because I'm happy to see you. I'll tell you what my mom always tells me. Plenty of rest, plenty of fluids, and you'll be better before you know it." She hugged him tight and kissed his cheek.

He grinned at her. "I'm happy to see you, too. I warned you about the germs, but if you don't mind, I sure don't." He kissed her forehead.

"You said an active murder investigation." She finally drew back and frowned. "So she was murdered?"

"Yes, all the injuries from the beating caused her death. Lewis wasn't sure how she even had the strength to give birth."

"He threw her in the trash." Jessie shook her head as tears stung her eyes. "Along with her unborn child. What kind of person would do such a thing?"

"I've been asking myself the same question. I hope we learn the woman's identity soon."

"Sit down." She gave him a nudge toward his chair. "I'll serve you." She nodded at the TV tray sitting next to his lounge chair.

"Are you going to eat with me? I would like your company for a while if you don't mind."

"I'm not going anywhere." She went into the kitchen to dish up his dinner. She placed a steaming bowl of soup, buttered bread, and a cup of hot tea with honey and lemon on the tray. She placed his meal close enough to his chair for him to reach and went back to the kitchen to get her soup. "Did I tell you Roger came into my store today?"

Matt frowned, his spoon poised in his hand. "You should have called me, Jess."

"He didn't stay long. Honestly, I believe he was testing me or something." She took a bite of her bread.

"What do you mean?" He put his spoon down and glanced at her.

She told him about the encounter. "I think he still hasn't found her. I hope she's far away by now."

"He's not far away, obviously." He sipped his tea. "I don't like him hanging around. We'll need to keep our eye on him." He gazed at her and smiled.

"What?" She looked away first.

"I like that you're here with me. The soup is great. Thanks for doing this." He took a bite of his bread.

"Of course." She laughed lightly. "You've done it often enough for me. I did make you something even if I can't take credit for the soup." She went into the kitchen and brought him a plate of homemade chocolate chip cookies. "Courtesy of me, your number one fan." She placed them on his tray and felt his forehead again.

He grabbed her hand and pulled her onto his lap. "I like you taking care of me, sweetheart. It's nice, real nice." He held her close, his hand rubbing her back. A few minutes later, he was asleep. His even breathing and occasional snore brought a smile to her face.

Jessie waited several minutes and then extracted herself gently, taking care not to wake him. She cleaned up the kitchen, covered him, and left him sleeping in his chair. On her drive home, the woman in the dumpster and Lily came to her mind often. How could one man be so kind and another be so cruel? Where was Roger now?

****

Matt awakened when the front door shut. He had fallen asleep while holding her. He couldn't believe it. She was peaceful to be around, and he felt better seeing and being with her. He grabbed his phone, checked his messages, and then called her.

"Hi, sweetheart, I'm sorry I wasn't better

company."

"You did exactly what I had hoped you would do, which is to rest. You didn't sleep very long." He could hear the concern in her voice and liked it.

"Jess, let me know if you see Roger or Lily around. We'll assume for now that the names are correct. This guy might be big trouble, and I don't want you alone around him." He stroked the stubble on his face. "If the two women are related in some way, then he could be our abuser, or they may know who is."

"I'll let you know if I see them again. Promise me you'll go to bed when you hang up and get some sleep. It might do wonders for you."

"I will, but it can't be any better medicine than seeing you, sweetheart. Good night, Jess, love you."

"The feeling is quite mutual, Mr. Parker." He could almost hear the smile in her voice.

Matt walked into his room and stretched out on the bed. Another ghost and another fine mess she had attracted. He grinned into the darkness. She sure had charmed him. Life was interesting with her; he couldn't complain. Now, if only they could find some answers before anything else happened, he would be a happy man. The victim's identity would be a nice start.

****

There were too many places for her to hide. Roger glared out the window. He would never find his wife at this rate. Most of the woods were too thick and dense to drive the motorhome in. She could be hiding anywhere. He would kill her when he got his hands on her. Damn! Roger hit the table with his fist. He had driven far enough today. She wasn't worth the trouble. No one left him unless he said she could. Lily was his property. She had cost him enough over the past few months. In the driver's seat, he started the motor and flipped on the radio to his favorite station. The RV made the turn toward Blue Cove. She had to be around there. Lily couldn't have gotten far; she was banged up. A frown creased his face. Roger hadn't meant to hurt her so badly. She made him so damn angry, talking back to him all the time. Her fault—all of it—he was a reasonable man. His hand tapped to the beat of the music. She was bound to get hungry at some point, and he'd be waiting to tell her he was sorry. He was. She shouldn't make him mad, make him hurt her when he really didn't want to. He shook his head. She'd come back. She always did. Just in case, he would keep his eye on the bookstore. Roger wasn't sure about that bookstore woman; there was something…sly…about her. If nothing else, she'd be a great replacement for the one who got away.

Chapter 6

Matt woke up with a jolt; his body damp with perspiration. He pushed up and sat on the edge of the bed. Rubbing his eyes, he tried to focus in the dark room. A strange noise. Was it real or a dream? There it was again, a cat maybe. No. He sat up straight. It sounded more as if someone were weeping.

Grabbing his gun, Matt slipped on his pants and went to investigate. He checked the doors, did a thorough search of the house and garage. All was secure. But the sobs were persistent and growing in intensity. Matt gazed out the window into the darkness. There was a woman sitting on the garden bench. Her form was barely visible; he needed to get closer. Easing the front door open, the cold night air stopped him when the chill hit his bare chest. Hurry. The woman's cries were real. He grabbed a jacket from the closet and put it on. By the time, he reached the garden, the crying had stopped, and the bench was empty. The search outside turned up nothing. Matt touched his hand to his forehead. It was cool. This was no hallucination. She had been there. He had seen her.

Whoever she was, her weeping had been genuine, and she needed someone's help. Call Jessie? He grabbed his phone and then placed it back on the table again. It was much too late to bother her. Matt pulled off his jacket and stretched out on the couch.

****

Jessie thought she was dreaming at first when she heard the woman's cries. It didn't take long for her to come fully awake. The heart-wrenching sobs were coming from somewhere close by. Jessie slipped out of bed and went to her front window to peek out into the night. On one of the benches on the garden path sat a woman. Jessie opened the door to listen. The night was instantly silent. She strained to hear, but there was nothing. Had it all been in her head? Jessie rubbed her arms as the goosebumps rose. The minute she closed the door, the anguished cries began again. From her vantage point at the window, she watched the woods come alive with hundreds of people. Were they alive or dead? Their tormented cries grew in volume to a deafening noise inside her head. She opened the door to make them quit. At once, there was silence. The blissfully sleeping world hadn't heard their cries. Why had she?

Jessie locked the screen, leaving the door slightly open. She wanted to talk to Matt, but when she saw the time, she sent him a text instead.

—When you see this in the morning, give me a call—

Her phone rang instantly, startling her.

"Are you okay, sweetheart?"

"Yes, I didn't think you would see it until morning. You're supposed to be resting."

"It is morning, kind of. I wanted to talk to you, but didn't want to wake you either."

"What's up?" Jessie asked him.

Matt described his encounter. She was stunned. "When I finally got outside she was gone. I searched the area but couldn't find her."

"Wait until you hear what I have to say." Jessie described her experience to him. "The second time I looked out the window there were lots of people crying. As soon as I opened the door, it became silent. It's still open right now. I'm afraid to close the darn thing because it was so loud."

"What are we looking at? I was sure she was real. This ghost stuff doesn't happen to me."

"Maybe she was real. It could have been Lily." Jessie began to pace. "Either way, there are real cries for help that go unheard. For some reason, we have heard some of them. Let's leave it for now. We have a murder investigation underway and a mystery to figure out. Besides, you aren't feeling well, which might have contributed to it." Jessie smiled.

"Are you saying I was hallucinating?" Matt sneezed.

"It could have been fever induced is all I'm saying. Either that or you caught my germs." Jessie tried hard not to laugh when he muttered a few choice words under his breath. "I imagine it could be Lily wandering around. She has no safe place. If it's her, I hope she shows up there again."

"What about our victim? Do you have any ideas?" She winced when he coughed.

"No, but I know somehow she's connected to Lily. The first time I saw her standing outside the door, I thought maybe she was Lily's sister." She frowned when he coughed again. "I don't know how they are related, but they're connected in some way. Yet to be discovered."

"Tell me when you come up with anything which

connects the two."

"Matt, you need to get some rest."

"That's not going to happen for a while. My mind keeps going over every detail I have so far, and I can't get it to turn off. It's either you talk to me, and we bounce ideas off of each other, or I'll be doing it alone."

"Okay, what is your theory so far?" Jessie asked.

"We have Lily, Jane Doe, and a strange phone call. If our Jane Doe and Lily aren't related, then we have a murderer we know nothing about. It would be easier if they were connected. I could arrest Roger, and it would all be over with." He inhaled. "It's never that easy."

"No, it's not. We might have to be patient with this one. It takes a lot for a woman to come forward because she fears for her life. People who know about it won't come forward either." She grabbed the notes she had written down. "Someone, somewhere, knows what happened to our Jane Doe. It may take a little prompting to get that person to come forward with their knowledge, though."

"I'm not good at being patient, as you know." He sounded groggy to her.

"Yes, I do know, but I love you anyway. Matt, you're ready to sleep now. Talk to you in the morning. Good night." There was a long stretch of silence, then the sound of his snore. She smiled.

Before she slept, Jessie sat at her computer and wrote a story for Max at the Blue Cove Sentinel. She described the dumpster find and the miracle baby. She would let Matt read it first, of course, before she submitted it. Her eyes teared up as she detailed the precious life found beneath the dead mother. In Jessie's eyes, their Jane Doe was a real hero. She had lived long enough to give her child life. She sent a copy for Matt to read and Sadie to edit. She stretched her arms over her head and yawned. She got up, closed the door, and it remained quiet. She wondered if Matt had seen her ghost or had he really seen Lily. In one way, for Matt's sake, she hoped it was Lily. But for Lily's sake, she hoped she was long gone. She checked her watch. Eight would come soon. It could wait until daylight. She stretched out on the couch and fell asleep.

Chapter 7

Had Matt seen her ghost? Jessie hoped for his sake that the woman sitting on his bench last night was alive and breathing. Matt wouldn't appreciate anything he couldn't logically explain. Jessie stepped into Joe's, closing the door behind her. She stifled a yawn, feeling the effects of her interrupted night. Matt accepted that strange things happened to her, he even seemed impressed by her ability, but he sure wouldn't like it if it intruded into *his* life. Not even a little bit.

"Hi, Jessie, do you want the usual this morning?" Molly smiled at her.

"Coffee only, please. No scone for me." She handed Molly her coffee mug to fill.

"Are you sure? I took your favorite out of the oven." She gave her a tempting smile. "They're fresh and filled with blueberries."

"I can imagine how good they are, but I have to have some discipline. I'm only allowing myself one pastry of any kind a week from now on." Jessie patted her waistline with a smile. "I have to be tough about this scone addiction of mine." Jessie poured cream into the mug of coffee that Molly had placed on the counter.

"What fun are you if you won't let me tempt you even a little?" Molly gave her back the change.

Jessie dropped a dollar into the tip jar. "I'm sure it will be replaced with some other special item before you know it. I can't seem to stay away from all your wonderful sweet delights." She turned to leave.

"I'll be over when I get a break to pick out a book or two. Kenny is either at his class at the academy or studying at home for the class every night. I have to keep myself busy when he's gone and out of his hair when his nose is buried in the books." Molly frowned. "Neither one is easy for me. I want his attention when he's there, and I miss him when he's gone." Molly's hand shot to her forehead in a dramatic gesture. "There's no help for me."

"Ah love, you never get enough." Jessie laughed. "Thanks, Molly." She waved as she went through the connecting doors into her store.

Jessie placed her coffee and purse down on the counter. A quick glance at the clock told her she had thirty minutes to relax before her day started. She looked around the store and frowned. Something felt a little off. What was it? There. Jessie pointed and frowned at the chair that was facing the wrong way. It hadn't been like that when she left last night. She would never turn it that way; it made the room look wrong. Her pulse quickened as she went over to it to move it back where it belonged. *Had someone been in here?* She placed her hand on the chair to move it back where it should be, and a strange sensation ran up her arm. She jumped back, removing her hand instantly. "I'm sorry to disturb you," Jessie mumbled automatically. "I need to turn this chair. It's blocking the bookshelf. Customers will be coming in soon." She felt foolish talking to what looked like an empty chair, but she knew who was sitting in it. "Your baby, a sweet little girl, is alive and doing well. I thought you might like to know. I hope you'll help us find out who did this to you. We will put him or her behind bars." Jessie found herself rambling on as she turned the chair without further incident. She walked to the back room, took her cash box from the safe, and got ready to open the store. Her morning ritual brought her little comfort this morning. She found herself often glancing to the chair and wondering whether her ghost was still there or had moved on.

Matt was standing at the door watching her with a silly grin on his face. She smiled and waved at him as she unlocked it. "How long have you been standing there?"

"Let's just say long enough to wonder what you were doing and who you were talking to." He brushed past her.

"It's a funny story, really. Do you have time to talk?" She grabbed his hand and laced her fingers through his.

"That's why I'm here. I can't seem to break this habit of needing to see you every chance I get."

Her lips curved into a smile. "Whatever you do, don't sit in the chair." She pointed to the leather chair. "You might get more than you bargained for."

"I'm sure I should ask you why, but I'll take your word for it. I don't care where we sit as long as I get to look at you."

"Aren't you sweet?" She kissed his cheek. "Are you feeling any better?" She noticed his red, watery eyes.

"I'm all right. The doctor said it's a cold, and I'll live." He pulled her down onto his lap. "Do you want to tell me what I saw?"

Jessie told him about the ghost she had been talking to most of the morning. She glanced over at the chair. "I'm not sure if she's still here or gone."

"I knew your answer would be different, but I wasn't expecting you to find a ghost sitting in the chair or moving furniture."

"I can't say I was either." She crinkled her nose. "To tell you the truth, I never saw her, but when I told her about the baby, I could finally move the chair." She looked at his puzzled face. "I know it's weird, but it worked."

"Jess, the woman last night was real; there was nothing ethereal about her. She wasn't ghost-like if you know what I mean. Her cries were real, and we need to find her before he does."

"It's possible Lily's wandering around with no place to go." She touched his face. "I thought she was probably real, too. You're too logical to travel down the crazy road I'm on." She frowned. "How is it that you can put up with all my strange baggage?"

"Easy, sweetheart, love is blind." He laughed when she playfully punched him. "You were as surprised by it all at first as I was. Admit it." He kissed her forehead.

"True." She glanced at the clock. "Why are you here?"

"Two reasons, I already told you one—I can't seem to stay away." He gave her a mischievous grin. "And I wanted to tell you about what Dave Lewis found on the victim." He described what he had seen to her, and what Lewis had told him.

"Occult, religious, what are we looking at?" She stood and shook her skirt out.

"It's too early to tell. I'll let you see the photos as

soon I get them. I'm going to send a set to Tom and let the bureau have a look, too." He stood in front of her. "I know it's time for you to open." He held her tight for a moment. "I'll call you later." He paused at the door. "No more talking to empty chairs, sweetheart. I understand you, but others might not." His grin widened, and he waved as he took his leave. She watched him until he was in his car.

He was right, of course, but she was the one that had to deal with it and at the same time, try to keep a certain amount of decorum, not him. She found herself laughing anyway. She must have looked all sorts of ridiculous to anyone passing by. Her smile lingered. He managed to make her day anytime she saw him. She opened the doors into Java Joe's and turned her sign on the front door to *Open*. Her day was off to another strange start.

Chapter 8

"Good morning, sir, this came from the coroner's office a few minutes ago for you." Kenny handed him a large sealed envelope.

"Thanks, Kenny." Matt took the folder and started back to his office. He paused and turned around. "How's your time at the academy working out?"

"It's a lot of work, but I'm doing well, sir." He gave Matt a serious look. "I'm keeping up with my studies."

"I'm glad to hear it. How's married life?"

"It's the best thing I've ever done." Kenny grinned. "Molly's terrific and fun to hang with."

"Keep up the good work. I'll be in my office if anyone needs me." He continued down the hall. Molly had done all right when she married Kenny. He was a good kid. *Kid?* He shook his head. Damn, he was feeling old. It had to be the damn head cold. He reached for another tissue.

Matt picked up his phone and paged the desk. "Kenny, get Tom Maxwell on the line for me. You can put him through to me the minute you reach him." Matt looked at the photos Lewis had sent over to him. It was beyond sick what the woman had been put through. Was it a part of a ritual or made to look as if it were? Looking intently at one of the photos, he shook his head. The baby's survival was even more amazing in the face of her mother's ordeal. The woman must have fought like hell to stay alive and bring her into the world.

Kids. He wanted to be a father. Yeah, he knew the risks of his job, but he still wanted to be a dad. He lifted his head to stare at the wall. Rescuing the baby from the trash had brought it home to him. He wasn't getting any younger. He couldn't put his life on hold for a job forever. His phone rang, pulling him from his thoughts. He picked it up and smiled at the greeting. "Hey, Tom, how's life in the city treating you?" He swiveled his chair to look at the window.

"Not bad. What's up?"

Matt told him about his murder case. "I have some photos of the symbols that were carved into her body. If I scan and email them to you, would you have one of your agents at the Bureau look at them? I need to know what I'm looking at."

"Sure. I hope it's not a ritual killing; that's a damn nasty business." Tom took a deep breath. "They can be tough to find unless you know of an active group. They blend in with normal everyday folks in the community. They don't walk around in costume. Once you know the woman's identity, you'll have to scour the background of her family and friends."

"I hope we'll have some information on her shortly."

"I'll get back to you as soon as I find out something for you."

"Okay, Tom, don't be a stranger."

"I've been looking for an excuse to head your way. I could use another amazing meal at the Inn." Tom cleared his throat. "I wouldn't mind seeing Katie again either. Call me crazy, but she's been on my mind a lot."

"Hey, man"—Matt felt his eyebrows rising—"I didn't see that one coming."

"Truthfully, neither did I."

Matt hung up the phone, smiling. Tom and Katie. He shook his head. Katie and Tom. Why not? Considering how short Katie was, Tom would have to stand her on a chair to kiss her. Matt smiled at the absurd visual in his head.

What would Jessie think about it? His phone rang, and he reached for it. She probably already knew, knowing her.

****

A light tapping sound at the back of the store caught Jessie's attention off and on during the morning. She had been too busy to check it out until now. She frowned as she went into the back room and pulled the back door open. Lily fell in.

Jessie jumped back with a gasp. She dropped to her knees beside her. "I'm sorry, are you okay?"

"I'm so tired of running from him," she mumbled, her face bone-pale. "Please let me hide back here for a few minutes."

"Would you like something to eat?" Jessie's heart was racing, and she could see the fatigue etched on Lily's face. She looked like she was ready to drop. She stood, got down a blanket that she kept on the shelf, and handed it to her.

"Yes," Lily whispered. "Anything would be great." She curled up in a fetal position and pulled the blanket over herself.

"He's been in here a couple of times looking for you, and he drives by several times a day." Jessie frowned and locked the back door. "You need to stay back here out of view."

"I will." Her eyes fluttered shut. "I hoped he would give up but no such luck."

"What's your name?" Jessie knelt beside her once more.

"My name is Olivia Bertelli, but he calls me Lily. He refuses to call me by my name. I don't know why."

"Another way he can control you, I guess. I'll get you something to eat."

"Oh, thank you. I'm hungry." She opened her eyes and looked up at Jessie. "I'll find a way to pay you back."

"Don't worry about it. I'd like to believe someone would help me if I ever needed it. You rest, and I'll get your food." Jessie got to her feet as Lily's—Olivia's—eyes closed again. Jessie closed the door of the storeroom behind her, went over to Joe's, ordered her a bowl of soup and a turkey sandwich, and asked Molly to bring it over. She needed to get Matt involved. Fortunately, this was a slow time of day, and the store was empty of customers. When Molly delivered the food, she carried the tray into the storeroom. Olivia was sleeping. Quietly, she placed the tray beside her.

She awakened with a start.

"I'm sorry," Jessie said soothingly. "I didn't mean to scare you."

"It's okay." She sat up and looked at the tray. "Boy, does this smell good." She reached for the bowl of soup and within a few minutes had devoured every morsel on the tray. "Thank you." She looked down at the floor once more.

"I would like to call my friend to come take you to

a women's shelter."

Her eyes widened, and she shook her head. "You don't understand. He pulled me out of a shelter the last time. I thought he would not only kill me but the lady who was shielding me. He seems to know where they are in every town."

"My friend can help you, trust me." Jessie put a gentle hand on her shoulder. "He's the chief of police."

Olivia's expression didn't change. "No one can help."

"I know he can. I'm going to call him." She watched her shake her head again. "Yes, Olivia. You can't do this alone. That's why you're in here, hiding from him. We need to know more about you so we can help you escape him for good." The bell on the door rang. "I'll be right back." Another customer followed the first one through the door, and they both had numerous questions for her.

Several customers later, Jessie finally got the chance to peek into the storeroom again.

Olivia was gone. Her heart sank as she relocked the back door. With a sad heart, she called Matt. "Guess who was here?" she asked him when he answered the phone.

"Your ghost friend," he replied.

"I forgot all about her to tell you the truth." She let her breath out in a sigh. "Lily was here. Her real name is Olivia Bertelli, and I bought her some lunch."

"Back up a minute. What do you mean Olivia was there. And you didn't call me?" She could nearly hear his frown. "Is she still there?"

"No." She sighed again. "That's my fault. I told her I was going to call you, that she needed help. It spooked her. A customer came in, and by the time I got back to check on her, she was gone."

She could hear Matt swear under his breath. "I hope we didn't lose our chance to get this guy."

"I tried, Matt. At least, I told her I thought you could help her escape him. She's wandering around town, hiding from him. She has no money and nowhere to go. I think she might have been your crying woman the other night. You can rest easier now."

Matt was silent for a moment. "I'll be by to take you to dinner tonight if you don't mind my red nose and a teary-eyed date."

"Even on a bad day, Mr. Parker, you're still the best-looking guy to me." Jessie smiled when he chuckled.

"Thank you kindly, sweetheart. Let's see if you still feel the same way when you see me. Besides, I have a little gossip to share with you."

"I didn't know you liked to gossip." A mischievous glint lit her eyes. "Another item to add to my list of why I love you."

"You keep a list, sweetheart? I'd like to read it sometime. While you're at it, be sure to add that I'm wild about you."

"I'll talk to you after work. Melinda is coming in the door." Jessie ended the call.

"Hi, Blondie." Melinda plopped down in the leather chair and shot back to her feet. "Is this an electric chair? The dumb thing shocked me." Melinda backed away from the leather wingback chair warily.

"Hi, Red, you wouldn't believe it if I told you." Jessie shook her head dramatically.

"Try me." Melinda tilted her head. "I've been

around you long enough to know you are a little strange." She threw her head back and laughed.

"I don't want to talk about it. I still can't believe it myself." Jessie walked over to her. "Sit in this chair, and you'll be fine. How are you doing?"

"I'm okay." She sniffed. "I still feel sad. I guess I should expect it."

"It will take a while." Jessie hugged her.

"Probably. I wanted to get a couple of books. Something happy please, I've had too much reality." Her arm brushed the chair, and she jumped. "Dang, what's up with this chair? Doesn't it like me or something?"

"It's nothing personal." Jessie tried to smother her smile at Melinda's suspicious expression. "It's occupied, and the inhabitant doesn't want to be disturbed."

"You're not kidding, are you?" Her expression was incredulous.

Jessie shook her head. "I'm serious."

"Who is sitting there, Blondie? Is it Gina our church ghost to the rescue?"

"No. I hope you're ready for what I'm about to tell you." Jessie leaned over the chair. "Melinda is the one who discovered you," she whispered to the chair's invisible occupant. "Red, meet the person who you found in the trash the other day. She's the mother of the sweet baby girl that Matt was able to rescue only because you were so quick to get help there."

Melinda slapped her hand to her head. "Well, I'll be. You're collecting these folks aren't you?" She plopped down in the chair again, but this time, she stayed there. When she realized what she had done, she jumped up again. "Oh, I beg your pardon."

Jessie smiled. "She doesn't mind now that she knows who you are."

"And I thought Gina was something. Do you suppose she's here to stay?"

"I have no idea. My guess is that her ghost will be here until she knows her baby is okay, and I hope she helps us find the person who did this to her."

Melinda stared at the chair and mumbled something under her breath.

"This is all new to me. Up until I moved here, I knew nothing about ghosts or had never seen one. All I can say is I'm thankful they've all been nice so far." She shivered in spite of her light tone. "I'm not sure I would want to have a run-in with an unfriendly one."

One eye still on the occupied chair, Melinda handed her the paper with titles of the two books she wanted. "I'll only tell Reba. No one else would believe or understand it." Her red curls bobbed back and forth when she shook her head.

"I appreciate it, Red," she said as she found the titles Melinda wanted. "I've already brought enough trouble since I moved here. The good citizens of Blue Cove might want to run me out of town if they heard about this. At the very least, they wouldn't want to shop here if they knew a ghost was sitting in a chair in my store."

"Well, it makes me feel good to know about her." Melinda's voice softened. "She didn't end in the dumpster." Melinda took her bag with the books, and Jessie squeezed her hand. As Melinda walked by the chair on her way to the door, she leaned over the arm and spoke quietly. She straightened and left, waving to

Jessie as she stepped outside. Jessie waved back. Matt would probably get a good laugh when he heard that Melinda was now talking to the empty chair, too.

Jessie finished out her day with a few more customers and her closing routine. Matt was waiting for her when she shut off the lights.

"Is Patterson's all right with you?" he asked when he held the shop door open for her.

"Sure." She placed her keys in his waiting hand.

"Let's walk." He locked her store, gave her the keys, and took her hand in his.

"I had a few funny things happen today." Jessie watched him out of the corner of her eyes as she recounted the story of Melissa and the chair. Matt laughed a big, booming laugh that made Jessie laugh, too.

"I have a bit of a story to tell you myself." His eyes took on a mischievous glint. "Tom Maxwell might be sweet on Katie. He told me himself, and he's headed here to stay at the Inn for a few days because he likes talking to her."

"Why, Mr. Parker, I believe you enjoy the whole gossip thing. I'll let you in on a little secret." She smiled at him. "I imagine Katie kind of likes Tom, too. But then Katie likes most guys who pay attention to her. Only time will tell if her infatuation with Tom is the real deal. I thought for sure that Jeremy was it, but they don't have a lot in common."

"You're right, of course, but it could be fun to watch."

She gave him a playful push when he opened the door to Patterson's. "You're full of surprises tonight."

"Why's that?" He leaned close as she walked past

him. "Can't fault a man for wanting his friends to be as happy as he is."

****

She had enjoyed their evening together. Matt was fun to be with and especially tonight. He had smiled, laughed, and charmed her with conversation all evening. When Liam and Connor showed up and invited themselves to their table, Matt wouldn't let Liam near her. She smiled every time she thought of how he had outmaneuvered Liam at every turn. If Liam got too close, Matt leaned closer and kissed her. When Liam grabbed her hand, Matt hauled her into his side draping his arm around her shoulder. Matt was certainly declaring her as his territory in some strange male ritual. Would she ever understand men? At least Matt tolerated Liam now, and in his own way was lending a hand to keep him in line. She smiled to herself. It was nice to have the attention of two great-looking guys, but Matt was the only one that mattered. She was hooked.

Jessie leaned her head back against the couch with a sigh. Sally would be here in a few days. They had been together all through high school, but it had been years since Jessie had last seen her. They rarely even talked. She frowned. Why was Sally coming here now? She fit into this scenario playing out in Blue Cove somehow. Soon enough, she would find out, she guessed. She turned off the TV and headed for bed.

Chapter 9

Jessie stood with Katie on the Inn's big wraparound porch. As soon as Katie heard Sally was near she could hardly contain herself. She bounced from one foot to the other. "The three of us together again." Katie's words bubbled out. "How long has it been? We had such great times. I hope she gets here soon. I can't stand it." She squealed as she saw Sally's car come into view.

Jessie didn't say anything. Katie didn't really expect an answer. She flew down the stairs when Sally's car came to a stop in front of the Inn and flung the door open, squealing with delight and wrapping Sally in a big hug as soon as she stepped out of the car. Jessie observed the scene tight-lipped and tried to see something of the Sally she knew in the woman caught in Katie's embrace. It was her, of course, with her thick chestnut hair that curled about her face and shoulders. But her velvety brown eyes seemed lackluster, without a glimmer of the merry twinkle that Jessie remembered so well. Even from where she stood, Jessie could see that Sally still had the incredibly long lashes that looked like miniature fans when she fluttered them. Everything else seemed wrong, somehow. Her once trim figure was bloated and doughy. Sally kept a fake smile plastered on her face. This was Sally, but…it wasn't. *Get a grip, Jessie*, she told herself firmly. *You aren't making any sense*. "Sally, I'm so glad you're here." Jessie determined to enjoy the moment, raced down the stairs, and joined in the hug.

"I have so much to tell you both. Where do I begin?" Sally grabbed Jessie's hand. "I know I have plenty of time to catch up, but I have to tell you both something before we go any further."

"Let's sit on the porch, and you can tell us whatever you need to." Katie led the way to a grouping of white wicker chairs away from the doors.

"I'm here because I need help. I had nowhere else to go. I'm not the person you grew up with." Shadows darkened her eyes as she looked from Katie to Jessie. "To be exact, I'm only a shadow of that girl. I've…I've lived in the background for so long I'm not sure how to begin to reclaim my life." Her lip trembled as she sat down.

Jessie sat down beside her and took her hand, squeezing it as Sally caught her breath. Katie was sitting on the other side of her, a stunned expression on her face. "Go on," Jessie said gently.

Sally gave her a grateful look. "Sometimes I get a glimpse of who I used to be, but then it's replaced with the reality of the hell I'm living in."

"Of course, we'll do whatever we can." Katie stood, her eyes wide. "I'll get us some refreshments, and then we can talk." She hurried to the door looking back at Sally over her shoulder.

Sally turned to her. "You've always been the serious one, Jessie. Sadie told me some of the things that have happened in your life. It's hard to believe, but you look well despite it all." She gave Jessie a faltering smile. "I need some kind of intervention. Look at me."

She shook her head as she stared out at the woods. "I saw you studying me. You hardly recognized me. I don't either. I'm overweight, I smoke, and I'm afraid to do anything about it."

"What happened?" Jessie held Sally's hand.

"I got married, which was my first mistake. And my husband turned out to be a bully. I've continued to let him bully me, which hasn't helped much either. He turned out to be a real nightmare, actually. There was no prince charming for me," she said bitterly. "Remember how we used to dream about the day our prince would come? I'll probably shock you, but hell, he turned out to be a mean SOB."

"It's strange that you should come right now." Jessie described the last few days to her. "Maybe you can help us understand what we're looking at."

Sally's phone alerted her to a text. "Speaking of my nightmare, that's him now. He'll be checking in on me so often it will make your head spin. I told him I'm out of town for work. You may have to back me up." She sighed. "I hated to get you involved, but I didn't know what else to do." She stood.

"I need to call him back, or he'll get suspicious." She walked around to the other side of the porch and made her call.

If Jessie had learned one thing since her days at college, it was that life could get mean. Dreams could be replaced by a horror story before you knew what had hit you. She had seen enough of it, living in New York. She had been touched, up close and personal, by that same truth, living in Blue Cove.

"Where'd she go?" Katie placed the serving tray down on the table. Three glasses of iced tea were accompanied by a plate of cheese and crackers.

"She's talking to her husband." Jessie pointed to where Sally stood shaking her head.

"I hardly recognized her, Jessie." Katie's eyes were round. "What's happened?"

"I don't know, but we are about to hear it from her." Jessie picked up a cracker with cheese and nibbled on it.

"I hope you girls are ready for this." Sally plopped down in the chair next to Katie and lit her cigarette. "Do you mind?"

Katie shook her head. "It's okay outside, but inside we're a smoke-free zone."

"I understand. I hope you guys will help me quit." Sally took a deep breath. "Here's the whole thing in a nutshell. I want to divorce my husband and see if I can find myself again. I need help, courage, and support to do it. I'm here because you two are my closest friends and if anyone can help save me from this awful life, you guys can." Sally took a puff and blew out the smoke. "We can talk more at dinner. I wanted you to know up front that this is more than a social call. Hell, I don't know if I even know how to be social anymore."

"You came at the perfect time, Sally. You're among friends, and we'll figure this out together." Jessie sipped her iced tea.

"I wouldn't put it past him to trace my phone calls and come looking for me." Sally looked troubled. "You have to be prepared. He can be frightful when he's mad."

"Let him come." Katie put her glass down on the table with a clang. "Jessie here is practically engaged to the chief of police, Matt Parker, and most of the police force are in love with her. Let him try something with them around." Katie doubled her fist and struck at the air. "Ka-pow!" Katie glared at her. "Don't give me that look, Jessica Lynn. You know I'm telling the truth."

"You're exaggerating as usual." Jessie rolled her eyes at Katie.

"Now, this is how I remember it." Sally's face lit up.

There she was. Jessie watched Katie and Sally banter back and forth. For a moment, the sparkle was back in Sally's eyes. It wasn't dead, only hiding. She sat up straight, her shoulders squared. Life wasn't anything if you couldn't help your friends when they were in need. She jumped into the center of the fun. The serious talk would come soon enough.

****

Jessie was dressed and waiting for Sally to come out of the guest room bright and early the next morning. She wanted to hear Sally's story and hadn't wanted to spoil last night's fun. When had the abuse started? Hearing her story might give Jessie some idea of how to help Olivia. The bedroom door opened with a squeak.

Sally greeted her and sat in the floral chair across from Jessie, positioning the pillow behind her back. "When am I supposed to meet Katie?"

"In about twenty minutes." Jessie smiled at her. "Did you sleep well?"

"I did." Sally smiled back at her. "For the first time in a long time." And she looked better today, Jessie thought. Not so doughy and pale. Sally cleared her throat. "I gather you have a man in your life. This chief of police." She smiled. "It's about time. Of course, I'm clearly not a good judge of men." She made a face.

"But from what Katie tells me, he's a keeper."

"He is." Jessie smiled. "Definitely."

"So why aren't you married to him? I've never known you to be serious about any guy. You went with Jake Perry in school, and all the while you drooled over Liam." Sally tugged at the pillow beside her twisting the fringe around her finger. "You had such a crush on him. I thought for sure you'd snag him eventually."

"I was crazy about Liam." She laughed, remembering. And Matt was still jealous of him, silly man. "He lives here now. Katie can fill you in on all the details. When it comes to why I'm not married to Matt…" She shrugged. "I'm not ready to be married yet. I still have a few things I want to do before I settle down." Jessie paused. "It's only a matter of time, though, because I love him," she said quietly.

"Wow, you must be serious." Sally's eyebrows rose. "Me talking marriage, that's a joke. I should be telling you to take your time and be sure before you take the plunge. I was in such a big hurry." She shook her head, her expression bleak once more. "All I got was a mess."

"Sally, what happened? You guys seemed so happy together." Jessie leaned forward.

"Things can be different when you're dating." Sally looked thoughtful. "Although when I think back on it now, I could see signs early on. Bruce always had a terrible temper, and I didn't want to believe it. Love can be so blind. My mom used to warn me about him." Her eyes were sad. "I was so sure she didn't want me to be happy, and I refused to listen. What a fool I was."

"Young and in love isn't always smart."

"You've got that right." Sally laughed shortly. "We

started out okay. The first couple of months were great. Then Bruce wanted to know where I was all the time. I swear he followed me." Sally scowled. "If I didn't account for every minute I was gone, he'd go ballistic on me. He…he didn't hit me at first." She avoided Jessie's eyes. "He called me awful names. He made me feel ugly and awful."

"Hit you? Oh, Sally." It was worse than she'd thought. "How could he do that to you? You were always one of the most popular and confident girls I knew."

"After listening to him for months, it was easy to stop believing in myself," she said bitterly. "If I ate dessert, he told me I would get fat. You know how I looked when I was young. I was a bean pole." She looked ruefully at her thick waist and ballooning thighs. "His constant harassment made me eat. I was so nervous. Food made me feel good, at least." Her lips twisted. "Look where that got me. Now he tells me I'm fat and disgusting. And I am." She looked at the floor, tears glistening at the corners of her eyes.

"No, you're not." Jessie paused. "Do you love Bruce, Sally?" Jessie asked softly, her heart aching.

"I once did. Love is the only reason I stayed, and why I made excuses for his behavior—to myself, my parents, and to all of our friends. I blamed myself. But love can turn to hate quickly." The tears rolled down her cheeks now.

"Why didn't you leave him?" Jessie asked her pointedly.

She shrugged but didn't raise her head. "I did in the beginning—many times. Then he would come crying on bended knee, begging me to take him back. It was like a sickness between us. He'd treat me great for a while, until the next time I did something to displease him…" Her voice trailed off, and she buried her face in her hands. "Oh, Jessie, I get disgusted with myself when I consider how much abuse I've taken. I've been too weak and scared to leave."

"Sally, you were so young, who knows what any of us would do under those circumstances." She put a hand on her arm, squeezed it gently. "Didn't anyone notice the marks on you?"

Sally shook her head. "I knew how to hide them. My parents always suspected there was a problem. My mom said she could see the sadness in my eyes. I was too embarrassed to go to them because they had warned me about him. I stayed with him and took it on the chin. Literally." Her crooked smile was bitter. "The first time he hit me, I excused it by saying I was to blame. He said it was my fault, too. It was hard to stop the self-recriminations."

"How did you do it?" Jessie handed her the box of tissues.

Sally took it and raised her head. "I don't know when exactly I woke up and realized I didn't deserve to be treated the way Bruce was treating me. No one does. I had listened to enough talk shows about domestic violence to know that I had been living in it for years. All I can say is, thank God I did. From that moment, I started planning how I would get away. When I told my parents what was happening, they weren't surprised and wanted to help me." Sally dabbed at her eyes and blew her nose. "I secretly opened up my own checking account. My parents helped me find a lawyer. Bruce should get served with divorce papers and a restraining order in the next few days. My lawyer wanted me to be gone when Bruce was served."

"I don't know what to say, Sally." Jessie smiled in spite of the pain she felt for her friend. "I'm so sorry for what you've suffered. I've covered stories like yours over the years, and I know how awful it is."

Sally's face took on a determined expression. "If I ever get out of this mess alive, I would love to help women in similar situations. There are enough of us out there."

"You will." Jessie took her hand. "All we have to do is get you through the next few weeks."

Sally stared off into the distance, her eyes flat and hard now. "I'm not going back there ever, and if he comes after me, which I know he will, I might have to kill him."

Chapter 10

Jessie clasped Sally's hand, the tick of the wall clock loud in the silence that filled the cottage. She didn't know what to say after Sally's pronouncement. It was usually the woman who died in domestic violence cases. If her husband did come after her and there was a confrontation, one of them or both might well die. This was another situation Matt needed to know about. Bruce would show up. There was no doubt in Jessie's mind.

"It's so beautiful and peaceful here." Sally walked the path that wandered through the grounds of the inn with her, pointing to the well-maintained trees and shrubs. "I can't believe Katie inherited the Inn from her uncle. I could see myself living here."

"You should see it when the gardens are in bloom if you think it's pretty now." Jessie motioned around the area. "It's gorgeous. From time to time, I pinch myself. I have my own slice of paradise in my cottage by the sea. Liam and Connor are moving into the other cottage on the property."

"I can't believe those two crazy guys are moving here, too." Sally smiled, shaking her head. "You can't really go back in time, but it would be fun to try. We had some great times together."

"We sure did. Although, I wouldn't want to go back. I'm enjoying this time in my life. You'll enjoy your life again, too." Jessie grabbed Sally's hand. "We'll help you get through this."

"I know, but I'm afraid I'm bringing trouble your way." Sally looked nervously over her shoulder. "I didn't know where else to turn, though."

"We'll manage. You're among friends now." Jessie frowned. "You can't bring more trouble than I've brought with me."

"I'm excited to find out what you girls have been up to." Sally gave her a hopeful smile. "I need to laugh, too. Katie could always be counted on for laughs."

"She's still the best."

"I hope so. I need to unwind. I've been on edge for so long, I don't know what it is anymore to relax, much less laugh. I'm dying to find out if I can reclaim my life."

"I'm speaking off the top of my head here, but I'm sure you can and will create a new you in the process." Jessie pulled Sally along. "Get a move on. Katie is waiting."

****

Matt hung up, shaking his head. Jessie was in the middle of it again, and he was concerned. Déjà vu. So far, they had managed to survive everything life had thrown at them. Sally had a big problem, and she was staying with Jessie. Not good, not good at all, on top of this current ghost-situation. If her husband decided to come after her, there was little either of them could do physically to stop him. Matt knew it in his gut he'd come, the same way Roger was still here looking for Olivia. A restraining order was hardly worth the paper it was written on as far as he was concerned. It did very little to protect the woman.

Frowning, he lifted the phone. "Jeremy, Matt here. Can you look into a few things for me?"

"We've had this conversation before."

"I was thinking the same damn thing."

"What's Jessie in the middle of now?" Jeremy asked. "Voodoo? Ghosts? I mean, what are we looking at?"

Matt filled him in on Olivia, the murder, and Sally. "I need you to find out what you can on Bruce Kingman."

"This case sounds almost normal." Jeremy chuckled. "No ghosts yet, huh?"

"Did I forget to mention the cult symbols carved into the body of the mother and the ghost that has taken up residence in Jessie's store? I guess I did." He smirked. "She likes to sit in the chair and zap anyone who tries to sit there."

Jeremy laughed. "Well, you can forget I ever used the word normal to describe one of your cases."

"There's nothing normal about it," Matt mumbled under his breath. "My concern is with Bruce. He'll be getting the divorce papers and restraining order in the next few days, and that's probably going to make him madder than hell." Matt took a deep breath. "I imagine he'll soon be on his way to Blue Cove."

"Not good, and you're probably right." Jeremy's tone was grim. "I'll see what I can find on him and get back to you as soon as I can. What about your murder victim?"

"No ID yet. I'll send you a name as soon as I find out one. As for Roger, I doubt it's his real name, but he's still hanging out around the Cove in his motorhome. He's been in the store twice. I hope he sits on the chair and gets zapped by the ghost."

Jeremy laughed wryly. "Never a dull moment, eh, Matt? You can't complain that your life is boring."

"True." Matt sneezed. "It's been interesting. I'll leave it at that."

"You'll hear from me soon. I might have to make my way there. My life is boring. Besides, I'm curious about Sally. Jessie and Katie are a handful. I can't imagine another one. I might have to find out for myself."

"Either way, we'll talk soon." Matt clicked off his phone.

Bruce would come, Roger would stay, and he had a murder to solve. It was never simple when it came to Jessie.

Chapter 11

"Matt, can you stop by the store after work?" Jessie didn't have a free moment to call until after lunch. The store had been particularly busy today, which was good. It distracted her from the newest worry. "There's something you need to listen to if you have some extra time."

"I'll be there in a few minutes. I was at the hospital checking on the baby and was going to stop by anyway."

Jessie smiled. "How's she doing?"

"Jess, she's perfect." His voice warmed. "They let me hold her, which was nerve-racking." He gave a half-embarrassed laugh. "She was so little, I thought I'd break her with these clumsy hands. We managed, however, and she even smiled at me."

"It's a reflex action with a newborn, or so I've been told. It still melts your heart."

"The nurse said that the agency has a couple in mind for her. She'll be adopted before we know it. Depending, of course, if they can find the woman's family. If they are innocent of her murder, her family will have some say in what happens to the baby."

"Extra good news, and boy, do I need it right now." Jessie frowned shaking her head when she noticed the chair was turned the wrong way again. She marched toward the offending chair. Maybe she should move it to a new place where it faced the window and didn't look so out of place.

"Are you going to tell me what's up or wait until I get there?"

"I'll wait." She scrunched her face. "You should enjoy the good before I give you the bad."

"See you soon."

Jessie stood by the chair and checked to make sure no one was watching her. "I hope you don't mind. I have a perfect place for your chair so that you can look out the window and keep watch."

Jessie moved one chair to replace it with *her* chair. Anyone who tried to sit there got up quickly enough. They might not know it was a ghost, but they were sure that it had some unusual problem. If she continued to keep her vigil, it was sure to become the talk of the town as the "haunted" chair in the bookstore. Jessie thought for a moment and then taped a *Do Not Sit* sign on the back. Hopefully, the problem was taken care of, and the bookstore wouldn't get a reputation for unruly furniture!

She shifted her gaze to the busy street outside. How long did they have before Bruce got here? Jessie got chills when she thought of the message he had left on Sally's phone. He had called her parents too. Sally's mother had called, worried sick, and wanted her to fly home immediately. Sally didn't want her parents in jeopardy and was talking about leaving to keep them all safe. Jessie shook her head and pressed her lips together. Matt would know the right way to approach this problem. She stood at the window, waiting to spot his car. "What's the problem with some men?" She shook her head and waved at Matt as he parked in front of the store.

"Okay, Jess, what's the trouble?" He spied the chair in its new position with the sign on it and started laughing. "I wonder if she'll leave it there?"

"I don't know, but I thought it was worth a try." She smiled at him. "You look like you're feeling better."

"I am." He kissed her. "No germs."

She led him to the table and when he was comfortable, she turned on the message from Sally's phone. "What do you think?"

Matt's eyebrows rose, and he nodded thoughtfully. "I'd say he's so angry he's not playing with a full deck. He was stupid to leave a message on the phone. This is all evidence against him if anything should happen to Sally."

"But you're not going to let anything happen to Sally are you?"

"Not in my town or on my watch if I can help it." His arms folded across his chest and his chin edged up. "As you know, sweetheart, there's always a risk. Her husband is madder than hell. You can hear it in his voice. He'll only get angrier when he sees her."

"He also called her parents. I guess they felt he sounded…threatening." She rested her hand on top of his. "They want her to fly home, but she's afraid she'll put their lives at risk. She's talking about leaving Blue Cove for the same reason. What do you suggest she should do?"

His expression didn't soften. "I think we need to get Sally in a safe house." He wanted her gone, too.

Jessie shook her head. "I don't know if she'll go for it. She wants to get her life back. She'll take off and go to some other town."

"If he catches up with her, she won't have a life." His hand curled into a fist at his side. "He could beat her or worse yet he could kill her and maybe anyone near her." He shook his head, his eyes tortured. "I know how you feel, but it's the same with Olivia. You can't get in the middle of this, Jess. If Roger knows she's been with you, he could take it out on you. The same goes for Bruce. We don't know how dangerous he is or if he's carrying a gun."

"I know you're right." She bit her lip and looked away. He had expected her to get angry at him, but he was only worried about her. And...he was speaking the truth. Domestic violence was the most dangerous part of police work. "I've...I've seen the change in Sally. She's not the same person. She won't trust you to keep her safe."

"Trust won't come easy. Even after a woman is safe, it takes a while to be whole again and to be able to trust a man. I get it." Matt stroked her hand. "Where is she?"

"She's with Katie at the Inn. They had some cooking project planned for today to keep her busy while I worked here." She reached over and touched his cheek. "Matt, I'm glad I met you. I realize how fortunate I am to have you in my life."

"I feel the same way about you, sweetheart." He raised his hand to cover hers.

"I know you're right." She smiled at him. "Seeing what Olivia and Sally are going through makes me appreciate how wonderful you are. Not to mention our Jane Doe. Even my father looks kindhearted in comparison. I have no right to complain about his caring about me, not after I've seen what these women have gone through."

"I know this is hard for you. Seeing your friend afraid of the person she married is a challenge to all notions of what marriage should be. I've seen it many times, and it's still hard for me to understand." Matt held her hand in his.

"What changes love into hate? I've written about it, I understand it statistically, but I don't get it." She frowned.

"Honestly, I don't know. Both are powerful emotions."

"Promise me you'll let me know if I ever make you so angry you want to hit me." She looked up to meet his eyes and saw his startled expression.

"You could make me mad, Jess, but I'm never going to hurt you." He squeezed her hand. "I would walk away first. I was raised by a father who was loving and tough. We never talked back to my mom. He taught us to treat a woman with respect. He showed the way by how he treated my mom. I'm glad you brought this topic up; it's too important to push under the rug. I'm never going to hurt you purposely. I may be a jerk, I might say something dumb, but I will never raise my hand in anger against you." His eyes held hers. "It's not going to happen."

She smiled, although she could feel the tears trying to come. Matt cared so *much*. "I guess I needed reassurance. I'm scared of what I've seen. It was always out there, I've reported on it, but it never hit this close to home before." She smiled at him. "Every time I look at that chair I'm reminded once again what anger can do."

"Don't let it stymie you. You're a smart woman. You can push back and give as good as you get." He grinned. "Maybe I should ask the same question, sweetheart." He grabbed her free hand as she threatened to swat him playfully. "I'll keep this with me for a while. If you don't mind." He held on to her hand and kissed each of her fingers. "I'll stop by after work to meet Sally. I'll convince her that the best place for her now is to get her to a safe house before he gets here. Which could be soon if he flies."

Chapter 12

During a lull in the afternoon, Jessie called the Inn. "It's me, checking in. What are you two up to?"

"We're cooking up a storm over here and expecting you for dinner tonight," Katie bubbled over the phone. "Of course, bring Matt along with you. Sally and I have created quite a feast if I do say so myself. Connor and Liam will be here."

"I'll ask Matt, but I'm sure he will. He wanted to meet Sally and talk with her about her situation." Jessie waved at a customer who walked in the door.

"Guess who else is coming down for the weekend." Katie sounded kind of excited.

"Could it be Tom Maxwell?"

"How'd you know?"

"Just a lucky guess." Jessie tried not to laugh. Matt's gossip might be right. "I wonder why he's coming."

"He told me he wanted to get away from the city and relax. I told him that until you moved here, Blue Cove was a great place to relax, but now not so much."

"That sounds like something you'd say."

"I couldn't help myself. You know it's true." Katie laughed.

"Whatever…" Jessie shook her head. "The only time Tom comes to town is when there's a big case, so I hope it's not an omen of what's to come."

"You're right." Katie sighed. "Maybe I should tell him to stay away."

"As if that would work. Maybe Tom could be coming to see you." She smiled. "I need to go; I have a customer. See you around six."

"What do you mean? Don't you dare hang up now."

Jessie laughed as she disconnected the call. As she rearranged the books on the display table by the front window, the motorhome was parked in the church lot again. Roger was still in town. Waiting frustrated her. Anticipating what might happen next kept her mind hopping. "Keep your eye on him for me," Jessie whispered as she walked past the chair.

****

"Matt, Lewis is on line two," Kenny told him.

"Hi, Dave. What do you have for me?" Matt opened his file on Jane Doe.

"Our victim has been identified as Larissa Young. She's on a missing person's report filed about five months ago. The strange thing is, the deputy who investigated her disappearance felt like the parents and the people he interviewed at the time were lying. He couldn't find any evidence to substantiate what his gut told him, but he thought her parents were somehow involved or knew who was and were covering for them. The report went on to say that the Youngs acted in an unusual manner throughout the process."

"Do you have an address for them?"

"They live outside of Blue Cove on some acreage. They're in the county's jurisdiction. It was Deputy Taylor Smith who signed the report."

Matt wrote Larissa's name in the file. "I'll have to

call the Sheriff's department and see if he can remember the case. Thanks, Dave, is there anything else?"

"The report mentions that several families were living together. The investigating officer found it odd. They seemed, to him, at least, to be covering for one another. I'm using his words loosely. They claimed the girl's boyfriend kidnapped her, but no one could remember the young man's name."

"Sounds fishy to me."

"I have the photos ready to head your way. Take a look at them and tell me what you'd advise in this situation."

"Will do. I'll call you if I have questions." Matt turned his chair around to look at the window. A religious sect—or someone trying to make it look like one—was a possibility.

Matt spent the next hour talking to Deputy Smith. He recalled the case easily and was saddened to hear about Larissa's murder. They went over his report line by line. Matt asked questions, but in the end, it was Smith's take on it that convinced him the parents and the folks around them had to be given a second look.

"They were covering something up. I'm sure of it. I couldn't get a search warrant. I had no evidence of a crime; all I had was this sense that something was off, way off, with those folks. My advice to you is free," Taylor said grimly. "Don't go out there alone. Make sure to take another officer or two with you."

Great, he had another bizarre case on his hands. Obviously, this couldn't be blamed on Jessie; Smith said the Young family had lived on the property for years. Still, between Olivia, Larissa, and Sally, it made him wonder. His cases had been petty stuff until Jessie had moved here. His life had been dull, too. He shook his head. Truth be told, the cases had been here all along, but no one had seen them before Jessie did.

He hoped Jessie wasn't too busy to talk. "Idle Time Books, may I help you?" He smiled as she answered the store phone.

"I sure hope so. I need to run some things by my partner. Is she around?"

"She is, as a matter of fact, and even has a few minutes to talk."

"Would you like to know the name of the woman who sits on your chair?" He heard her quick intake of breath.

"Yes, I've been talking to her most of the morning, and it would be nice to call her by her name even if I can't always see her."

"Her name is Larissa Young."

"Larissa…" Jessie said the name aloud followed by her quick squeal. "Uh, give me a minute, Matt, I seem to have a little situation here."

"Jess, Jess—" Matt yelled into the phone.

"It's okay, Matt. Larissa was letting me know she was here."

"How was she letting you know, or should I ask?"

"By way of a flying book," Jessie replied with laughter in her voice.

"Hell, I *shouldn't* have asked. Did the book hit you?"

"No, not even close. Larissa, my ghost is happy I finally know who she is."

"I was talking to the deputy who investigated her disappearance months ago. Taylor told me he was sure her parents were lying. We need to do a little investigating ourselves. How would a long run through the woods later this week sound to you?"

"Interesting. Will I be running alone, or will I have company?"

"Company, definitely." Matt could almost see the wheels turning in her head.

"Sounds like a perfect date to me."

"I'm not sure I'd call it a date. It's more like work to me."

"I should mention to you that Roger's motorhome was parked in the church's parking lot most of the morning, but I saw him leave a few minutes ago."

"Did he come into the store?"

"No, which is strange. Hey, Matt, your little piece of gossip about Tom being sweet on Katie might be true."

"Did Katie tell you something?"

"Only that Tom is coming to spend a couple of days at the Inn this weekend. He needs to get out of the city and relax, he told her. I'm impressed with your skills. If I ever need to know what's happening in town, I'll be sure to check in with you first."

"You won't get much out of me." He chuckled. "I'm usually oblivious to what's going on. I have another call coming in. See you, sweetheart."

"Matt, there's an Agent Kimble on line one."

"This is Chief Parker." Matt listened while Kimble talked. After his lengthy explanation, Matt knew his answer. "You can count me in on this plan."

"This is top secret; no one, I mean no one else can know."

"I understand. I'll arrange everything on this end."

Matt wrote a few notes from their conversation.

"We'll talk again soon."

****

"See you tomorrow." Jessie waved at Molly who was standing in the open doors between their businesses.

Molly nodded. "I'll close these for you. Enjoy your evening, I'll be leaving myself in a few minutes."

"Larissa, look after my store. I wish you could tell me what happened to you. Matt doubts your parents are telling the truth. If anyone can find out, he will. He's the best." Jessie shut off the lights, pushing things around in her purse until she found her keys. Money was in the safe, the safe was locked—she went through her mental checklist as she went out the back door to her car.

Brrr. Jessie pulled her coat tight around her. The wind was chilly. She started the car and turned the heater on full blast. She couldn't wait for Sally to meet Matt.

The drive to the Inn didn't take long, and Jessie parked her car in its familiar spot. Getting out, she paused for a moment to gaze into the sky. The stars were out in force without one cloud to hide them. She took a deep breath. Cool with a hint of spring in the chilly air and the promise of warmer days ahead. Soon, the gardens of the Inn would be alive with color. Already the daffodils and tulips were pushing their heads out of the thawing ground. She walked a few feet and paused again to take in the quiet beauty.

"Have you made up your mind?" Matt's deep voice took her by surprise.

She turned around to find him standing on the top

step. "What do you mean?" She found herself breathless.

"Are you coming or going? You looked like you couldn't make up your mind." He walked down the steps. "I've been waiting for you." He stopped in front of her, his hand reaching out to touch her hair.

"I'm heading that way but taking my time." She covered his hand with hers. "It's so quiet, like the calm before the storm. I wanted to enjoy it for a moment."

"Quiet is nice." His fingers moved to her cheek. "Alone with you is even nicer." His gaze dropped to her lips.

Jessie leaned closer to him and then stopped when her phone started ringing. She shrugged at Matt and rolled her eyes as she reached for it. "This is Jessie."

"Where are you two? Dinner is ready, and we're waiting for you." Katie's voice sounded loud in the silence.

"We're coming up the steps right now." Jessie grabbed Matt's hand and pulled him along.

Matt put his hand on the doorknob and leaned close to her. "We'll pick up where we left off soon, sweetheart."

From the moment they walked through the door, they found themselves in a whirlwind of activity. Jessie introduced Matt to Sally, dinner was delicious, and Liam, along with Connor, were entertaining as usual.

After dinner, Jessie left Matt and Liam to question Sally about her situation while she helped Katie with cleanup in the kitchen. She had put the leftover salad in the refrigerator when Matt grabbed her elbow, pulling her out of the kitchen.

"We need to talk." She tried to shake his hand off,

but he wasn't letting go. He pulled her into the study, his face grim, and closed the door. "We are going to put Sally in a safe house. I don't want you in the middle of this. Bruce is trouble, Roger is too, and you don't need to be anywhere near them. I saw the pictures of what Bruce did to Sally, and you saw Roger's work firsthand. Liam is in full agreement with me."

Jessie stared at him. "Okay." She liked this side of him.

"I'll make all the arrangements for her care. I want her out of town." Matt hugged her. "Until she's gone keep your eyes open. I don't know when her husband might get here."

"I will." Jessie stood in the circle of his arms and sighed with contentment. "What brought this on?"

"I saw the pictures Sally has from the hospital. They convinced me."

"What's your plan?"

"Right now? I know for a fact that Sally is going for coffee with Liam." Matt waggled his brows at her.

"Do you have a plan on how to use the free time?" She reached up and whispered in his ear.

"I sure do. Let's go to your place, and I'll show you." He grinned.

"Sounds tempting to me." She laughed when he tugged her toward the door.

Chapter 13

Matt's plans to get Sally out of town were falling apart quickly. The shelters at Rocky Pointe and Harrisville were both full. Neither place would have space to take her for at least a couple of days. His search for another home for the interim came up empty. The shelter needed to be equipped to handle Sally's situation, which might mean a bigger city. He got Kenny busy checking places in New York, hoping Bruce didn't get to her before he could get her moved. He glanced at his watch. In two hours, he would be running in the woods with Jessie. Not much of a date, but a least it was time alone.

The weatherman said it would be cloudy with a chance of fog, which suited him fine. They didn't need to be seen by the group living on the Young's land. Smith's report, which he had read over several times, interested him. Another strange case that had made its way to Blue Cove on the heels of Jessie's arrival.

He tapped his pencil on the notepad. Jessie was feisty and always ready for a challenge. Matt tried to imagine any of the women he had dated who might have been willing to run in the fog, in the middle of nowhere, and call it a date. It never would have happened.

"Hey, Matt, what's got you smiling?" Dylan knocked on the open door.

"Jessie, what else?" Matt noticed the new janitor sweeping the hall.

"Something good, I take it?" Dylan leaned against the door frame.

"Yeah, you could say that." Matt's smile broadened.

"Where are we in the Larissa Young case?"

He handed Dylan a copy of Smith's report to read. "Jessie and I are going to snoop around the family compound later on."

Dylan scanned the report. "So they're blaming it on the boyfriend, but they don't know his name? Sounds damn convenient to me." He folded his arms across his chest. "How can your daughter date someone, and you don't even know the kid's name?"

"I'm not sure what we'll find or what we're looking for. A quick jog around the area might give us a reason to request a search warrant, though. For now, we'll be a couple out for an evening run in the woods. We won't go on their property, only watch them from a distance and hope we'll stumble onto something."

"I'll be on call if you need backup." Dylan gave him a crooked smile. "Whenever Jessie is involved, it's not simple."

"True, but it's not boring either." Matt grinned, and then his smile faded. "There are too many similar things taking place in our town for this to be a coincidence. It's been brought to our attention in a dramatic fashion."

"What you mean?" Dylan walked in and sat in the chair in front of Matt's desk.

"We have a murder, but we also have two women who are being stalked and threatened by husbands, and who have both connected themselves to Jessie." Matt frowned. "It's never good to be in the center of domestic cases."

"Not my favorite case to handle, too dangerous." Dylan looked at the report again. "What do you think about the cult angle?"

"Our victim had some symbols carved into her body. They're being analyzed now by an expert in the field. We don't know if they're real or a poor attempt at a copy."

"This report becomes more interesting with that piece of evidence." Dylan frowned.

"Agreed. Add to it a compound with several families, and I think you get the picture. It may be real or only contrived. All I know is that Larissa is hanging around Jessie's store and doesn't seem to be in any hurry to leave."

"Damn, that part of Jessie's life is still strange to me. A ghost…how does she deal with it? I know every argument for why it can't be real, but she blows them all out of the water." Dylan shook his head.

"I keep thinking I'll come up with a logical explanation. I can't, and neither can Jess."

"You be safe out there and call mc if you nccd me."

"Dylan, it might be a good idea if you followed us out to the area." Matt frowned. "Smith warned me to take backup and not to go to the area alone. I should listen to him and play it smart."

"I'll follow you. What time?" Dylan stood.

"I'm picking Jessie up at five when she closes the store."

"Don't leave until I get there," Dylan said as he

walked out the door.

"We'll wait."

****

Jessie had worked at the church all morning. She walked back to the store, her mind racing as she went. What had happened to the woman who had called and hung up several times? She hadn't called again on Jessie's shift. Had she called during Audrey's time at the church? She made a mental note to ask Audrey. Was the woman somehow tied into the case? Another question she needed to find an answer to.

Larissa could throw books to get her attention. Could she get a response out of Larissa if she talked about her parents? She would mention it tomorrow and see if another book flew her way. Throwing a book was a strange attempt at communication. Heck, what was she thinking? She smiled and shook her head. A dead person trying to communicate with her in any way was weird. Whatever, Larrisa was in her life for now, and she would know soon enough why. Another new normal.

Jessie waved at Molly, said goodbye to Audrey, and hello to Larissa. The few customers in the store kept her busy most of the day.

"Hi, Blondie." Melinda stood in the doorway between the coffee shop and the store. "How's it going? Is our friend still here?" Melinda's red curls were pulled up in one of her precarious, lopsided ponytails on top of her head.

Jessie turned and nodded. "What are you up to?"

"I needed coffee, and I want to buy a book. I see you moved the chair." Melinda pointed toward the chair. "The sign adds a nice touch, too, I think."

Melinda grinned as she stepped into the store.

"I had to move it because she kept turning the darn thing to see out the window. I have no idea what she's looking for. The sign is there for the safety of my customers. The chair, as you know, gave a few folks a bit of a jolt when they sat in it." Jessie bit her lip to keep from laughing at Melinda's expression.

"I remember, Blondie." She rubbed her backside. Then she softened her voice to almost a whisper. "Do you know who she is yet?"

"Her name is Larissa Young," Jessie told her.

"Larissa," she repeated it until it rolled off her tongue like a song. "What a pretty name." Melinda headed to the shelf where her favorite books were.

Jessie watched her look around, stop at the chair, and begin to chat. Perhaps it was therapy for Melinda. She was the one who had found the body, after all. What does anyone really know about life after death? Jessie knew what she had learned growing up, but lately, since moving to Blue Cove, she had more questions than answers. The ghost thing was happening, and that was all there was to it.

It was time to get busy. Jessie shook her head. "Here are a couple more books by the same author." She pointed them out to Melinda and then picked up her feather duster and went after the shelves.

****

He scrambled up in the tree. If his wife was around, she couldn't see him. Parking outside of the area, he had walked in. There were plenty of places to hide with so many trees around. He lifted the binoculars and scanned the area. A nice surprise was waiting for his dear little woman when he finally found her. It was a perfect night to get three for the price of one. Thought she could get away from him, did she? Well, the joke was on her. He swore to himself. "Keep them in their place," his daddy used to tell him when he was growing up. His mother was docile enough. She had been hit plenty of times, and she never left his dad until the day she died. "Don't let them mouth off or get away with anything. That's how they like it. Women want you to be rough, that's why they're so sassy." His woman sure as hell didn't like it. He hadn't seen it coming when she'd left him this time.

Chapter 14

Jessie closed the store, changed her clothes, and waited for Matt. "Keep watch for me, Larissa." She locked the store behind her when Matt arrived.

"Hi, sweetheart." He held the car door open for her.

"Thank you." Her hand touched his when she got into the car. "How far out of town do we have to go?"

"It's about a twenty-minute drive from here. Dylan is going to follow us. I might have even convinced him to run with us too. Smith told me to be sure to take backup when we went. It seemed like the smart thing to do."

"Dylan running...I don't think I've *ever* seen him run. Does he?" She smiled at Matt.

"I guess we're about to find out."

Dylan parked behind them and got out with his running gear on. "Do you mind if I ride with you two? I'm not sure of the area; I don't remember ever being there before."

"I had to look it up myself. It's not too far, but it's several miles off the main road in the woods. I haven't been there either."

"Switch places with me, Dylan. Your legs are too long to be stuffed into the back seat." Jessie opened the door and got in back. Dylan closed the door for her.

"Thanks." He latched his seat belt. "Matt, I told

Collins where we were headed in case we called in for backup. He said you had already told him and given him the location. I should have known you would. You always cover all the bases."

"I have no clue what we'll run into out there. I wanted to make sure someone knew where we're headed."

"It's better to be safe than sorry," Dylan replied.

"You've got that right." Matt chuckled. "You're the one who made me think of it when you told me earlier that our cases took some unusual turns whenever Jessie was involved." Matt signaled and pulled onto Main Street.

"My exact words were that it's not simple when she's involved." Dylan turned and winked at her.

"Yeah, unusual." Matt made a U-turn at the intersection and headed out of town.

"You can both knock it off. Seems to me it's this town that has the problem, not me. I never had any issues until I moved here." Jessie sighed. She tapped Dylan's shoulder. "Are you going to run with us or are those clothes just for looks, pretty boy?"

Dylan laughed. "I'll leave you in my dust."

"He can talk the talk, Matt, but can he keep up? That's the question."

"You'll find out soon enough." Matt chuckled.

"This I've got to see." She smiled. "You wouldn't want to place a wager on how far you make it, would you? I have a ten spot in my pocket and would love to double it."

"Now, Jess, quit picking on Dylan. He's here to cover us. He could sit in the warm car and refuse to help at all. Be nice, sweetheart."

"You know, Jessie, I run more than Matt does. He doesn't like to jog, and I actually do." He turned and winked at her. "I'm more like you than you know."

"Do you hear voices and see ghosts, too?" Matt laughed.

"Nope, I can't say that I do." Dylan turned back around. "So what's the plan for tonight?"

"We carry our weapons and cell phones. I'm not sure what the coverage will be, but we should still carry them." He handed them each a small light attached to a band. "They're great to wear on your forehead. You'll have enough light to see the path in front of you."

As they talked, Jessie listened for a while. She was nervous, and she didn't know why. It didn't help that the fog had started rolling in. The night always seemed a tad more spooky when there was fog. Matt had used the words *cult* and *strange*, several times in the last few minutes, which didn't help. "How close will we get to their property?"

"As close as we can get without actually stepping foot on it." Matt turned off onto a dirt road. "A hiking trail owned by the state runs along the property line on one side. We'll stop at the trailhead and run along the path. With this fog bank, we'll have to keep each other in sight."

The closer they got, the more Jessie's nervousness intensified. The atmosphere was charged and not in a good way. She had reservations about being in the area at all. Why? After teasing Dylan, she would have to get out, run, and keep her mouth shut.

"You're quiet. Is everything okay?" Dylan turned his head to look at her.

"My mind is in overdrive."

"You aren't thinking of backing out are you?" Dylan teased her.

"No, but I believe we need to be careful. There is definitely an abnormal feeling in the atmosphere here."

Matt pulled into one of the parking spaces at the trailhead. "What do you mean by *abnormal*?"

"You know these feelings I get." She watched him nod. "I can't explain it exactly, but we need to be on our toes."

"Now do you see why I thought I should come along?" Dylan started to open the door. "The two of you keep together. Jessie, you need to stick to Matt like glue."

"I will. Don't worry."

****

It had all started out innocently enough. They kept a nice pace, conserving their energy and within sight of each other. The closer they got to the property line the more apprehension Jessie felt. A huge light marked the corner of the property. A chainlink fence with barbwire at the top ran the length and width of the land as far as her eyes could see. Jessie nearly lost it when a huge, ferocious dog hit the fence, growling and baring his teeth. The dog ran the fence line with them, growling the whole way. When the path veered away, she was happy, but it was short-lived. The sound of shots exploded in the dense air, and the bullet scuffed the ground in front of them. Matt grabbed her hand, pulling her off the path and through the trees with Dylan running beside them. The next bullet splintered bark on a tree to the right of them, sending it flying in their direction. Jessie kept her head down and ran as fast as she could. Matt let go of her hand for a moment to draw his gun. Dylan shot out the light. In all of the confusion, she thought he told her to keep running. She did, and now she was lost. The barking dog sounded like he was getting closer. Was she running toward him or had he jumped over the fence? She paused, bending over to hold her sides and suck in air. It was hard to hear anything in the thick, dense fog. The sound of Matt's voice or Dylan's would be nice about now. *Keep moving*, she told herself.

She pulled out her phone. Blast, no bars, no service, how would she ever find Matt in this murkiness? Hold on, she could see the outline of something ahead. Her eyes focused on a small structure in the midst of the trees. Its outline emerged through the spooky mist as she ran closer. What she saw stopped her in her tracks. Sinister in appearance, gothic in nature, its small spires and gargoyles stood watch and seemed to be staring at her. Creepy, and the fog didn't help. The gate creaked as she opened it to go inside. The building was smaller than it looked from a distance. Was it a small chapel? It didn't feel like any church she had ever been in. Maybe it was someone's tomb. She shivered. A strange odor met her when she opened the door. Incense, perhaps. The light from her headlamp told an eerie story as it danced on the walls. It settled on a strange stone slab in the center of the aisle, which had something smeared all over it. Oh, this was worse than she had thought. She slumped to the floor. She had stumbled into something awful and didn't want to be trapped here. Where were the dog and the person who had fired the shots? "Get hold of yourself, Jessie," she whispered. A quick check of her phone told her she still had no service. *Run, get out of here*, her mind screamed. Matt would want to see the place, and she had no idea how to tell him where it was located. Back outside, she took a deep breath, gasping for air. She couldn't believe this place was actually here in the middle of the woods. She checked her phone again. *Please let this work.* She held it up to snap a picture, then slipped out the gate and ran. The spots from the flash blinded her for a moment as she ran through the thick vapor.

****

"Where is she? I was holding her hand and then she was gone." Matt glanced over his shoulder.

"She kept running. She couldn't have gotten too far ahead." Dylan kept pace with Matt. "The problem is, you get turned around in the fog." He checked his phone. "I don't have any service, or I'd call her."

"With backup and daylight, we'll be paying the Youngs a little visit," Matt said grimly. "We have sufficient cause to question a few folks." Matt was weaving through the underbrush and swatting at tree branches in his way.

"Hell yes, you can't shoot at people on the trail even if it is near your property. Makes me wonder what they were doing." Dylan kept pace with Matt. "The dog wasn't very welcoming either."

"To tell you the truth I'd rather deal with the dog any day than his crazy owner shooting at me when I can't even see where he's hiding. The dog can bite, but a bullet can kill." Matt paused to listen. "Do you hear anything?"

"Besides our heavy breathing? I don't hear anything but Fido's barking." Dylan stopped beside Matt.

"More like Brutus than a Fido if you ask me." Matt started to jog again. He headed parallel with the property, hoping to close the distance between them and the trail as they moved away from the compound.

"We should be getting near the path. There aren't as many trees."

"Do you hear that?" Matt motioned for Dylan to stop. The sound was louder.

Dylan stopped. "Whatever it is, it's getting closer."

The fog made it hard to tell where the sound was coming from. Matt stood silent, trying to catch sight of any movement. Someone burst from the fog, slammed into him, and he found himself on the ground with Jessie sprawled on top of him.

"Ouch." She rolled off him. "You're like hitting a brick wall, but I'm sure glad it's you I ran into."

"Me too, sweetheart."

"If you two are finished?" Dylan chuckled and extended his hand to help Jessie up. "Where have you been?"

"I thought one of you told me to keep running, so I did." Jessie pulled her phone out of her pocket to see if the picture was on it. "You'll never believe what I found." She held up a fuzzy picture for him to see, and went on to tell him about the makeshift altar, the incense, and what looked like fresh blood. "It was hard to tell in the limited light I had. You'll have to find it at some point. Whatever it's used for is not good. I know what I felt and what I saw. It was bad."

Matt could hear the apprehension in her voice. "Could you find it again?"

"I have no idea. I don't know how I discovered it, to begin with, or how I even located you. I was trying to work my way back to the car."

"If it was the car you wanted, you were headed the wrong way. You were on your way back toward the Young's property. I'm sure you don't want to go back there tonight."

"No way, not with a shooter and a dog guarding it."

Matt grabbed her hand. "I'm not letting you out of my sight again. If we're lost, we'll all be lost together."

"Sounds good to me. It's spooky out here. I don't care if I never see that place in the dark again."

"If we keep heading this way, we should intersect with the trail fairly soon. At least, I hope so. I'm hungry. Whose stupid idea was it to run tonight in the fog anyway?"

"Yours," Dylan and Jessie said at the same time.

It took another fifteen minutes, but he had been right. They found the path, which took them to the car. The evening hadn't gone the way he'd planned.

"We'll have to get a team out here and scour the woods in the daylight. Is anyone besides me up for a late dinner?"

"I am," Dylan said eagerly.

"Me, too." Jessie patted Dylan's shoulder. When he turned to look at her, she handed him a ten dollar bill. "You won the wager, fair and square. You do know how to run." She smiled.

Chapter 15

"Matt, Jeremy is on line one." Kenny stuck his head in the door.

"Thanks." He reached for his phone. "Jeremy, what do you have for me?"

"I found Olivia in the Missing Person's database. I'm sending a picture over to see if she's the girl. She will look a little different now. This picture was from a few years ago when she was fifteen. Still, you should be able to tell if it's her. She grew up in Tampa Bay. Her parents said that at the time she went missing, their daughter seemed to have a fascination with someone she had met online." Jeremy paused.

"I've heard the same story a few times with different players."

"It happens often enough. I wish the Internet came with a warning for kids to be wary of any unknown person they meet online. It might spare them a lot of heartaches."

"It wouldn't hurt for parents to be Internet savvy, too. They need to know the pitfalls out there." Matt wrote Olivia's name on his notepad. "She's been gone for a little over a year. I have no proof the guy she's with now is the same one she was interested in. I would love to haul his sorry ass to jail, but I have nothing to pin on him. I haven't even talked to Olivia yet. He's hit her, but I have no proof other than what Jessie's told me."

"I know from working on domestic violence reports with Jessie in the past that women don't usually turn the guys in. They're too afraid of the man to do anything. Most of the men are like Sally's husband in society."

"How's that?" Matt asked.

"Bruce Kingman looks like a model citizen by all accounts. No display of temper, no trouble on the job or with the police until a few weeks ago when he was arrested for domestic violence. He was released a few hours later with a slap on the wrist. The only other mark on his record was the restraining order that showed up a few days ago. Her father told me Sally finally called the police the last time he beat her, but only after her lawyer forced the issue."

"I'm glad the lawyer pushed her to do it," Matt replied.

"So is her dad. Her attorney also told Sally to get to the hospital and be sure that the ER personnel documented the bruises which could be used as evidence."

"I've seen those photos. It's a good thing they have them. Bruce doesn't look quite as good when you see what he did to her."

"Still he'll have folks who will stand up for his character if he's well liked. Plus only one arrest makes it look like a single incident," Jeremy said.

Matt didn't like where this was headed. "Could her husband have a friend in the police department? There has to be someone with knowledge of the abuse besides her parents. A girlfriend, a co-worker, or one of his friends."

"I'm not sure. I'll ask Jessie to find out." Jeremy paused. "Sally seemed to be really popular, but people I talked to at her job had noticed a big change in her the last few years. She had become more reclusive and withdrawn. She went home right after work and didn't participate in social activities. It fits the scenario of someone being abused."

"Did you talk to anyone else about her?"

"Her mother had plenty to say, and none of it was nice when it came to Bruce. According to her, it's been going on for a few years. Sally was afraid of him. They saw their daughter change before their eyes, and they felt powerless to stop it. He was a good manipulator and always talked Sally into coming back. They were afraid he would do it again if he didn't kill her first."

"Another familiar story." Matt turned his chair around to look at the window. "Did you find out anything about the Youngs?"

"The Youngs, according to all the records I searched, don't exist. There are no electric bills, social security numbers, or tax records available. They must be totally off the grid." Jeremy took a deep breath. "I find that to be a scary proposition in this day and age."

"It's unusual all right." Matt frowned.

"There is the report on Larissa, but that's it, nothing more. It's as if they don't exist. Which makes me wonder if they are covering up something besides their real identity."

"An angle to consider. We were running near the property last night on state land, not theirs, and got shot at. I'd say something is definitely going on out there. When Jessie got separated from us, she stumbled upon a crypt somewhere in the woods with a bloody altar in it. I've requested a ride-along with the Sheriff when he goes to question them about the shots. I wasn't pleased with their welcoming committee. I have a team who will be searching the area tomorrow while we're keeping the Youngs too busy to shoot, hopefully."

"If I had a photo to scan I might be able to do something with facial recognition to find out who they really are." Jeremy cleared his throat. "Of course, I'm speculating. Maybe they're really off the grid, but I find that hard to believe."

"I'll try to get you a picture, even if I have to use my phone. Thanks, Jeremy, this helps a lot. I'll give the info to Jessie about Olivia. Jessie might be able to use it to rescue her."

"I'll keep searching. Hopefully, I'll find something on the Youngs. I'll stay in touch. You should have the picture in your email."

"Okay, Jeremy, thanks." Matt opened up his email and printed a copy of the picture. Only Jessie would know if this looked like Olivia.

****

"Hey, Jessie." Molly stuck her head in from Joe's. "I wanted to stop by earlier and tell you that when I opened up the coffee shop, there was a woman hanging around at the back of your store. When I asked her if I could help, she shook her head and walked away. I don't think she was trying to break in or anything. She seemed lost to me."

"Thanks for letting me know, Molly." Jessie suppressed a sigh. "I know who it was. I've been helping her out when I can."

"I thought maybe it was something like that, but I thought I should let you know." Molly turned back to the coffee shop. "She seemed down on her luck."

"If you see her again give her something to eat. I would be happy to pay for anything later. She has to be hungry. Can you keep it a secret that she's here? Her life may depend on it."

"Of course, I can. I thought the woman appeared desperate to me." Molly turned back, her face full of concern. "I wanted to help, but she left the minute I asked her if I could."

"She's fleeing from an abusive situation. I'm trying to talk her into going to a shelter. Her name is Olivia, and she's afraid her husband will find her. I have no clue where she's sleeping or how she's eating." Jessie wanted to pull her hair in frustration. Why couldn't Olivia let her help? "The baby she's carrying needs her to be well."

Molly shook her head. "When I hear about a situation like this I realize how fortunate I am to have a great man like Kenny in my life."

"I know. I feel the same way about Matt."

"We'll take care of her together." Molly raised her hand as if in a pledge. "I want to help."

"Thank you, Molly, it might take both of us to help her. The man looking for her comes into my store, and I've seen him in the coffee shop. He drives a motorhome, which is often parked in the church parking lot."

"Oh, I think I know the guy you're talking about. A clean-cut man that seems wound tight."

"That's the one." Jessie's smile broadened. She was excited that someone else understood the situation. "Don't let him know that you've seen her."

"You can count on me." Molly glanced into the

coffee shop. "I have to go. I have customers. Keep me in the loop."

"I will."

Jessie noticed the chair sliding jerkily across the floor to a new location. She moved quickly to stop its progress. "Oh, no you don't." If anyone saw it, what would they think? Larissa had a mind of her own, whimsical with a bit of a temper. Jessie sighed and bent over to pick up the sign that was now lying on the floor. A tug of war ensued until Jessie threatened to put her and the chair in the backroom. As if she had any control over the actions of a ghost. She turned the chair exactly the same way it had been before and stuck the sign back on it. "Behave yourself." Jessie knew what was coming next as she walked away. She ducked in time as the book sailed over her head, barely missing her. It skidded over the counter and onto the floor with a thud.

Wouldn't you know it, a temperamental spirit had picked her store to wait in. "I wish you could tell me how to help you." Jessie went into the back room and carried out a stack of new books.

There had to be a better way to communicate with Larissa. And no, she wasn't about to have a séance or use an ouija board. She was having a hard enough time accepting all the weird stuff happening to her as it was.

Chapter 16

Jessie tossed and turned all night. She knew, without a doubt, Larissa was at her shop for a reason. The first chance she had today, she would mention the Youngs and see what happened. Larissa was more temperamental than Gina had been so it could get interesting. *Prepare for anything* was her new motto. Jessie parked her car behind the bookstore, intending to walk across to the church. Everything changed the moment she saw Olivia huddled against the back door.

Jessie moved fast and reached for her. "Let's get you inside before anyone sees you." Jessie helped her stand and held onto her as she swayed on her feet. Unlocking the door, Jessie opened it to let her in. She eased Olivia against the wall long enough to grab a chair for her sit in. "You have to accept help, Olivia. You can't keep going on like this. If all this running doesn't kill you first, it can harm your baby."

"I know." She faltered. "I'm ready now. I'm too tired to run anymore, and I have nowhere to go." Tears spilled from her eyes, and she started sobbing.

Jessie called Matt and told him to get there quickly and come to the back of the store. She also arranged for Audrey to take her place at the church. Jessie sat next to Olivia, handing her one tissue after another. "The body of a woman showed up at the church in the trash. I'm telling you this because she had also been abused, and I don't want the same thing to happen to you."

"Do you know who she was?" Olivia stopped crying long enough to look at Jessie.

"Her name was Larissa Young."

Olivia wrapped her arms around herself, and she wept more earnestly. "No, please, not Larissa." She said it over and over again as she continued to weep.

"Do you know her?" Jessie watched her closely.

"Yes," she gasped.

Jessie moved to unlock and open the door when Matt knocked. "She knows Larissa." Jessie spoke softly as she leaned close and whispered in his ear. "Olivia, this is Chief Parker. He can help you if you let him. He's also a close personal friend of mine, and you can trust him." Olivia nodded, her eyes opened wide and scared.

He sat beside Olivia and waited for her weeping to subside enough to talk. "Jessie told me you knew Larissa. Can you tell me how?"

She sniffed. "She's my cousin. Her mother and my mother are sisters. Oh God, I can't believe she's dead. How...what happened?"

Jessie took her hand and looked at Matt.

"Murdered." Matt paused. "It wasn't pretty." He handed her another tissue. "Do you have any idea who could have done this to her?"

Her voice was quiet but steady. "It's a long story, but I need to tell someone. Maybe it will help you find her killer."

"We have time to listen. Start when you're ready." Matt turned on his pocket-size recorder.

Olivia closed her eyes. "I met Roger online. I was only seventeen at the time. He was handsome, charming, and flattered me. I ran away with him. I had no idea where we were headed or what my life would be like, but I was in love. At seventeen, that's all that matters. Not even the sorrow I would cause my parents could have stopped me." Her expression was gloomy. "I know—sad, huh? Roger promised to marry me as soon as we reached our destination. I left a note explaining it all to my parents and promising to contact them as soon as we got there. After being on the road for several days, I found out we were headed to my cousin's family. I should have told my parents then, but Roger convinced me they would send the police to take me back. I never called." A tear slipped down her cheek.

"How did Roger know about the compound?" Matt jotted a few notes.

"Roger's best friend, Adam, was living there and wanted him to come. He had told Roger he had found the answers to life, and that it was the perfect place to raise a family. I should add that Roger was a perfect gentleman the whole trip. He never touched me in any way, which at the time, I found a little odd." She sniffed.

"Before you continue would you like a bagel and tea?" Jessie could hear Olivia's rumbling stomach.

"Please?" Her weary eyes brightened. "I'm so hungry."

"How long has it been since you last ate?" Jessie put the teabag in hot water.

"I'm not sure. Maybe a day or two." Olivia started wolfing down the bagel as soon as Jessie handed it to her.

"Continue when you're ready." Matt waited

patiently as Jessie handed her an apple when she had finished off the bagel. She wiped her mouth with the back of her hand.

"In the beginning, everything seemed okay. One thing I found strange was that my aunt didn't want me to tell my mom where I was. They wouldn't let me communicate with my parents in any way—not even to ask them to my wedding. For all my parents knew, I could be dead. Randy Phillips took my phone my first day there and smashed it. He said my family would be able to track the GPS, and they couldn't let that happen. They wouldn't let me use the radio they had at the compound; they said it was only for emergencies." She smiled tentatively. "As soon as I can, I want to call my mom."

"You can call her today," Matt told her. "Why didn't your aunt want you to talk to your mom?"

"I don't know. My aunt was really nice to me when my uncle was around, but when he wasn't near she kept telling me my mom would try to take me away from Roger, so it was best she didn't know where I was. It confused me. Over time, I began to understand, though."

"What did you come to understand?" Matt sat forward in his chair.

"It was a strange place. My uncle controlled everyone, along with another group of men. They were called the Chosen Elders. Everyone had to work on the compound. Women were basically subservient to the men. We couldn't wear pants, and we had to be submissive. Roger loved it, and so did Adam. It was definitely better for the men. In time, Roger became like all the other men there. He beat me to keep me in line. More than once he told me it was because he loved me."

"That's a different take on love." Matt glanced at Jessie, shaking his head.

"I know Larissa hated it. On more than one occasion she told me she was going to run away. She had grown up in the compound and had her own horror stories to tell." Olivia paused to wipe her nose. "You know what I find strange?"

"No, what?" Jessie found herself mesmerized by her story. She could also see Larissa standing behind Olivia's chair.

"I find it hard to understand why folks who are supposedly religious can sometimes be so mean to others and yet consider themselves better."

"*Better* is questionable," Jessie blurted out.

"Mean in what way?" Matt looked at his notepad and scribbled his thoughts on it.

"Most of the families had several kids. They even have their own school. Believe me, no kid ever wanted to goof around in their classes. They wouldn't be seen for a few days if they did, and when they came back, they didn't talk about it. You could see the black and blue marks if a sleeve inched up. I know. I saw it up close and personal. My job at the compound was as a teacher's assistant." She frowned. "Larissa suffered the most. They made an example out of her. She loved music and was a gifted singer. Her voice was a thing of beauty. They always called her rebellious because she listened to music on the radio she had hidden and sang the songs. The leaders would lock her up somewhere for days. I never found the place, but I tried. I would have let her out for sure." She took the tissue Matt handed her. "I asked Adam once why, if they had found the answers to life, were they such a stern and unhappy group?" Her voice trailed off.

"What was his answer?" Jessie looked at her watch. It was almost time to open the store. Jessie saw the sad expression on Larissa's face as she moved around Olivia.

"He never answered." Her lips trembled. "Roger blew up at me, and I was marked as a troublemaker from that day on. One thing I was happy about; I was there long enough to see Larissa run away. Her father had to answer to the elders the way he had made so many others do. I thought she was free of the place. They must have caught up with her. I ran away a couple of times, too, but Roger always found me and took me back." She shuddered deeply. "I can't go back there ever again."

"Do you have any idea who might have killed Larissa?"

"Who knows?" Her expression was bleak. "It could be anyone. Adam said he was in love with her. Maybe it was her father or one of those who measured out the punishment. No one that I know of ever died from it before, though."

"Is Adam still at the compound?" Jessie asked.

"As far as I know, he never left."

"I want to take you to the station with me. You'll be safe there, and we will contact your parents. The best thing we can do is get you back home to your family in Florida and out of the area. Does that sound good to you?" Olivia nodded her head. "Jessie's store will be opening soon, and I don't want anyone to see you who might be able to tip them off to your location."

"Did you know Larissa was pregnant?" Jessie stood. It was time open the store.

"No." Olivia's eyes widened. "And she wasn't married. Her parents would be plenty angry about a pregnancy out of marriage. It would make them look bad. It could be the reason she is dead. Did the baby die too?"

"Her baby survived." Jessie put a gentle hand on her shoulder. "She managed to give birth before she died. The baby is a little girl and what Larissa did to bring her into the world was truly courageous."

"Larissa was kind to me." Tears had begun to leak from her eyes again. "I will miss her, and the world will miss getting to know a brilliant singer." She stood and hugged Jessie. "Thank you for helping me. I knew I could come back, and you'd know what to do." Olivia looked at Matt. "I'm ready to go. I hope my parents will let me come back until I can get on my feet."

****

Jessie watched Matt and Olivia drive away. She locked the back door and went out front to open the store for the day. "Well, what do you think of your cousin now, Larissa? We are one step closer to finding who did this to you. I'm sorry for all that you suffered in your life. It's hard to imagine that there are still groups out there like this. Larissa, we need your help to narrow this down."

Jessie felt a whoosh of cool air brush past her. Larissa passed by her again as Jessie opened the doors into the coffee shop, and again when she opened the front door. "Are you trying to tell me something? I wish I understood. Did I tell you, Larissa, I went running out by your parents' land? Someone shot at us, which was bad enough, but I got turned around in the fog. I ended up in a creepy place that looked like someone's tomb in the woods." Jessie watched fixated as books suddenly spiraled up from the display table, zipping in every direction like a disturbed hive of bees. Reba walked in the door as a book plopped to the ground in front of her.

Reba picked up the book, eyed the others swirling in the air, and slapped her hand to her forehead. "My, oh my. What is going on here?"

"I believe—at least this is my take on it—that I have an angry ghost named Larissa trying to tell me something. The problem is I have no idea what it is."

"What were you talking about when this erupted?" Reba ducked quickly before a flying book hit her.

"A crypt in the woods. I haven't had time to tell you about it yet."

"Larissa, dear, you need to quit making such a fuss. We will figure out what you're trying to tell us, but you must quit this *now*." Reba's voice rose a notch, and all the books fell to the ground at once.

"How did you get her to stop?"

"I told her to."

"Yes, I know that." Jessie let her breath out in exasperation. "Why did she listen to you?"

"Because I meant it." Reba edged past Jessie to stand in front of her. "You'll learn soon enough, dear."

"I hope I learn fast. This is getting ridiculous." Jessie picked up the books and arranged them once again on the display table. Hopefully, no one else had seen the floating books. "This has been some morning, and it's only beginning."

"Why don't you sit down and tell me all about it, dear. You could use a moment to compose yourself before you have to greet customers."

Jessie told Reba about their run near the Young's property, finding the spooky crypt with its blood-stained altar, and finding Olivia this morning. She repeated the story Olivia had told them.

"My goodness, you've had an eventful few days. Now to figure out what it all means and what you need to do about it."

"I forgot to mention that my friend Sally is here, and she's also being abused by her husband. Who, unless I miss my guess, is on his way out here to get her. Soon our town will be filled with angry husbands looking for their wives." She managed a shaky laugh. "I'm sure they'll blame me. That's how it works."

"No time for self-pity, young lady. We must devise a plan." Reba smiled to take the edge off her words. "I'm sure you'll have a run-in with a couple of them. I do want to caution you, though. The answers to this case will seem obvious, but they're not. You'll have to dig deep for the truth, and it may be found where you aren't looking."

"What does that mean?" Jessie frowned, shaking her head.

"It might have started with Larissa's family, but there're more people involved in it now. Keep your eyes and ears open, my dear, and you'll figure it out."

"I'm more confused than ever."

"You'll solve it. You, and that nice Mr. Parker, of course. Here's my list of books that I've come for. I do enjoy my reading time whenever I can get it."

Jessie helped her find the titles, rang up her purchases, and walked her to the door. "Enjoy your books. You left me with a lot to think about."

"I will. Jessie, wait for the answer." Her eyes softened, and she smiled gently. "It'll come to you when and where you least expect it. With it will come some positive changes to Blue Cove and a happy event, too. I'm excited to see what will happen to our town because of this case." Reba waved as she stepped out the door.

Chapter 17

Jessie mulled over Reba's words whenever she got a chance. Nothing was ever as it seemed. She couldn't wait to tell Matt about Larissa and her swirling books. It still amazed Jessie that Larissa tried to communicate. Jessie smiled, still speculating about how Reba had managed to stop Larissa. She had actually behaved when Reba told her to. No more goofing around. She nodded emphatically. If Jessie had to live with this strange stuff, she'd better figure out how to get a handle on it, too. She saw Larissa watching her. In Palm Springs, those snake-like creatures had obeyed her when she told them to leave. Her hand went to her forehead. Of course. She smiled. She did know what to do, and she had better start acting like it. This wasn't the time for a mental vacation. People's lives depended on her, that's why they were here. Her ringing phone sent her searching for it again. This time, it was found under the counter.

"Hi, sweetheart, I wanted to let you know that Olivia's parents were thrilled to hear from her. They want her home ASAP. They are coming here to fly home with her."

"What was their reaction?"

"Her mother cried, which I suppose is normal under the circumstances. She was also stunned to hear that Olivia had been with her sister the whole time.

Angry might be too mild a word for her reaction when she found out that her sister wouldn't let Olivia call."

"What's up with her and the sister?"

"Good question. Olivia's mother promised to tell me more when she gets here. For tonight, Olivia will be staying with Joe Collins and his wife. They'll keep her safe."

"At least she won't be wandering outside." Jessie paused. "Matt, be sure she eats soon. She needs to keep up her strength."

"She's doing that right now. Marcy's making sure she goes slow and easy, so she doesn't make herself sick. I couldn't help noticing earlier how fast she ate that bagel. I have a doctor coming over to check her out this afternoon, too. We want to make sure she's well enough to fly."

"Good idea. I'm glad you thought of it." She swiped at the dust filming the counter.

"Oh, and by the way, it was her outside my house that night I heard the woman crying. She has been wandering around town the last several nights and hiding during the day."

"I'm glad one mystery is solved at least. I was concerned that my weirdness was rubbing off on you." She smiled. "It's comforting to know you're okay, and I'm the only strange one in town. Although, Reba may be a tad weirder than me." Jessie told him about her morning. "She told Larissa to stop, and she did. Just like that." Jessie snapped her fingers. "I'm still in awe of her."

He laughed. "Jess, sweetheart, you are in a league all of your own. Did anyone else happen to see the swirling books?"

"Good heavens, I hope not. I'll become the 'haunted bookstore' for sure, and nobody will dare come here! Matt, if I were you, I would think twice about this whole relationship thing. If you married me, all this stuff might be happening in your home on a regular basis. It's something for you to thoroughly consider."

"You can't scare me off that easily." He sounded amused. "I've always liked a good challenge."

"Yes, I remember. You've told me often enough." She had to smile. "But don't say I didn't warn you."

"Duly noted; I'm not going anywhere."

"Not to change the subject, but Reba did mention that while it all might have started with the Young family, there are now more people involved. She told me that the answer isn't the obvious one."

"Of course not, it couldn't be an easy case." He chuckled. "We'll get to the truth eventually—with a little luck."

"Hopefully, I'll find a better way to communicate with Larissa, and she'll help us out."

"It would be nice, but we don't need her help to solve the case. Before I forget, I need to tell you a couple of things. I'm going with Deputy Taylor to pay a little visit to the Youngs tomorrow morning. He's going to introduce me as the person in charge of their daughter's murder investigation."

"Have they ever been questioned in regards to her murder?"

"No, that's why I'm going with Taylor. The property is in the county's jurisdiction, but the body is in mine. We're trying to get a peaceful foot in the door. When Kip and Dylan went out to tell them about

Larissa's death, an armed guard met them at the gate and called for the parents. Dylan said they showed minimal emotion. Larissa's father told him they figured she'd probably wind up dead soon enough because of the way she was living. The mother didn't say anything, but there were tears in her eyes. She stood behind her husband the whole time."

"Is it legal to have an armed guard?"

"If they're on their own property, protecting their own land, and not menacing, it's legal in most areas. And if they have a license to carry, it's legal. The man had one; Dylan checked. He never threatened them or pointed the gun at them. The FBI tracks different groups like this all over the country. Tom is looking into the Youngs for me to see if they are on a watch list."

"We don't know half of what goes on around us, do we?"

"Probably not."

"Thanks for letting me know about Olivia." She glanced out the front window. "Uh-oh. I'm about to get real busy. A bus parked across the street and people are headed to the coffee shop and hopefully into my store from there."

"Do you have to entertain Sally tonight?"

"No, she's having dinner with Liam to discuss her legal options for dealing with Bruce. Speaking of Sally, did you find a place for her?"

"Not yet, but if a spot doesn't open up soon, I have someone who will take her in for a few days. It's best you have no idea where she will be. I'm almost positive Bruce will pester you about her location. For a while, you really won't have any idea."

"That's fine." She kept an eye on the door that led to the coffee shop. "I know it's for her safety."

"I'll stop by after work, Let's go to dinner."

"Sounds good to me. See you later."

****

Matt updated Olivia's file. The events of a few nights ago replayed in his mind. Had the shooter been on the Young's property? He wasn't so sure. Between the confusion of the moment and the dog hitting the fence and making a racket, the truth was that the shooter could have been hiding anywhere. It didn't make sense the Youngs would jeopardize their low profile by doing something that stupid. Groups like this wanted to fly under the radar. They didn't want anyone involved in their business, especially the police.

He checked his watch. Ten minutes until he met with Dylan and Kip. Matt had a good idea about what he wanted them to check on. Stepping out into the hall, he made his way to the fresh pot of coffee and filled his cup. *Do your job,* he chided himself. *It's too early to be tired.* Back at his desk, he scribbled a few notes on his notepad while he waited.

Kip arrived first and sat, followed by Dylan a few minutes later. Matt laid his pencil down on the desk. "Do you want coffee? There's a fresh pot."

"None for me." Dylan took a quick look at his phone messages while Kip got a cup. "What's on your mind?"

"What do you think about the possibility our shooter wasn't on the Young's land?"

"It sure seemed like it was coming from there to me."

"The more I consider it, the more I think it was

someone hidden in the trees outside the property. There are too many things that don't add up."

"Like?" Dylan's brow rose.

"They're off the grid. Jeremy couldn't find anything on them at all. Why would they do anything as stupid as to shoot at runners on state land? We weren't trespassing. I don't believe they'd want the attention that comes with breaking the law."

"Okay, suppose you're right." Dylan frowned. "Who *was* doing the shooting, and where were they hiding?"

"That's what I want you both to check into tomorrow. Go back to where we were when the shots were fired. Search the area for any sign of the bullets or casings that might have been left behind. Something isn't adding up." Matt clicked his pen on and off. "The Youngs have been careful to stay under the radar up to now, and I don't think they are involved in this. Their daughter's murder is a different story. We're meeting with her parents tomorrow regarding her death."

"We'll take care of it. Do you want us to see if we can find the crypt Jessie talked about?" Dylan asked. "It might be easier to find during daylight."

"If you have time, go ahead. When Jessie mentioned stumbling upon it to Larissa, she wasn't happy."

"How can you tell whether a ghost is happy or not?" Dylan chuckled.

"Trust me, you wouldn't want to know." Matt grinned.

"Our cases have gotten a helluva lot more interesting since she moved to town."

"I agree. And dangerous." Kip frowned. "I used to

give out traffic tickets and make arrests for vandalism. Not exciting, but not hazardous either."

"My gut tells me we have to watch out for Jessie. Bruce thinks Sally is with her, and he'll logically blame her for Sally leaving him. If Roger suspects Jessie lied to him and helped Olivia, he'll take it out on her. We have two angry, irrational men looking for someone to blame for their problems, and Jessie has a target on her back." Matt handed them each a copy of his notes. "Read these, and we'll discuss more after we get back tomorrow."

"Is it possible Bruce is already in the area? Could he be our shooter?" Dylan looked over the page of notes Matt had handed him.

"Or Roger, for that matter?" Kip asked.

"It could be anyone, including someone on the Young's property," Matt responded. "I get the distinct feeling someone knew who we were and wanted us out of the way. A few of the shots were too close for comfort."

Dylan nodded. "Add Larissa's murderer to an active shooter, and I'd say we've got our hands full." Dylan stood to leave. "We'll get back to you after we finish tomorrow."

"Did you find a place for Sally?" Kip stood to follow Dylan.

"If a shelter doesn't open up, I've secured a place for her in a few days. She'll move in with Joe and his wife. I didn't tell Jessie where she'll be. I don't want her to know any details because Bruce will certainly be watching her."

"We'll keep our eyes open for strangers in town. Do you have pictures of either man?"

"I'll try to get their photos to you before the day is over. I don't have any on file, but Jeremy should be able to get a photo of Bruce from the Internet and with any luck, one of Roger, as well."

"Sounds good."

"We'll meet again tomorrow before the end of your shifts." Dylan nodded at Matt as he walked out of the office.

Kip stopped at the door. "Chief, do you have any idea of a suspect yet?"

"Nothing firm, Kip." He frowned. "I have a theory I'm working on but no firm evidence. Tomorrow will either point me in that direction or nix it."

"I hope it points you toward the murderer. I can't help thinking about Larissa and her little girl that she'll never be able to hold. It was a shock to see her in the dumpster like a piece of trash." Kip shook his head. "I want to do everything I can to help find her murderer. You can count me in until we find him."

"Thanks, I know I can count on you." Matt eyed him, noticing the shadows beneath his eyes. "Do you need to talk to someone about it?"

"I might." Kip chewed his lip. "I've seen the crime scene in my mind several times over the last few days. Coming on the heels of our last case, it's...it's unsettling. I...need a way to get past it."

Matt handed Kip a business card. "This is the doc I go to."

"You?"

"Yes, me. Look, Kip, this stuff isn't easy." He put a hand on Kip's shoulder. "No one can brush it off, and if they say they can, they're fooling themselves."

"Thanks, Matt." Kip stuck the card in his pocket.

"I'm going to call."

"Good, you'll be glad you did."

****

The store was quiet for the first time in several hours when she finally closed the doors into Java Joe's. Clicking the lock on the front door brought on a happy sigh. Jessie's prediction had been right. It was a busy day. Two bus tours had brought many customers to the coffee shop, and quite a few had wandered into her store. She had a nice surprise when she added up the sales for the day. Time to restock! She grabbed a stack of books in the back room and carried them out front to replace the ones she had sold off the table.

With the last of her closing routine done, Jessie sat in the big leather chair to wait for Matt. Dinner out sounded much better than cooking. Her feet would be happy to do no more standing tonight. Jessie found it odd that she hadn't seen Roger's motorhome for a few days. Maybe he had decided to move on. From the sounds of it, the best thing he could do would be to get away from Larissa's family, but people rarely did what was best for themselves, herself included. She smiled and turned to Larissa.

"Keep watch over the store for me." Jessie shook her head. "I always tell you the same thing every time I leave." She frowned at the chair. "Do you stay here after I'm gone or do you roam about? I guess I never thought about what you do while I'm not around. It's strange enough to think about you being here at all." Jessie saw Matt pull into the parking space in front of the store and got to her feet. "Goodbye," she said as she opened the door. Admittedly she was glad to be out from under her ghost's watchful eyes. Jessie dropped the keys into Matt's open hand. He locked the door for her.

"Is Patterson's okay? It's too nice not to walk tonight."

She nodded. Her feet complained the whole way, but Jessie wasn't going to say a word about them. She enjoyed walking hand in hand with Matt in the quiet of the moment. She wasn't alone with him after all, she discovered. From the corner of her eye, she could see Larissa moving along beside them. One of her questions was answered anyway.

Chapter 18

The next morning Matt grabbed a coffee from Joe's before heading out of town. He was meeting Deputy Taylor at the turnoff near the Young's compound in an hour. Jessie was standing behind the counter in her store with a perplexed look on her face. He grinned and tapped on the door. "Good morning, sunshine," he said when she opened the door to let him in.

"I swear!" She stood back to let him in. "I hope this crime is solved soon, and Larissa can go to wherever she needs to be." She placed her hands firmly on her hips. "She does this to get a rise out of me."

"Does what?" Matt was baffled by what had her so riled. Everything seemed normal to him.

"Can't you see it?" She looked stunned.

"See what?" He looked around and didn't see anything strange.

"She has rearranged everything. We don't have the same design ideas at all. Can't you see the difference?" Matt shook his head. "Men," she mumbled. "How can you not see it? The books I had out on the display table last night have all been replaced by ghost stories. Not everyone who comes in here likes ghost stories." Her chin rose along with her voice.

Matt gave her a lopsided grin. She was pretty when she was upset. "I'm sorry."

"I'm glad *you're* enjoying this. To add insult to injury, my favorite abstract painting was in the back room this morning, covered with a towel."

Matt laughed aloud; he couldn't help it. This was the most absurd conversation he had ever had. "I don't know what to say." He sputtered out the words between laughs.

"Did you know she was beside us as we walked to Patterson's last night? No, how could you? I'm the only one who can see her." She gestured toward the chair. "You can wipe that silly grin off your face. She was there the entire time we ate. I felt like I was being spied on." She pointed her finger at his chest and jabbed it a couple of times. "You'd better get this guy soon, or I might have to take matters into my own hands."

Matt saw the hardback coming and grabbed the book out of the air before it hit her. "You might want to keep only small paperbacks near her. She throws well for a ghost." His booming laugh filled the air along with Jessie's peels of laughter. Another crisis deterred in Blue Cove. He smiled. "Do you think you can handle her today? I'm headed out to her family's compound to talk with them."

"I work at the church this morning. Audrey will be here. Larissa's usually quiet when others are around. You wouldn't want to take her with you, would you?"

Matt shook his head. "Dylan and Kip will be looking for the crypt while we keep her parents busy. Wow!" He ducked and managed to grab the small hurricane lamp before it beaned him.

"Larissa, stop it." Jessie faced the chair, fists on her hips. "If you're going to stay here, you have to stop now."

"Let's hope she listens." He placed the lamp on the counter. "I'll let you put this where you want it when I'm gone."

"I hope she behaves. If not, I may have to call Reba." Jessie walked with him to the door. "I'm sorry; you get all this crazy stuff along with me."

"I'm happy to have you." He tilted her face up and kissed her. "Stay safe, and remember to move hard objects away from where she's sitting. She has a great aim." He grinned and kissed her again. "Jess, when this is over, you and I are going out of town for a few days. You need it, and so do I."

"Sounds divine." She traced his firm jaw. Her hand lingered a moment on his cheek, then she sent him on his way.

****

Jessie waved as Matt drove away. What a morning. She smiled at Audrey as she walked in. "You know where to find me if you need me." Jessie put on her jacket.

"I'm sure I won't. See you in a while." Audrey waved at her.

Jessie walked across the street to the church with a plan formulating in her mind. She wanted to talk to Pastor John about it. She had finished her article on Larissa for Max and her old boss, Neil. It brought up so many memories of interviews she had done on the subject of domestic violence. She couldn't stand by any longer and do nothing. If Sally could get her life together, this would be the perfect place for her to work at helping women.

Jessie stepped through the door of the church and moved down the hall toward the office. A sudden sense of being followed filled her. A quick search around of the area showed no one. Still the feeling lingered. Unlocking the office, she placed her purse on the desk and paused to answer the ringing phone.

"First Community Church, may I help you?"

"Is this the lady who owns the bookstore?" The woman's voice was barely audible.

"It is. How can I help you?" Jessie leaned against the edge of the desk. It was then that she saw Larissa. She was watching Jessie from the hall.

"I don't have much time; he'll be back. Please, I need help. I don't want to end up dead." The woman began to cry.

"What's your name? Do you want to talk to a pastor?"

"No. When I can, I'll come to you." The woman gasped, and the phone clicked off.

She was more resolved than ever to talk to Pastor John. Jessie had never seen Larissa here before, so why was she here now? Jessie made a pot of coffee, turned her computer on, and waited for the pastors to arrive.

"Hey, Blondie." Melinda walked in and plopped down in the chair. "It's always good to see you sitting behind the desk."

"Good morning, Red." Jessie smiled when she saw Melinda's familiar pencil sticking out of her curls on the top of her head.

"So much stuff has happened since you came to work here, the quiet days are hardly bearable anymore. How's our friend over in your store?" she whispered.

"Actually, she's standing in the hall." Jessie pointed to where she could see Larissa.

"If that don't beat all. Has she ever followed you

here before?" Melinda asked.

"Not that I've ever noticed."

"And you would have seen her." Melinda slapped her knee with a hoot. "You have your own ghoul following. I wonder what's up." Melinda pushed her glasses back up on her nose. "Whenever one shows up here, they seem to attract others."

"Let's hope this time it doesn't happen."

"I rather like it, to tell you the truth."

"Good heavens, why?" Jessie sputtered.

"It's hard for me to explain, but I find comfort in them being around."

"You can keep Larissa if you want. She's been upset all morning."

"Has she zapped someone again?"

"No, but she rearranged my store and threw a few books to make her point."

"You live an exciting life." Melinda chuckled. "Or a charmed one, in the magical sense of the word."

"I'd rather it was ordinary. Quiet would be nice and without flying books." Jessie enjoyed the range of emotions playing out on Melinda's face.

"I bet she's here to get Gina to join with her in finding her killer." Melinda shook her head in frustration. "Would you listen to me? As if I would know. This is more up your alley."

"I'm the new kid on the block. You're the one who first told me about Gina. You might want to consult Reba. She's the one in the know. The rest of us are amateurs in comparison."

"True, our Reba is in the know. She's always been the way she is. I used to think she was odd, but I like her a lot now."

"What changed for you?"

"She cares about folks and takes the time to understand things. Reba goes out of her way to be kind to people who are different. Folks like me." Melinda's expression changed. "I'm different. I know it. People teased me all the time growing up, but Reba saw the real me hidden inside. No one else took the time. I'm not stupid like I've been told." Melinda swatted at the tear running down her cheek. "You're a lot like her in that respect. You've always been nice to me and willing to listen."

"I could say the same thing about you. From the day I walked into this church to work, you've been nice to me. You made me feel welcome."

"Listen to the two of us." Melinda shook her head. "We'll be crying all over each other if we keep this up." She gazed out into the hall. "I was wondering what our mutual friend is doing here."

"Well, I hope she didn't follow me to make a mess here in the church. Although, I do like Larissa. The more I learn about her, the more I like her."

"She's waiting for Gina, but I could be wrong." Melinda stood. "I better get to work, so the boss doesn't see me sloughing off." She waved when she walked out the door.

Jessie smiled at her. Melinda was a bright spot in any day. Ghoul following. Funny, she was getting used to the idea. It didn't distract her like it once had, nor did it overwhelm her. What did that say about her? It was a subject to be pondered for sure but not now. She heard the pastors talking as they walked down the hall. She wanted to get their opinion on the idea rolling around in her head. Something had to be done about all these men who thought it was okay to hit their wives or girlfriends.

Jessie left the church upbeat after talking to the pastors. Pastor Kevin was excited about her idea of the church hosting a forum on domestic violence. Ever since Larissa had been found in the church dumpster, he had been talking to Pastor John about the need to do something in the community to bring about awareness of the crisis. Jessie assured him she was eager to help. She knew of some great speakers from her days in New York, and she would make the necessary contacts for him. Jessie smiled. Living in Blue Cove was turning her into quite the activist. Who knew? She opened the door to the familiar sound of the bell. At least her dream of owning the store was a reality, even if her anticipated "quiet life" wasn't happening.

****

Taylor and Matt had questioned several people from the compound and were down to only a few left. They were a hard group to read, and so far, the leader— who did all the talking—hadn't given them much to go on. Something strange was going on. The group seemed to be living in some kind of time warp. Nothing appeared to be normal.

Matt couldn't take his eyes off the large, burly man walking toward him. His dark beard was streaked through with gray. Wrinkles etched his face and formed a permanent frown. But it was the cold, steely stare he gave them when he walked into the room that caught Matt's attention. No doubt about it, this guy didn't want to be there.

"Let's get this over with. I have work to do and this ain't getting it done." He sat in the chair, slumping forward.

"Please state your name for our report," Taylor told him.

"I'm Randy Phillips, and I'm one of the head elders here."

"So, you're the enforcer that Olivia was telling me about." Matt saw the quick spark of anger in his eyes.

"You can't believe anything Olivia tells you. She's a liar as far as I'm concerned. Where is she anyway? She hasn't done her chores the last several days, and her husband is looking for her."

"Where she is right now is none of your concern. I'd hate to think you had anything to do with the bruises all over her body." Matt stood and leaned close to Randy's face.

"Not me." He shrugged, unmoved. "Once they're married, it's the husband's job to keep them in line."

"Nothing is off limits? Is that what you're telling us, Randy? Is that how you keep them in line, as you call it?" The deputy frowned at him.

"How a husband deals with his wife is not up to me." He shrugged again. "I have no say in it. My job is to watch over and train the children and young people. I tell them what's expected of them and how they should act."

"You do more than tell them; you measure out punishment when they don't. Isn't that right?" Matt raised an eyebrow. "I was told you punished Larissa on more than one occasion. She was even locked up for a few days. What do you have to say for yourself? A big man like you picking on children." Matt waggled a finger at him and sat down again.

"How we teach our children obedience is up to us.

Larissa had problems you wouldn't understand." He narrowed his eyes, his jaw set. "We were trying to save her."

"If you are abusing children while you are "training them," then it is the law's concern. Especially, since one of your children ended up dead and dumped in the trash in my town." Matt leaned back in his chair. "Your training methods and lives will be under scrutiny until we find Larissa's murderer. It's how society works."

Randy's lip curled. "You've stated the exact reason we have chosen not to be a part of society as you call it. We follow a law that is higher than yours."

"You may believe you can do as you please, but you live in this state and in my county. The laws of the state and this county apply to you, too." Deputy Taylor stood with his fists clenched at his sides.

"I haven't seen Larissa for several months." Randy shrugged, his expression now sullen. "She ran off, and we let her. Larissa was willful, rebellious, and self-indulgent. The leaders told her to leave and not come back unless she wanted to live by our rules. She left, and I said good riddance."

"I don't know about you, Taylor, but I think Phillips here doesn't sound like the type of man who should work with children. He doesn't have the temperament." Matt studied the man sitting across from him. "We're through with you for now, but I'm sure we'll be back."

Randy stood. "Larissa had parents and a young man here who loved her, but it wasn't good enough for her. She broke hearts and was a bad influence, so no, I wasn't sorry to see her leave. I'm not sorry she's dead, either." His eyes fixed on Matt. "But I didn't kill her, I give you my word on it."

"Nice sentiment. Trust me, we'll find out who did. The DNA under her nails and on her clothing will give us answers. Oh, and Phillips, you might want to let Roger know that we're looking for him. Beating your wife isn't legal in this state anymore. It hasn't been for quite a few years."

****

"Do you see what I mean about these people?" Taylor asked him as they walked to their cars.

"They're definitely different." Matt shook his head. "And they're hiding something. The only one who was remotely truthful was Phillips, and he wasn't nice. No wonder Larissa wanted out of here. It would be hard to live under the oppression of those leaders."

"Any ideas?" Taylor leaned his hip against the side of his cruiser.

"I need to mull it over in my mind for a bit. I might be wrong about this, but I don't believe any one of the leaders was involved. You saw how they reacted when you mentioned the shooting. There's a reason they've lived off the grid. They sure as hell don't want the attention this murder is going to bring them."

"Keep me in the loop with the investigation." Taylor got in his car.

"I will. Don't be a stranger either," Matt said as he opened his car door.

He wrote a few notes in his notebook and then started his car. This case was getting interesting. There was something about Larissa's father. Matt wasn't sure, but he thought he had seen his face before. Maybe on a wanted poster. He grabbed his ringing phone. "Dylan, what's up?"

"Are you done? Can you talk?" He sounded excited.

"Yeah, we just wrapped it up here. Did you find something?"

"You were right about the shooter not being on the group's property. We found where our shooter was hiding. You're going to want to see what else we found. Jessie wasn't kidding when she said that crypt or tomb didn't feel right, and she didn't want to be in there. It gives me the creeps in the light of day. I can't imagine what it was like at night."

"How can I find you?" Matt asked.

"We'll be waiting at the trailhead to the park where we were the other night. We had to hike through the woods but not too far." Dylan exhaled. "And Matt, whatever has been going in this place can't be good."

"I'll be right there." Matt reversed his car and headed out to the highway. If this required a search warrant from the county, Taylor was going to have to be a part of it. He reached the highway and turned. Dylan had sounded excited enough. Matt couldn't remember Dylan ever saying he was creeped out. It must not be good. Jessic had a way of stumbling on to the weird and the bizarre. What was it this time?

Chapter 19

"Let's see what you've found," Matt said as soon as he got out of his car.

"We thought we'd show you where the guy was hiding. It's on the way to the crypt." Dylan motioned to them and started walking.

"The place is deceptive. It looks almost like a tiny cathedral out in the woods, only a lot creepier looking. You know gothic." Kip walked beside Matt. "I can't believe Jessie went in the place at night to check it out. Most anyone I know would be freaked. I was. This whole place doesn't seem right to me."

"Jessie has a tendency to jump into things," Matt stated. "It's the reporter in her. After it's over, she realizes the danger she was in. I guess she's like us in that regard."

"Yeah, you're probably right. Still, I wouldn't want to see this place at night, especially after being shot at. It would be a scene right out of a horror movie."

They were nearing the Young's property. Matt could hear the dog barking and could see the fence up ahead. Before they reached it, Dylan veered off to the right, heading toward a large stand of trees.

"We found the casings here." Dylan pointed at the ground. "You can see the footprints all around the area. I figure he was hiding up in this tree." Dylan tapped its trunk. "We ran the opposite way to get out of his line of fire. I'm still trying to figure out how Jessie stumbled onto the crypt. She had to have run a crazy pattern to make it to where we're going next."

"How she did it without running back into the line of fire is beyond us. You'll see what we mean." Kip and Matt followed Dylan, as he started moving again.

The area was thick with trees, dead undergrowth, and low-hanging limbs, which had to be swatted out of the way. Matt tried to imagine her running through this without having any idea of where she was. After walking for about fifteen minutes, they came into a small clearing in the midst of the trees. There it stood. The opening gate screeched and groaned with the slightest movement.

"From the looks of this place, you wouldn't think anyone had been to visit it in years. That's only a first impression. If you look around closely, there are footprints of all sizes everywhere." Dylan pointed to a few of them. "All of them fresh."

"What's inside, or is it locked?"

"Unlocked. As to what's inside, you'll have to see it to believe it." Dylan led the way. He pushed the door, and it creaked open.

The interior was damp, musty, and dark except for the sunlight that spilled through the single beveled window onto a large stone slab in the center of the crypt. "Is this a grave or some kind of altar? This looks like blood to me, not paint." Matt moved closer to get a better look.

"We were thinking the same thing." Kip nodded.

"It'll have to be tested to see if it's animal, human, or something else." Matt noticed the symbols carved on the stones around the building and took a closer look at each one. "Damn, some of these look like the ones carved on Larissa's body."

"We wondered if they were similar. It seems our Jessie made quite the find. How she did it has left me scratching my head." Dylan shook his head.

"You and me both. Destiny, fate, kismet, call it what you will. She heard Abigail when no one else could. I guess it was meant to be. We're too logical to figure out the path she ran." Matt took a closer look at the symbols engraved in the walls. They were etched along the base of the stone slab too. Who was using this place? Footprints were fresh, and they weren't all Jessie's shoe size. "If she hadn't discovered this, we would have never known it was here. We will need the county to issue a search warrant. We might also have to do a few nights of surveillance around the area."

"It makes you wonder what kind of folks might show up." Dylan pointed as the sunlight reflected off something shiny. "Would you look at this?" He bent down and opened a trap door on the floor. Stairs led down into a huge underground room.

Matt followed Dylan down the stairs. The room was large. The symbols they had seen upstairs were painted around the hard earthen walls. At one end of the space there appeared to be some kind of altar. At the other end were several wooden cabinets. "I wonder what is in these." Matt tried the handles, but they were all locked.

"There are a lot of fresh prints indicating this room has been used recently." Dylan pointed at the ground. "I wonder what these are used for." He flipped one of the metal rings that were anchored into the wall on one side of the room. "Torture maybe? This place gives off a bad vibe."

"I would say it's unnerving." Kip started up the stairs. "Are you guys coming? I need some fresh air."

"I'm right behind you." Matt followed Kip. "I've seen enough to know we need to take a closer look at what this place is used for. It gives us all something to think about on our way back into town."

****

Jessie had finished her closing routine around the store when her phone rang. She didn't recognize the number. It could be a vendor. "Hello, this is Jessie."

"Jessie, this is Bruce. You remember me, don't you?"

"Sure, I was at your wedding if you recall." Her voice sounded sarcastic even to her.

"I don't mean to bother you, but I'm worried about Sally. She's not answering or returning any of my calls. You wouldn't happen to know where she is, would you?"

"No, I don't." She crossed her fingers behind her back. At least, at this very moment, she wasn't lying. She didn't have a clue where Sally was hanging out.

"If you see her or talk to her, let her know that I'm trying to reach her. Tell her I have the tickets for our second honeymoon." He sounded saccharine sweet.

"If she calls me, I'll let her know. Have a good evening." What a weasel. She hung up and gave Jeremy a quick call.

"Hey, sweetheart, it's been a while since we talked. What's up?"

"I was wondering if you'd run a number for me and tell me the location where the call was made."

"It may take a few minutes, but I can get you the

info."

"Thanks, Jeremy." Jessie gave him Bruce's number from her phone's log. "Let me know what you find out. Sally's husband, Bruce, called me from this number, and I'm trying to find out how far away he is from Blue Cove. I want to make sure Sally is in a safe place before he shows up."

"I've done a little work for Matt on the subject of Bruce. I'd be happy to check this out for you." Jeremy sounded grim. "I'll get back to you as soon as I find out."

"I'd appreciate it." Jessie grabbed her purse from under the counter and shoved her phone into it. She was ready to call it a day. "Well, Larissa," she said as she started toward the front of the store to check the door, "I wonder what Matt found out today at your parents' compound. I wish you could write or talk to me in some way." The lights of a car pulling up in front of her store caught her attention. "Speaking of Matt, there he is now. I know you can throw books, but can you find a way to tell me who killed you?" She waved at Matt as he stepped out of his car.

"Do you need to get home, or can you have dinner with me?" he asked when she opened the door.

"Dinner sounds perfect." She smiled up at him. "You'll have to bring me back to my car."

"Let's take yours; it's a sweeter ride." He locked the door and followed her to the back of the store. "How was your day?"

"It was a good one. Did you find out anything?"

"It was interesting. Yes, I'd say it was definitely interesting." He took the keys from her hand and opened the car door for her. "You have Dylan and Kip in a quandary. Me, too, if I'm honest about it."

"What do you mean?"

"None of us can figure out how you came across the crypt, given the direction you were running."

"I don't know how I did it." She frowned, trying to remember. "I just did."

"And your feet were on the ground the entire time? You didn't have any ghostly assistance?"

"Are you teasing me?" She glanced at him with a puzzled expression.

"No, I'm serious."

He did look serious. Jessie shrugged and smiled. "I can never tell with you. I was running, and there it was."

"The thing is, Jess, it was located in the opposite direction of the way you ran. You either cut real close to where the shooter was hidden, or you took an extremely long way around. We can't figure it out."

"Like everything else going on around me right now. It doesn't make sense." She frowned, trying hard to recall every moment of that awful night. "To be truthful, I don't know how I found you again. I was so turned around in the fog, I'm lucky to have run into you at all. Did you learn anything else or only find more proof about how strange I am?"

"We found out a few things. The crypt, by the way, was like you said. Only we found something I'm sure you never saw." He explained about the secret room below.

She shuddered. "My instinct was to get out of there quick. What do you think it is used for?"

"I have no idea, but I can imagine. There were lots of fresh prints in the area, indicating some kind of

149

recent activity there."

"Whew, that's a little creepy." She exhaled and adjusted herself to see him better.

"Honestly, I'm more perplexed than ever about the case including Larissa's parents. That's where you come in, sweetheart. I need to bounce this stuff off you. My logical mind is getting in the way." He frowned.

She gave him a look. "I'm not sure if I should see your need to talk to me as a compliment or an insult."

"Definitely a compliment to the strange world you live in." He grinned at her. "What new things happened in your day since I caught the hurricane lamp this morning?"

"Larissa went to the church with me this morning. Melinda said I had a ghoul following, and Pastor Kevin wants to do a forum on domestic violence at the church." She paused. "Not to worry you or add to your concern, but Bruce Kingman called me looking for Sally. I have Jeremy tracking down his location when he made the call. I need to know how much time we have to get Sally to safety."

"Something tells me I need to ask how your day went more often. I might be missing a lot of detailed information." He pulled into a parking spot in front of Mindy's Waterfront Grill. "Did Jeremy find out anything?"

"I'm still waiting for him to call."

"We'll eat dinner and wait together. You know what the strangest thing about the day was for me?"

She shook her head. "Stranger than what you've told me so far?"

"Yes," he said. "Larissa's father looks familiar. I've seen him somewhere before. I keep wondering if he is wanted for something. I know I need to investigate this further." He reached across and took her hand. "Let's put all the pieces we have so far out on the table." Matt took his notebook out of his pocket.

"We know Larissa was murdered. It all begins with her."

"Yes, and we know that strange symbols had been carved into her body. Symbols which we found carved into the stones on the walls inside the crypt, by the way."

"Oh, that's new, I didn't see the carvings." She tapped his hand. "Of course I was at somewhat of a disadvantage with it being so dark and all. Add to it the fact that I was alone, had been shot at, and was maybe a wee bit scared." She grinned at him. "You can see where I'm going here. I was lucky to see the blasted place at all."

"Jess, if hadn't been for you, we wouldn't have a clue about where to begin." He drew a line under a statement on the page. "We know we were shot at by someone outside the compound, not inside. I'm glad one of my theories panned out today."

"Another new piece of information." She frowned. "I could have sworn it was someone on the property."

"It still could have been, but that person was not on the property when they shot at us. As strange as the Youngs are, I'm not sure how they're involved in the shooting. They seem to be in hiding and would rather not draw attention to the compound—which might be wishful thinking on my part. From what Olivia's mom said, she hasn't seen her sister in years. She's always blamed her brother-in-law for the mess they were in, but she's not sure anymore after Olivia told what her aunt did to her. Mrs. Bertelli is ready to go to battle with Rose for not telling her where Olivia was all this time. She'll be back, and Rose Young is going to get an earful."

"I'm sure I would do the same thing. How awful to let your sister worry needlessly about her child. If it were me, I'd be in her face, and she would have some major explaining to do."

"I'm sure you would make her do it, too." Matt chuckled and shook his head.

"What?" Jessie tilted her head.

"Ghoul following. I just got it."

"Melinda seems to think she's there to get Gina's help." Jessie tapped her fingers on the table.

"Have you seen Gina again? She has shown up in several of the cases you've worked."

"Not yet, but I can't say I'm looking, either. I hope Jeremy has some information soon. It would be good to know where Bruce is. I don't want him to suddenly show up and cause problems for Sally."

"Jeremy will call when he has the information. He's good at what he does. I'm trying to convince him to move here and join the team."

"He talks about it, but I'd be surprised." Jessie shook her head. "So many organizations call on him in New York. He'd get bored if he lived here full time. Although, if this crazy stuff keeps happening, maybe he wouldn't." She watched a couple walk into the restaurant. "As much as it saddens me to say this, Katie and Jeremy as a couple aren't working. She's overwhelmed by how smart he is, and they have nothing in common. I think my lovely, flighty friend has moved on to Tom."

"You're right. I wouldn't be surprised by anything. Who knows? Maybe Tom will end up on our team."

"I guess like everything else we'll have to wait and see."

"My policy, especially when it comes to you, but…" He leaned across the table and kissed her. "I'm stepping up my assault. I'm ready for a change."

"I'm glad," she whispered and gazed into his eyes.

Chapter 20

Jessie wasn't going to tell Matt, but he had already won. He would know it soon enough. His charm campaign had worked its magic, and she was definitely under his spell. She thought about him most of the time and missed him as soon as he left. He was nothing like her father, and that made him worth keeping in her book. Simply put, she enjoyed being with Matt. He was one great-looking man and—wonder of wonders—he loved her.

She smiled at him. "Thank you for dinner."

"Anytime." He opened the car door for her and bent to kiss her once she was in the car.

"Why is it your phone always rings when I'm busy?" He smiled, closing the door as she rummaged through her purse to find her phone.

"Hi, Jeremy."

"Hey, sweetheart."

"Did you find the information?" She put her phone on speaker. "Matt's here so he can hear, too."

"Matt, I sent you a photo of Bruce by the way."

"I'll check out my emails and thanks."

"Sure thing. Bruce made the call outside Columbus, Ohio. He should be in your neighborhood in the next few days, depending on how fast he drives."

"Then I need to get Sally out of here and to a safe place soon."

"A good plan," Jeremy stated. "Jessie, sweetheart. Don't deal with Bruce on your own if he shows at your place. He's not a nice guy. Matt, keep her safe."

"I will. Did you get the pictures of the Mr. Young and the compound that I sent you?" Matt asked.

"I'm tracking him down now and running a facial recognition scan on Young, now. I'll let you know as soon as I have something concrete," Jeremy replied.

"Okay, we'll talk later." Matt glanced at Jessie. "I'll make calls when I get home. We'll find a place for her; don't worry."

"I never doubted that you'd take care of it." Jessie unbuckled her seat belt when Matt pulled in behind his car in front of her store. She got out and went around to the driver's side. "See you."

He kissed her goodbye. "Keep your eyes open."

****

"How was your evening?" Sally asked when Jessie walked in the door.

"It was nice." Jessie hung up her jacket. She plopped down on the sofa and turned to face Sally. "I had a call from your husband today."

Sally's face paled. "How did he get your number?" She fidgeted with the remote in her hand.

"I was wondering the same thing. I'm sure Bruce could find the information easy enough if he tried. With the Internet, it's simple to locate almost anybody." Jessie repeated his message about his attempts to reach her and the tickets for a second honeymoon.

"I knew he was coming, but this makes it real. Jessie, I'm scared." Sally muted the TV.

"I had Jeremy, a friend of mine, find out where Bruce was when he made the call. Jeremy traced him to

Springfield, a small town less than fifty miles outside of Columbus, Ohio. Bruce should be here soon, and Matt promised to get you somewhere safe before he can get here."

"I know Bruce will be angry when he doesn't find me, but I can't face him." Sally stood and started to pace. "I've put you at risk. I should've never have come here. He won't believe you when you tell him I'm not here, or you don't know where I am. He won't leave you or Katie alone."

"It'll be okay. Matt won't let me know where you'll be. That way I can't accidently leak any information."

"You have no idea how he gets." Sally had gone pale. "When he's angry, he can get mean. His fists have done a lot of damage to my body, but he's done even more to my mind. I…I don't want him to hurt you both." She was trembling.

"We'll be fine." Jessie reached for her hand. "You need to concentrate on yourself right now. Keeping you safe and away from him is all that matters."

Sally frowned. "I know you're right, but I feel bad about leaving Katie and you to clean up my mess. I walked into this marriage on my own, and I walked away from it." She straightened her shoulders. "I'm the one who should have to face it."

"Under normal circumstances, I would say that's true, but this is different, Sally." Jessie twisted the tassel on the pillow. "Domestic violence is serious, and more often than not, the woman is the one who ends up injured or dead." Jessie jumped when she heard the knock at the door. There was no way he could be here yet. She peeked out the window. With relief, she opened the door to Dylan. "Hi." She motioned him in. "Why are you here?" Jessie closed the door behind him.

"I've come to get Sally. We have a place where her husband won't find her." Dylan glanced at Sally. "You might want to get your stuff together; I want to get you out of here as soon as possible." Sally left the room. "Matt is going to have Kip watching your place and the Inn for the next couple of nights. He'll be close by in case Mr. Kingman happens to show up a touch angry."

"I knew Matt would take care of it." Jessie smiled. "Sally is scared. It took courage for her to leave him. It's a hard thing for a battered woman to do. I'll go help her pack," she called back over her shoulder. "Make yourself comfortable. You'll find iced tea and soda in the fridge."

Sally was shoving stuff into her suitcase when Jessie entered the guest room. "No more feeling sorry for myself. I need to be strong if I'm going to make it out of this alive." She grabbed her makeup from the nightstand and shoved it into her overnight case. "Will you write me or call?"

"I won't know where you'll be for a while. You'll probably be without a traceable phone, too. The main thing is to keep you safe until Bruce is no longer a threat to you."

Sally looked at her for a moment, her eyes glistening. "When this is over, I would like to come back here and have you both help me get my life back together."

"We'll be here waiting." Jessie handed Sally a gift bag. "I brought you some books in case you get bored."

"Thank you, you've been kind to me." Sally reached for Jessie and hugged her. Sally grabbed her suitcase and went into the living room.

"Mrs. Kingman, I'll take that for you." Dylan took her suitcase.

"Out with the man and with his name too. From now on, it's Sally Mansfield." Sally smiled at Jessie as she walked out the door. "I'll be back to reclaim a better version of me, hopefully soon."

Jessie nodded. Sally would be okay. She had to be. Jessie watched them leave and waved at her when she turned around.

****

Sally's old cell phone sat on his counter. She had received several throwaways in exchange for it. Sally could use them to call her parents and friends, but she wasn't to give out the numbers, and they wouldn't be able to contact her. Matt would be able to monitor her incoming calls from Bruce. From what he was learning about Bruce, he was not a man to be trifled with.

Jessie was never far from his thoughts. "Hi, sweetheart," he said when she answered the phone.

"You didn't tell me that Dylan was coming for Sally tonight." She sounded as if she'd been crying.

"Are you okay?"

"You know me, I always cry."

"I'm sorry. I didn't mean to take you by surprise, but it all came together after I left you tonight. The only thing I will tell you, for now, is that Sally is out of Blue Cove and headed to a safe house."

"I'm glad. Since Bruce called earlier, I've been worried about her."

He heard her sniff. "I knew you would be."

"Maybe Bruce will leave once he finds out she's not here."

"How many of these stories have you done over the years?" Matt could imagine her expression.

"A few. Why?"

"You know it doesn't work that way. The angry husband doesn't give up and walk away. This stuff festers in them until they explode, which brings me to why I called you."

"Make your lecture short and sweet."

"Jess, this isn't a lecture, but a warning to keep your eyes open. The fact that he called you makes me believe he thinks she's on her way to see you. He'll think you, at the very least, know where she is, and you're holding out on him. He won't be nice, believe me."

"What's new? I haven't exactly been given the welcome mat since I moved here. As a matter of fact, I've heard it rumored that a few townsfolk believe I've brought more than a fair share of trouble to town with me."

He wanted to be there in person to comfort her. "I'd say the folks here know only a few of the things that have gone on. Those who know you, love you, and even if they don't, it doesn't change anything where I'm concerned. You're not going anywhere, and you need to keep your eyes open for Bruce. Call me if you see him."

"I will."

"Did you tell Katie that Sally is gone?"

"Not yet, I needed to get my tears over with first."

"Do you want me to come over and hold your hand? I'll even let you cry on my shoulder."

"You're sweet. I'd like that." He could hear the smile in her voice again.

159

"I'll be over in ten, and if you don't need my shoulder we can find some other way to amuse ourselves."

"Sounds perfect to me. I love you, Matt."

"I'll be there in a few."

Matt turned on his laptop and downloaded the picture of Mr. Young from his camera. He had captured it with care on his phone as he tried not to draw attention to himself. Matt had seen Young's face somewhere before, he was sure. If only he could remember where. Most likely, the Young name was an alias. He could sense there was more to the man than met the eye. Honestly, he understood Reba's theory. Larissa's problems might have started with her family, but it went beyond them. His thinking, exactly. He shook his head. Seeing eye to eye with Reba was downright strange. The case began to take shape in his mind. Jessie would love that he had a plan. He couldn't wait to tell her. It was more like a trap to bring a killer out of the shadows. Jessie might not be the bait this time, but she would set the trap.

Matt grabbed his keys and went to the car. He liked hearing her say she loved him. His campaign was moving along quite nicely. He had the ring picked out and ready—as soon as the right moment presented itself. As much as he'd like to, he knew he couldn't rush things. Right now, their heating romance was enough.

Chapter 21

With a little encouragement from Matt, Jessie began to unknowingly set the trap. She wrote an article about Larissa for the local paper. She wrote about what it was like to be abused by a person who had promised to love and honor you. The article prompted many discussions around town and calls to the police station. Jessie also sent a copy to Neil in New York, in case he was interested. He was. Larissa's death had some unusual elements involved in it, and the baby's survival also added a happy twist to the story.

Jessie was nervous about Bruce. So far he was a no-show. She couldn't let her guard down—by no means—but she was happy not to have to deal with him. With a little luck, he would hopefully stay away.

She unlocked the door to her store and turned on the lights, locking it behind her. Roger and his motorhome hadn't driven by lately. Maybe he had left when he couldn't find Olivia. He probably hadn't, but one could hope.

"Good morning, Larissa." A smile lit up her face when she saw the chair had once again been shifted ever so slightly to the right. Jessie was getting used to the strange morning ritual of moving the chair back to where she had left it the night before. Every morning brought something new. Jessie was never sure how Larissa would rearrange her store after she left. They were playing some kind of game. Jessie glanced around the room. Two of the paintings had been swapped. "I see you've been busy overnight, haven't you?" That's when she noticed the table. "Honestly, Larissa, you and I are going to have to come to terms about this. Leave this table alone." She wagged her finger at the chair. Jessie sorted through the books on the table pulling out several books. "These are bestsellers not ghost stories. I'm trying to help you find your killer. The least you can do is work with me." Jessie shook her head and reached for her ringing phone. "Idle Time Books, may I help you?"

"I don't have much time," a woman's voice came over the line, "but I wanted to warn you to be careful. Your store is being watched, and so are you."

"Who is this? Who's watching me?"

"It doesn't matter. I don't want you to end up like Larissa."

"Do you know who killed Larissa?" Jessie asked.

"I have an idea, but no proof. It wasn't supposed to happen. I was promised it wouldn't, but it did anyway."

"Who promised?"

"I can't talk now. Please be careful." The phone clicked off.

It was the same lady who had called the church. Jessie was sure of it. Was it Roger who was watching the store or someone else? Jessie noticed that Larissa was watching her. "I wish you could help with this." Larissa edged closer to her. "Does your mother know who did this to you? Is she being hurt the same way?" Larissa reached her hand toward Jessie. "Your mother does know, doesn't she? Did your parents try to protect you?" Jessie knew from Larissa's actions she was getting close to the truth. Maybe her mother's life was in danger, too. How many times had Larissa witnessed her beatings? She was scowling. No wonder Larissa wanted to be free from her family. Maybe both parents were guilty. They'd figure it out. Jessie called Matt and got his voicemail. She repeated the events of the morning and then got busy with her morning routine at the store. It was turning out to be a busy morning, and the store wasn't even open yet.

Katie was the next call. "Hey, Jessie."

"What's up?" Jessie sighed and gave up on trying to shelve her shipment of new books.

"Tom's coming into town tomorrow night for the weekend. Why don't you bring Matt and come to dinner?"

"I'll check with him and get back to you. I'm not sure if he has plans. If he can, we'll be there."

"Sounds good. Has the new Corrine Clark book arrived yet?"

Jessie smiled at her eager tone. "They're on order and should be here any day now."

"As soon as you get it let me know. Better yet, bring me a copy, and I'll pay you. I can't wait to read it. I read the review on the book this morning, and it sounds like another good one."

"I will. I'm looking forward to reading it myself."

"Even if Matt can't come, you should. I'll see you tomorrow night. Bye." Katie hung up before she could respond.

Her watch said she had fifteen minutes before the store opened, and that's when she noticed Reba standing at the door about to knock. Jessie went over to let her in. What news was she about to get now? She tossed her hair over her shoulder. This morning was off to a crazy start, and it wasn't even nine yet.

"Hello, dear girl. I wanted to stop by for a quick chat and to see how your guest is behaving."

Jessie told Reba about her morning of rearranged pictures, the chair, and of course, the books on the best-seller table that had been swapped out for ghost stories.

Reba chuckled. "You might have a bored ghost on your hands. Either that or she's playful. She was, after all, far too young to die or to be a mother. Every time I consider what happened to her, it breaks my heart."

"I know. I feel the same way. I wonder what her mother thinks about it." Jessie frowned. "A woman keeps calling me. It happened again this morning." She told her about the strange call she'd had earlier. "Afterward, when I asked Larissa if her mother knew, I got the sense that she did know what was happening to Larissa. The woman this morning said she had been promised Larissa wouldn't get hurt, but she did anyway."

"You are communicating with Larissa? How?" Reba looked surprised.

"I can see her every now and then. Today when I questioned her, Larissa responded by reaching her hand toward me and by the expressions on her face. She frowns and gets agitated when she's upset. At times she looks sad and soulful. What can I say? It's strange, I know. Some days I wonder if I'm just making it up because I want to help her so bad." Jessie sighed.

"Oh, Jessie, if that were only the case. You could walk away from all of this, but I fear you'll actually see it happen. You'll always be helping someone from now on. I'm sure about it." Reba gazed away, a sad expression on her face. "It has interrupted my life more times than I can say. Lawrence still doesn't know what to make of me at times, but thankfully, I know he loves me. This gift nearly ended my marriage in the beginning. He didn't know what to think of his strange young wife. Lawrence wondered if I was making it all up. He's come to trust my instinct, but it was touch and go for a while. I have to admit I thought I was crazy, too. There was no one to help me through it."

Jessie reached over and patted her hand. She had never seen Reba like this. "I'm glad you've been there for me. I've wondered about myself a few times, too. I couldn't have made it without you."

"I may be older, but it doesn't make it any easier. I know people in town think I'm eccentric, and that's putting it politely." She gazed out the window. "You are fortunate that Matt trusts your abilities, even though I know he doesn't understand them. He's logical, and this side of you twists him inside out. But…he's a rock when it comes to you."

"Yes, but I don't think it's fair to him to have to put up with this madness every day in his home, too." Jessie felt herself tearing up. "That's why I'm so hesitant to jump into this relationship. I don't want him to get so frustrated by this side of my life. It's a lot to ask of him. Look, you're stronger than I am, and it impacted your marriage." She had to turn away. "I can't imagine how he feels."

"You have to. Matt isn't going anywhere—I can tell by the way he looks at you. You need Matt like I needed Lawrence. He brought a normalcy and stability to my life."

Jessie shook her head. "I want to believe you, but I

don't want Matt to wake up some morning and wonder what he got himself into."

"Oh, honey, every married man does that one day, anyway." Reba chuckled. "You're a woman, and your emotions alone could make him wonder. You know there aren't any guarantees, but it sure helps when they're head over heels for you, and Matt is."

"I needed to hear this, I guess." Jessie smiled in spite of herself. "I get lost in these cases sometimes and forget the other things I want. I do want to be loved, and I need things to be normal, if only once in a while."

"Of course you do, dear. It sure doesn't hurt either when your man knows all the right buttons to push—if you know what I mean." Reba smiled, fanning her face.

"Yes, I believe I do." Jessie laughed. "And Matt's good at it."

"You may as well jump in, my girl. There's no sense in hanging on the edge of what might be one of the greatest highs in life. Love, passion, it's all great. This other stuff will always be here; you can't bring it or make it go away. All you can do is go with it when it comes. Matt gets it. Lawrence does, too. We're both lucky girls in that regard."

"I couldn't agree more." Jessie smiled at her.

"I think my job is done here. Oh, your friend Katie—I do love that spunky girl—she's about to have an adventure of her own. It'll all work out the way it's meant to."

Jessie walked Reba to the door and watched her drive away. It was time to open for the day. Jessie flipped the sign around. She unlocked the doors into Joe's Coffee Shop and waved at Molly who had a line of people waiting for their morning coffee. Routine, she liked it. There was something safe and normal about it. A break every now and then was nice, but there was a lot to be said about the little daily things in life. She took a deep breath. Funny, how a few words from Reba could set her world back in place. She couldn't imagine doing this alone and hoped she wouldn't have to try.

A truck pulled up in front of the store. The new book order was here. Jessie watched the man unload the boxes onto the hand truck. She knew him and waved. "Evan, how's Adriana?" She held the door open for him.

"She's great. The baby is due any day."

"It's been a while since I last saw you." Jessie smiled at him. "You can put the boxes in the back room."

"You'll be seeing me more often; Blue Cove will be a part of my permanent route. Adriana told me to be sure to tell you hi, and we'll bring the baby by to see you as soon as she's born."

"You're having a little girl? How nice." Jessie dabbed at her eyes.

"Yes, our own little Jessica Lynn, named after the lady who saved her life. It was either that or Radar, which didn't seem appropriate." He grinned at her.

"I'm honored." Jessie signed the places he had marked on the paperwork. "Be sure to tell Adriana hi from me too."

"I will. See you soon…" Evan pulled the hand truck out the door.

Jessie waved as he drove away. Well, in some way she had helped people. Everything wasn't entirely weird. A baby girl named after her. She dried her eyes again.

While she stood there, Roger's motorhome pulled into the church parking lot. Speak of the devil and there he is, she mused. Jessie watched him get out and cross the street. He passed by her door and went into Joe's. She was standing behind the counter when he came through the open doors from the coffee shop. If Jessie had any doubts in her mind about him, they all went out the window when Larissa saw him. Out of the corner of her eye, Jessie saw the large dictionary sail through the air and fall at his feet with a loud bang. He jumped.

"I'm sorry, I must have knocked it off the counter." Was that the best she could come up with? Really! Larissa was circling him, anger etched on her face. Even from behind the counter, Jessie could feel the sudden shift to a cold, clammy atmosphere. She shivered.

He waved it off. "I thought about getting my wife another book, but I'll come back when I have more time to shop." He raced toward the door, glancing back at her with a strange look on his face.

Chapter 22

Larissa, I wish you could talk, Jessie mused. If she was any judge of the situation, Roger was guilty of something besides beating Olivia. Whether he was actually involved or was a not-so-innocent bystander, Larissa was angry at him. She placed him on her list of possible suspects.

Jessie called through the door to Molly, "Come over when you have a minute to talk."

"Do you want me to bring coffee with me?" Molly asked as she handed the lady in line her change.

"Yes, please." Jessie nodded.

Three ladies walked into the store. The tallest of them went to the display table, reminding Jessie there were new books to go through. Corrine's book had to be in one of the boxes delivered this morning. Jessie opened the first box, grabbed a large stack of books, and groaned as she carried them to the counter. Darn, they were heavy. She smiled thinking about how easily Matt could have lifted the same stack or even the whole box. He was a sight to watch. Her face flushed. With any luck, she had grabbed the books she wanted in her first attempt. She sorted through the pile. No books by Corrine.

"Do you have this book?" The woman handed her the title scribbled on a post-it note.

"Yes, I do." Jessie led her to the shelf where the

author's books were located. She left her to look and went into the back room to pull more books from the box.

Molly tapped Jessie's shoulder to get her attention. "I can see you're busy, so I placed your coffee on the counter along with a new treat. You'll have to try it because it's my gift."

"A scone perhaps?" Jessie asked.

"Not this time." Molly shook her head.

"I give up. What did you bring me? A better question might be how long will I have to exercise to work it off?" Jessie laughed.

"No counting or worrying about the calories." She winked. "Just enjoy it, please. It's a wonderful strawberry cream croissant. I love them, and I know you will too. We have similar tastes." Molly tilted her head. "Did you want to ask me something? You said you wanted to talk to me."

"Yes, but I can't remember what it was. Come over when you get another break. Maybe the thought will pass back through my mind." Jessie took a bite of the croissant. "You weren't kidding. Mmm. I love it. Is this one of your creations?" Molly smiled and nodded. "This is simply amazing." Jessie closed her eyes, running her tongue over her lips. "I bet Katie would love to have them as part of her breakfast menu from time to time. You should ask. Between you and Katie, I won't ever go hungry. You are my incentive to keep running so I can enjoy all your goodies guilt free." Jessie licked the yummy creamy filling off her fingers as she pinched off another piece of the strawberry cream delight. "Well, almost guilt free."

She saw one of the women watching her. "If you

like strawberries, then you simply have to try this."

"I might have to. Watching your expression sold me." She followed Molly into the coffee shop. "I'll be back. Do you happen to have Corrine Clark's new book?"

"It should be in one of the boxes that were delivered this morning. Maybe by the time you get back, I'll have found the right one."

The woman's friends followed her. "We'll be back for our copies, too," one of them told her.

Jessie sipped her coffee and took another bite of the yummy croissant. She went through the second box and pulled out three copies of Corinne's new book. She knew what she'd being doing tonight when she got home. She would be reading and dropping off Katie's book. The next few nights would be filled with their chatter about the book—something they had done together many times over the years.

****

Matt's morning was busy. He noticed that Jessie had called but didn't have time to return it. He listened to her voicemail as he walked into his office and his next meeting. Dylan had a coffee cup in his hand, and Kip had his notepad ready. Matt sat in his chair. "Do you have any ideas about that crypt?"

"I checked to see if we had any active coven or neopagan groups practicing in the area."

"What made you think of a group like that?" Matt glanced from the file to Dylan.

"I thought it had to be one of those groups." He shrugged. "Who else would want to hang out under a tomb as a meeting place?" Dylan took a drink of his coffee.

"Smart thinking. What did you find out?" Matt grabbed a pencil.

"I found one active coven that mixes in neopaganism. Believe it or not, they had an ad on the Internet."

"Everyone is on the Internet and social media," Kip stated.

Dylan nodded. "It's the way of it. The leader, a Bethany Albright, said they were a group of white witches. They're considered to be a peaceful group, and they only dabble in white magic. They use their spells only for good, she told me."

"What does that mean?" Kip's eyebrows rose.

Dylan shrugged his shoulders. "Damned if I know. I can only tell you what she told me."

"Did you ask her about the crypt specifically?" Matt tapped his pencil.

Dylan nodded. "Their coven has used the crypt in one form or another for many years. They have written permission, and she said she would fax me a copy today. Bethany said they meet in the lower room so as not to disturb the dead. The tomb belongs to their one-time leader and the founder of the coven. She mentioned how several members had noticed the blood stains or perhaps paint at their last gathering. Albright told me she had reported it to the county sheriff's office because those stains hadn't been there when they'd used the place the previous month. She thought maybe vandals had desecrated it."

"Interesting, I'll check with Taylor to see if she actually filed that report. Anything else?"

"I asked about the locked cabinets. Bethany said she'd be happy to meet us there whenever you want to open them. They keep their books, magic potions, and powders in them."

"We'll have to take her up on that, of course. Have her join us there tomorrow to unlock them." Matt paused. "I would rather they unlock the doors than for us to break the lock and possibly damage the cabinet."

"I'll call her as soon as we're done. Albright was fairly sure that no one else used the tomb besides them. The stains made her wonder if someone was trespassing, though." Dylan scanned through his notes. "No one else has permission to use the crypt, and their group only gathers once a month at the most. Some months they skip it altogether so she couldn't say what might happen between their meeting times. They'd never noticed anything unusual until their last gathering when they found the stains."

"Great info. Sounds like Albright will be a good source." Matt picked up the legal document. "The judge gave me the search warrant for the crypt. Deputy Taylor will be in on it along with the county's crime lab. I also got permission for Frank to bring Radar. I want to see if he picks up Larissa's scent in the area. It might eliminate the site as our crime scene or place it squarely at the crypt."

"When does the search take place?" Dylan placed his cup on the corner of Matt's desk.

"Frank has some free time in the next few days. He'll arrive this evening, so we'll search the premises tomorrow morning. Taylor will meet us at the site. You can see why it would be good for Bethany to meet us there tomorrow. I want both of you and Marcy to come, too. We'll leave town at eight-thirty sharp."

"Sounds good. Do you need me for anything else?

If not, I have to do a follow-up on a vandalism call." Dylan shrugged. "Someone has been slashing tires near the Seaside Village neighborhood."

"Yeah, and Mrs. Ferguson has complained again about her noisy young neighbor for the umpteenth time. Joe handed me the complaint when I walked in the door." Kip grinned. "I'll be happy when Kenny can take her calls. It's the same thing every time I go. She's lonely and wants someone to talk to. I could be wrong, but I have yet to see this noisy neighbor that she's always complaining about. Plus she always has coffee and fresh cookies ready when I arrive."

"Give me the coffee and cookies any day." Dylan stood. "I used to take her calls, and trust me, you'll miss those cookies when you don't get them."

"If you say so." Kip rolled his eyes. "It's a little difficult hearing Ferguson's stories about her kid's escapades over and over again. I try to remind myself she's lonely, and I nod when I'm supposed to."

"You're a good cop, Kip. We've all had to spend some of our early days in the department with the Mrs. Fergusons of the town or handing out traffic tickets." Matt took his glasses out of his pocket and slipped them on.

"Ah, the exciting life of a small town cop. That is until Jessie came to town. Eh, Matt?" Dylan laughed.

Matt grinned. "We're finished here; you're free to go." He grabbed his phone and called Jessie. "Hi, sweetheart. I got your message. It sounds like you've had quite the morning."

"You only got the beginning on your voicemail." She proceeded to tell him about everything that had taken place.

"I don't like the idea that Roger was there again." Matt frowned.

"Larissa didn't like it, either. She almost nailed him with a dictionary. It took some quick improv on my part to cover her toss, and he still gave me a funny look when he walked out the door."

Matt chuckled. "Having seen Larissa's aim first hand, it had to be a close call."

"It was." He heard her laugh. "Tom is coming in for the weekend, and Katie wants us to come to dinner tomorrow night. Does that work for you?"

"Sure, Frank may need to come along. He'll be in town later today. We're doing a search on the crypt tomorrow morning."

"Wow, that happened fast." He could hear the excitement in her voice.

"Yeah, we need to do it before we lose evidence. Do you think you can work it out to come with us? I want to get your take on it." Matt tapped his pencil on the desk.

"I'll try to arrange it." He could hear her smile.

"I'm taking Frank out to dinner. Do you want to come along?"

"Of course. I always like to see Frank. I need to run, Matt. I have a customer coming in the door."

"We'll talk later." He ended the call and made one to Deputy Taylor. Taylor confirmed that Dylan's informant had indeed reported the blood stains, so at least that part of her story was true.

Matt opened Larissa's file. He studied the pictures of the symbols that had been carved into her body. They were poor copies of what he had seen on the wall. Had they been done to cast guilt on the coven who used the crypt? His gut told him an angry man was involved in her murder.

Chapter 23

It was official—her mind was on overload. Molly had popped in twice to see if she had remembered what she was going to ask her, and she couldn't remember.

"Maybe you didn't want to ask me anything. It could be you were sending me a subliminal message to bring you coffee and that croissant." Molly smiled as she checked in again with her.

"You could be right. Your delectable creation was so good." Jessie pushed her hair out of her eyes as she laughed. "You should give me a couple to bring to the Inn so Katie can try one. I know she'll love it and badger you for the recipe." Jessie shook a finger at her. "You'll need to hold your own and make her buy them from me. I'm serious, it makes good business sense. If you have one left over, wrap it, and I'll give it to Katie when I drop off this book later."

"I have a few left, and I'll bring them to you before you leave." Molly got up to return to the coffee shop. "Speaking of business sense, I heard through the grapevine that the owner wants to sell Joe's. I've been talking to his realtor. Kenny and I had a meeting with the loan officer at the bank, and it looks like a real possibility that I could be the new owner. I know it will be a lot of work to make it turn a profit, but I have a few ideas for marketing some of my creations." She smiled dreamily. "My father said he would front us the down payment."

"Oh, that's great news, Molly. You'd be perfect neighbors. I love the idea."

"Keep your fingers crossed. We are negotiating it now."

"I will. I hope it helps." Jessie smiled.

"We'd like to keep the name if the seller will let us." Molly frowned. "Every time I come in here, I've meant to ask you if they're making any headway in the murder?"

"I'm sure they are, but it takes time to build a case." Jessie's hand went to her forehead. "Oh, Molly, thank you. Now I remember what it was I wanted to ask you. Did Olivia's husband say anything to you earlier?"

"He asked if his wife had been in to get her coffee yet or if I had seen her in your store. I told him no, of course. He's an odd, tense sort of man. You could feel the anger radiating from him."

"I get a distinct feeling that he doesn't trust me, and he's checking up on me to see if I'm telling the truth. Be careful with him. He's got anger issues. Of course, I did lie to him, but I'm hoping he doesn't know it." Jessie laughed.

"I agree, one look at his wife told me all I need to know about him. As much as he was angry at his wife, I think he's angrier at you, so watch out for him." Molly glanced over her shoulder. "I have someone at the counter. I'll be back with the croissants soon. One for you and one for Katie. You can have it for breakfast."

Molly was right; Roger didn't like or trust her. Jessie finished unpacking her boxes. She arranged Corrine's latest book on the table and the shelf so they would be noticed. She also placed a popular paranormal mystery in front of Larissa. "Here, this is for you to enjoy, but please leave the other books right where they are." Jessie shook her head. If only she would listen. What would the store be like in the morning?

At five, Jessie said goodbye to her last customer and locked the store. She hadn't seen Frank since their last case, and she was looking forward to seeing him at dinner. Checking her watch, she had enough time to stop at the Inn with the book and croissants before Matt picked her up.

****

Jessie walked in the back door at the Inn. Katie was standing at the stove, stirring another one of her fabulous dishes. With a colorful apron tied around her waist, Katie looked perfect standing there. "I've come bearing gifts." She smiled when Katie turned around. "I brought you Corrine's new book and something yummy you're going to love." Jessie sniffed the air. "What smells so good?"

"I'm trying a new recipe for apple glazed pork chops and roasted sweet potatoes. It is pretty darn good if I do say so myself." Katie took a clean spoon out of the drawer. "Taste this sauce."

"Yum. Is that apple cider I taste?" She licked the spoon clean.

Katie nodded and smiled. "You're getting good at this. It's apple cider along with a few secret ingredients."

"This is definitely a keeper. I swear you're getting better at cooking all the time."

Katie curtsied with a grin. "I know. Do you want to stay for dinner?"

"I wish I could, but I'm going out with Matt. Frank

is in town to help with a case, and I'll get to see him, too. If he's still here tomorrow evening, we'll bring him with us—if that's okay with you?"

"Of course." Katie picked up her new book and flipped it over to read the blurb on the back. "Sounds exciting. You know what this means?"

"I sure do. We'll be having late night conversations for days. I'm looking forward to it."

"Me too, it's tradition." Katie glanced at the receipt inside the book. She grabbed her purse and handed Jessie the money she owed her. "When I'm done, this will go on the shelf in the library. My guests like to read when they have down time. In the winter, they're in by the fireplace in the evenings, and in the summer, it's in the garden during the day."

"I would do the same." Jessie pulled the croissant from the bag. "You have to taste this while I'm still here. I told Molly you might want to order some for your guests on a weekly basis. It's a small taste of perfection." Jessie watched Katie taste the strawberry cream-filled, flaky croissant and knew what was coming next. Jessie braced herself.

"I wonder if she'll give me the recipe. These are scrumptious."

"She won't. I made her promise to hold out against you."

"Why would you do that?" Katie frowned at her. "I can learn to make them myself."

"Molly might buy the coffee shop. They're in the negotiating process. Like you and me, she'll need to turn a profit. I figured you would want to help a new business get off the ground in Blue Cove." Jessie smiled and played her trump card. "Besides, Molly is our friend and newly married to boot. We should support her any way we can."

"Okay, Jessica Lynn, I see what you're doing. I'll buy them and not beg for the recipe for a while. Beyond that, I make no promises." Katie took another bite. "They are good and worth every penny she'll charge, but don't tell her I said that. I'm going to try and work a deal. I wonder how she makes the cream mixture." Katie licked her lips.

"Now, now, that's Molly's secret." Jessie touched Katie's hand. "You know, you have a good heart, my friend."

"You won't always get me to comply without a fight. I'm also a business woman who must turn a profit." Katie took another bite of the croissant.

"I know, but once a week won't break your bank. Besides, you can't expect Molly to give away the secret to her yummy creations so soon. I know you wouldn't."

Katie waved her hand at her. "Whatever. You tricked me into agreeing, but I can live with it."

Jessie looked out the window. "Matt's here. I'll read the first couple of chapters tonight so we can discuss it tomorrow night."

"Sounds good." Katie followed Jessie to the door. "Don't forget dinner tomorrow night. Tom is coming, and I'm nervous. I think he may be coming here to see me."

"Of course, he is." She hugged Katie. "You'll be fine. What's not to love about you?"

Katie smiled. "I can think of plenty of stuff." She gave Jessie a playful push. "You'd better get going. Matt's waiting."

Jessie stepped out onto the back porch as Matt got

out of the car. She walked down the steps waving at him. "I'll be right there." She looked back at Katie. "Don't worry, Tom likes you already, or he wouldn't be coming here to stay for a few days."

"I hope you're right." Katie waved at Matt. "I wish dreamy eyes could see me," she whispered to herself.

Jessie waved as she walked to the car. She slipped into the back seat when Matt opened the door. "Thank you." She smiled at him. "Hi, Frank. How's it going?" She fastened her seat belt.

"Things have been good, at least for me. Matt tells me you're in the thick of things again."

"You heard right." Jessie ran her hand through her hair with an exaggerated sigh.

"I want to hear all about it, especially about the ghost hanging out in your store." Frank turned in the seat.

"I can oblige you with details." Jessie began rattling off the facts of her ghost saga as Frank laughed.

"You could never call your life dull. I'm glad it's you and not me. I'm too old for that kind of excitement." Frank grinned and shook his head.

"What sounds good to you, Frank?" Matt drove into town.

"You pick the spot; I can find something I like anywhere." Frank scrolled through the messages on his phone.

"You should take him to the fifties diner where Franny works. Best homemade rolls and pie around. And if Franny is there, it's worth the ride just to see her." Jessie saw Matt smile in the rearview mirror at her.

"The fifties diner it is."

Chapter 24

Jessie had made the arrangements so she could go with the team. She slipped her gun into her holster and put her badge in her pocket. The mirror didn't lie. Jessie groaned. Those worrylines and dark smudges under her eyes were signs of her restless night. She ran the brush through her hair. It would have to do. Another brief look, a little more concealer and lip gloss, and she threw her hands up in surrender. With a spritz of perfume, she grabbed her jacket out of the closet and headed to the kitchen.

Jessie filled her mug with coffee and screwed the lid on tightly. She cut the strawberry cream croissant into three slices. She would share a piece with Matt and Frank. Word of mouth was important to any new business. Jessie was ready when Matt knocked on the door.

"Good morning," she said as she opened the door.

"Hi, sweetheart. Are you ready?" He leaned close and gave her a sweet, delicious kiss.

"I am." She took a deep breath, fanning her flushed face. She picked up her coffee and the bag with the croissant slices and preceded him out the door. She slipped into the backseat when Matt opened the door. "Hey, big fella. How are you doing?" Jessie pushed a treat through the slats in his crate. Radar turned his soulful eyes on her. "While I'm handing out treats, I have something for each of you to taste, too." She latched her seat belt and handed a slice of croissant to Frank along with a napkin. She gave one to Matt, too.

"What's this?" Matt turned to look at her.

"One of Molly's creations. It's delicious. Did you hear that Kenny and Molly might be buying Java Joe's?"

"I did. Rumor has it that Jason and Joe have to liquidate a lot of their holdings to pay court costs after their involvement in the Collector's Club and the Palm Springs case. Molly will make a much better neighbor for you. At least you won't have to worry about her spying on you."

"True." She saw Frank take a bite of the croissant. "Do you like them, Frank?"

"I'd buy them in a minute. I should take a few home to my wife when I leave."

Matt took a big bite and started the car. "You can tell Molly, I said they're good." He licked the strawberry cream off his lip.

"I'll let Molly know you both liked them. Word of mouth is how you build a good business. That and social media, of course."

"You should know all about it," Frank said. "Your business is doing well, isn't it?"

"It is, thanks to the tour buses and the coffee shop next door. Everyone in town has been very supportive. Of course, they don't know there's a ghost hanging out there. I'm not advertising it, either." Jessie took a sip of her coffee. "I didn't think to ask you whether you wanted coffee."

"We have it. I wouldn't let Frank go to work without his morning coffee—not decaf, but the real stuff." He winked at her in the mirror.

****

Matt pulled the car into a parking space at the trailhead. Dylan and the others were already there. While Frank got Radar ready to do his job, Jessie stood next to the car rubbing the back of her neck. They needed to get started. He gathered everyone together.

"We have some distance to cover to reach the site. I've asked Dylan, who knows the way, to lead our group. If you have any questions, Deputy Taylor and I will both be available." The team started walking. Matt slowed down to let Jessie and Frank catch up to him. "Are you okay?" he asked. "You seem a little nervous."

"I'm all right. I don't know what to expect." She glanced at him.

"You were alone that night; I understand your apprehension. This time, you'll see it in the day and have others with you. You'll do fine. If you get a chance, talk to Bethany Albright and tell me what you think about her." Matt gave her shoulder a pat.

"I will. You don't need to look after me. Go ahead with Taylor and do your job. I'll walk with Frank." Matt nodded and moved ahead on the trail.

****

"Matt said you came upon this place at night after having been shot at." Frank slowed his pace to talk.

She nodded. "I was separated from Matt and Dylan when I started running away from the gunshots. I ended up all turned around because of the fog. No one can quite figure out how I stumbled onto this place. It was a scary night." Jessie shuddered. "Matt thought maybe I had a little help since I was running in the opposite direction. Who knows? I don't think I did. My feet were on the ground at all times." She smiled at him. "I guess I'll get to see how strange it was that I found it."

"What's your take on all the crazy stuff that has happened to you since you moved here?" Frank asked her.

"It's been baffling and a tad bizarre, to say the least. I moved here to have a quiet life, which hasn't been in the cards so far. Although, Matt is a great perk." Jessie glanced at him. "Reba has told me my real reason for moving here was I wanted my life to make a difference. I don't know if I ever said it aloud, but I might have thought it. I guess, in some strange way, I'm helping others."

"Gina's parents and Abigail's would say you are." Frank gave Radar a treat. "Abigail is home with a happy ending, and Gina's parents were free to grieve and help their grandchildren pick up the pieces."

"I guess you're right." She pressed her lips together.

"Not to mention Adriana and Liam, who would no longer be with us if it hadn't been for you. Do you get the picture?" Frank tugged Radar's leash to keep the dog at his side.

"I'm starting to." Jessie smiled at him.

"We all learn to work with what we have. I have a dog that knows how to find the missing and bring people home to their waiting families. You have a strange group keeping you filled in." Frank chuckled. "We always want a family to find their loved one no matter what. Happy ending or sad. They need closure."

"Of course, you're right." Jessie crinkled her nose. "I think that's why Larissa is here. She needs the closure for the sake of her family and daughter. Then she can rest in peace. At least that's what I always thought, but Gina keeps showing up. I wouldn't call it resting for her."

"Didn't you tell me once someone at the church said she believed Gina was looking out for them? Maybe she is. Who knows? I can't say for sure she's not. Can you?"

"I never thought about it before, but it doesn't stop me from thinking about it now. All the time." Her eyebrows rose. The rest of the group was stopped near a group of trees ahead. She came to a stop as soon as they reached them. "I guess we are supposed to stop here," she whispered. Frank nodded.

"Our shooter was in this tree. We found bullet casings on the ground at the base of the tree," Dylan explained. "He had a clear shot at the path we were running on and plenty of light, although the fog might have distorted it. It wasn't dark in this area because of the lights on the perimeter of the Young's property."

"If you wanted to see your target on the path, this was a good spot to sit and wait." Deputy Taylor nodded at the tree. "Someone had to know you were coming, which gives you all something to consider."

"The tomb's about fifteen minutes from here." Dylan started walking.

Matt approached Frank. "I thought we should get to the clearing near the crypt and then let Radar get to work. I brought a scent article. Larissa was wearing this shirt on the day we found her. I'm curious where the dog will take us. She may have never been at this site, but my gut tells me she was. I hope Radar can make it clear."

"He should be able to." Frank patted Radar's head.

While Matt continued to talk with Frank, Jessie moved ahead and introduced herself to Bethany Albright. Bethany had kind hazel eyes and a sweet smile. Jessie liked her. Bethany told Jessie more than she had ever wanted to know about their group. One thing Jessie knew for sure, Bethany was not involved with Larissa, nor was anyone from her group. She was a nice lady, normal even, in a far-out way. Although she did have some unusual ideas, they were alike in some regards. Jessie rubbed her arms. She knew the crypt had to be close. Her skin crawled as if tiny spiders were walking up and down her arms. Apprehension was coming over her, bringing with it the fear of that night.

Chapter 25

Matt stopped the group. "We'll let the dog go first." He handed Frank Larissa's clothing for the dog to smell.

Frank took off the dog's leash and put on his line. "Big guy, it's time to get to work." Radar sniffed the item. With his nose to the ground, he began to track. His ears brushed back and forth across the dirt bringing the scent into the air. He went to the gate, and Frank pushed it open. Radar moved around the crypt and then went inside. The first place he stopped was at the center, where the tomb rested. "She was here at some point. You might want to check to see if this is her blood." Frank pointed at it.

"Take a sample," Taylor called out to one of his team.

Radar went over to the trap door and began to paw at it. "Is there another area below here, Matt?" Frank asked him.

"Yes." Matt lifted the door, and the dog went down the stairs. He sniffed around the area and sat, indicating that Larissa had been down there at some point. "Okay, we know she's been in both of these areas. We can let the team in to do their work. Before we see where else Radar takes us, I want Jessie's reaction to this." He called up to have Jessie come down and kept his eyes riveted on her.

****

Jessie came down the stairs. She stood in the center of the room with her eyes closed. The color drained from her face, and she wrapped her arms around herself. Images flashed through her mind. Larissa was begging them not to leave her alone. Larissa's fear was physical. Jessie started to cry.

"Jess, tell me what's happening?" Matt stood beside her, careful not to interrupt her.

"Larissa has been here. Isolated and locked in the dark. Why? To teach her some kind of lesson. She had no way to know if it was day or night. Alone. Underground. Beneath someone's tomb. What kind of people would do this to a young girl? No wonder she ran away. It must have been a horrible life for her. What if she heard noises above her?" Jessie shivered. "The last time Larissa was here it wasn't good. She begged them not to hurt the baby."

Matt put his arm around her shoulder. "Do you want to stay here or follow Radar?"

"I want out of here." Jessie stumbled toward the stairs. Her breath caught in her throat.

"I thought you might. I'll put Dylan in charge of our group, and we'll see where Radar goes from here." He followed Jessie up the stairs.

Jessie was elated to be outside. She inhaled and lifted her face to the sun. "I can't imagine what being locked down in that room could do to a young girl's psyche. It freaks me out to think of it."

"I'm a grown man, and I wouldn't want to be locked in there, either." Frank stood beside her. "I've seen the harm people can do to each other firsthand, but I can't say I understand the why of it all."

Jessie watched Matt talking to Dylan. Matt was in the zone. If anyone could solve this case, it would be him. Larissa would have justice because Matt wouldn't give up until he found her murderer. "What's next?" she asked when he approached.

"I want to see where Radar takes us from here if he takes us anywhere else."

"Sounds like a good idea to me." Jessie watched Frank prepare Radar. "The way Frank handles his dog fascinates me." She leaned toward Matt and spoke softly.

"Are you ready?" Frank asked Matt as he knelt beside Radar.

Matt nodded. "We're ready."

"Fella, let's get to work." Frank let him smell the scent article again and then stood. Radar went through his routine. He surprised Matt by taking them the opposite way from the compound. The dog tracked into an area overgrown with underbrush and dense with trees. A bumpy, rutted path was the only road into the area. It was possible that a pickup or four-wheel drive could move over the pathway, but Matt doubted anything else would make it.

Radar was pulling hard. The dog came to a place in the center of a group of trees and sat down. Frank pointed to a ring of rocks. "A campfire was built here not too long ago."

"I wonder how long ago." Matt bent down when he noticed a spot that had clumped on the ground. He put on his rubber gloves and scooped the clump into the bag with a spoon. He sealed it. "Possible blood evidence." He found a few more stains around the area.

Radar went to work again, this time leading them

to the gate of the compound where he stopped again. "Our victim had to have been here." Frank noticed a small stain in the dirt.

"I wonder if it started or ended here for Larissa." Jessie paced in front of the gate.

"Hey now, what are you folks doing there?" A man's deep voice startled Jessie. "This is private property," he growled. The stranger was tall and menacing and carried a rifle.

"The dog is tracking for the County Sheriff's office and the Blue Cove PD." Matt showed the man his badge. "We have a search warrant." He handed him the piece of paper.

"Well now, I don't see this property listed on this here paper so you'd best move along." He handed Matt back the paper.

"Right here it says wherever the dog's track might take him. So far, that's here. If he wants to go inside, then we'll be going inside." Matt pointed to the search warrant. "You can stand down and open the gate. If he goes in, so do we."

The gate swung open. "I'll be going with you if you come in."

"You can follow as long us you don't impede the dog's movement or our investigation." Matt turned to Frank. "Wait to start him. I'm calling for backup."

"Good idea. From the looks of that guy, we might need a few extra hands." Jessie zipped her jacket. "He's not happy to see us." The man shut the gate.

"I was thinking the same thing." Frank stood beside her. "I wonder if Radar will go through the gate. I'm betting he does. What do you think?"

"I'm sure he will. Larissa used to live here. I don't

know how long it's been since she was home, but if I had to guess, I'd say it hasn't been very long." While they waited, the man watched them. Jessie noticed he didn't say anything, but he never took his eyes off of them either. "How long until he gets here?" Jessie turned so she didn't have to see the man or his gun.

"Taylor has to get back to his car and then drive over. It'll be at least twenty minutes. I'm willing to wait." He eyed the man with the rifle. "I want backup. I have no idea what Radar will find, and I'm not inclined to risk it."

"You'll get no argument from me. I agree." Frank let Radar lie at his feet. "I have a feeling he's going to go through the gate. We need to be prepared for whatever awaits us."

"Jessie, if you get a chance to talk with Mrs. Young give it a shot. I doubt you'll be given much of an opportunity, but if you are able to, seize it."

"I'm on it." She saluted him, her lips in a tight line.

"Who lives here anyway?" Frank stood next to Matt.

"The land is owned by a Mr. Young, who is Larissa's father. They are a religious group living off the grid."

"Seems strange that they'd suddenly draw attention to themselves in this way." Frank frowned.

"I agree. We wouldn't have known about this group if our victim's body hadn't shown up." Matt shifted the dirt with his shoe.

"Do you think they are involved?" Frank asked.

"I'm not sure if they murdered her, but some of the group's practices are questionable and might have led to her death."

"Like locking her up for misbehaving?" Frank shook his head.

"Yes, and beating her, too." Matt leaned against the car. "We know their discipline of the children is abusive. We are building a case with an eyewitness now."

"Beliefs are important in life, but some people take it way too far in how they control the lives of others." Frank crossed his arms. "Is control an issue here? If it is, the women and children usually pay the highest price. I've seen it before."

"So have I. Women and children don't fair well in human trafficking, either. They're usually the victims." Jessie frowned. "A good portion of crimes happen to women and children, including domestic violence. I get angry thinking about it."

"Control is a major issue with this group. The women are subservient and do a lot of the work. It beats me how, in this age, groups like this can still exist." Matt shook his head.

"Innocent people get trapped somewhere between wanting a simpler life with meaning, and a dominant person's dream to create their idea of a perfect world." Frank shoved his hands into his pockets. "People will freely give up their right to critically think in exchange for a moral code to live by."

"It all seems to start out innocently enough," Jessie said. "At least in the groups I've interviewed. Most people don't realize how many freedoms they have relinquished until something happens to them or another person. Even then, it's hard for them to turn on the perpetrator or to leave the group that has become their family," Jessie added.

"The question is, will they go as far as to murder someone to keep their way of life?" Matt turned to watch the cars approaching. "I think someone did. Maybe her parents, one of the leaders in charge, or even one of the overly zealous followers."

Matt walked over to Taylor, Dylan, and the others as they got out of their cars. "As I told you on the phone, I'm not sure if Radar will go in, but we didn't want to risk it without backup."

"I'm in agreement with you, Matt." Taylor grabbed his radio. "Let's see what happens."

Frank knelt beside Radar, held the scent article for him to smell, and gave him the command. Radar went back to the gate and pawed at it. "He wants to go in."

"You heard the man. Open the gate." Taylor looked at the guard, who complied.

They followed the dog through the compound, drawing a crowd of men as they did. Jessie was shocked when Radar picked Mr. Young and Randy Phillips out of the crowd. "These men will need to be questioned. They were near enough to her that their scent was on her clothing," Frank told Matt.

Taylor took the two men into the compound's dining hall for questioning. Radar continued his track to another building, where he sat. "What is that building?" Matt questioned the man standing beside him.

"It's our infirmary," the man replied.

"Who looks after the people who come here?" Matt looked around the group.

"I do." An older, distinguished-looking man stepped forward.

"You'll need to come with me." Matt escorted him to where Taylor held the other two men.

****

Jessie and Frank sat down on a bench outside the small infirmary. "Wow, he picked them out, just like that!" Jessie snapped her finger. "I've seen him in action before, but still, it's rather amazing."

"He was on today. Whether these are the men who killed your victim is yet to be seen. There might still be someone else, and Larissa came here for help. I'd love to be a fly on the wall to hear what's going on in that room."

"Me, too. Matt wanted me to talk to Mrs. Young, but I'm not sure who she is. If I start asking around, I could get her in trouble." Jessie patted Radar's head.

"Maybe if you sit here, and I move away, she'll come to you. I'll stay close enough to help if you need it." Frank leaned close to her to murmur his suggestion.

"It might work. Especially if she's the woman who has been calling me at the church. Don't go too far, though. I don't like being here alone."

"I won't. I'll be able to see you, I promise." Frank and Radar walked away and left Jessie sitting there alone.

Jessie went through the alphabet in her head and sang a song or two before a woman sat on the far end of the bench. She had been standing with a group of women who had stared at Jessie for several minutes. The drab clothing they wore seemed to be relics from the past. Jessie glanced at the woman.

"It's a nice day, isn't it?" Jessie saw her nod. "I'm Jessie."

"I know." The lady cast her eyes downward. "I'm Rose Young." She moved closer to Jessie on the bench. "I loved my daughter, and so did my husband," she blurted out.

"You have a strange way of showing it." Anger flashed in Jessie's eyes. "How could you let them lock her up alone for days without helping her?" Something didn't feel right to Jessie.

"How did you know?" Rose fidgeted with her hands in her lap.

"Olivia told me." Jessie's chin edged up.

"You don't know what it's like here." Her voice softened.

"No, I don't. Tell me, because as I see it, you or your husband could have stopped this before she was killed by simply calling the police."

"We can't use the phone without being monitored. The elders wouldn't let my niece even call to tell her parents that she was alive. I have to be careful talking to you now. If I'm caught, I shudder to think what will happen."

Jessie frowned. Was she being played? "If Larissa were my daughter, I would have found a way to call the police." Jessie gripped the armrest on the bench. "You should go. I don't want to put your life in jeopardy." She glanced at the woman again, anger rising in her.

"The men are too busy talking to worry about me right now. I need to talk fast, though." She moved a little closer to Jessie. "I'm the one who called the church."

"I thought so," Jessie said. "You could have told me to call the police."

"I called because I was worried about my niece Olivia and my daughter. I wasn't free to talk; someone was always around." She paused. "Olivia questioned everything, and I knew the leaders would be hard on her. Because she was married, they put pressure on Roger to deal with her. I saw what happened to my daughter over and over again. I was powerless to stop it." She stood. "I need to go. I'll find a way to talk to you again."

Jessie had her doubts about what Rose was telling her, but she didn't know why. "I find it hard to believe you were concerned about Olivia. You knew she was underage, and he was over twenty-one. Yet you let him marry her without her parents' approval." Jessie saw a worried look pass across Rose's face.

"I knew she was, but I couldn't stop the wedding." She looked down again. "It doesn't work that way here. Not even my husband could have stopped it."

"But you called me, and you could have called your sister to tell her Olivia was alive. You could have phoned the police and saved your daughter." Jessie tapped her foot.

Rose's shoulders slumped. "I wish I had done many things that I didn't. I'll live with it forever and never get to hold my grandchild in my arms. Nor will I ever see my beautiful Larissa again. Fear kept me from helping the one person who meant the world to me. I'm sorry, I need to leave." Tears ran down her cheeks, and she stifled a sob as she walked away.

"Take care." Jessie wasn't moved.

"You have no right to make our Rose cry. You need to keep your nose out of our business, or you'll wish you had." The man had come up silently and now stood with his legs apart and his arms crossed. "We don't answer to man's laws."

Jessie jumped at the harshness in his voice. She was happy to see Frank and Radar coming toward her.

"Boy, am I glad to see you," she called to Frank. The man's menacing stare gave her the creeps.

"I'll stay right beside you. Let's hope the brute gives up and walks away," Frank told her quietly. He patted Radar's head as the dog growled at the man. With a scowl, the man turned on his heel and stomped off.

"I thought he'd never leave. Thank you, big fella." Jessie glanced at Frank.

"Me, he could intimidate, but I don't think he wanted to tangle with this guy." Frank rubbed Radar's head.

Chapter 26

Matt and the older gentleman walked into the hall. Matt closed the door behind him. Phillips and Young were already sitting at one of the tables. Larissa's father was slumped in his chair, his face resting on his hands. Phillip's arms were folded across his chest, and his chin jutted out. Matt motioned for the man with him to sit. "You have some explaining to do. I want to know how your scent came to be on the clothes that Larissa was wearing when she died. You'll either talk now, or I'll take you in for questioning." Matt lowered his eyebrows, his face hot.

"You're in some serious trouble here, and right now, you're the lead suspects in Larissa's murder. Start talking!" Taylor growled.

"Larissa was here, and I tried to help her, but she needed more help than I was capable of giving her." The older gentlemen rubbed his temples. "Ours is a small clinic, and she needed a trauma center. I told Randy she needed to get to the hospital right away. I was told to go home to my wife; he'd take care of her. I assumed he had." He pointed accusingly at Randy.

"What's your name? Are you a doctor?" Taylor took out his notepad.

"Glenn Crawford, sir. I'm a doctor and have a license to practice in the state."

"We'll need to have a copy of it." Matt's face

tightened. "Tell me what you observed that night."

"She had several broken bones with multiple cuts and bruises. She was in the early stages of labor and should have had an emergency c-section. When I read the story of her giving birth and dying in the dumpster, I was appalled. I couldn't do the surgery here for obvious reasons. Hers was a life threatening situation, and I didn't have the help or equipment."

"Mr. Young, where were you and your wife while this was going on?" Matt's nostrils flared. "If this had been my daughter, I would have done anything I could have to save her life. What were you doing?" Matt's fist hit the table.

"I was watching the doctor. Randy and I had carried her in from the gate where she had been dumped." Mr. Young hung his head. "She was hurting something awful, and I didn't understand our moving her probably made it worse. I wanted to get her help. My past had caught up to me." Tears welled up in his eyes.

Matt waved off his emotional speech. "But you didn't call an ambulance or make sure she got to the hospital? My God, man, this was your daughter." Matt shook his head and studied the two men sitting in front of him. They were not so cocky now. "What were you thinking? I ought to arrest you. Even if you can prove you didn't beat her or have a knowledge of who did, you did nothing to save her. You're both guilty of neglect."

"Randy told me to go home, that he'd take care of it. You see, he was trying to protect me. He knew if the police got wind of the fact she had been here you'd ask questions. Randy was afraid what we had built together would be destroyed. It doesn't matter anymore. I don't blame him, though. You're right I should have done something even if I had to carry her to the hospital myself. I've been living a falsehood and seeing my little girl broken...well now, nothing matters any longer." Young waved off Randy, who was trying to shush him.

"I'd be careful if I were you, Randy." Taylor's voice was hard. "You've been busy abusing youngsters including Larissa, whom you locked in the crypt for days at a time. I can see that you're shocked we know. That's abuse, plain and simple, Mr. Phillips, and the county frowns on it. We have laws, you know, and you've broken them." Taylor pointed at him.

Matt looked at Glenn. "You're free to go for now. You'll need to stay around. I'm sure we will have more questions for you. Don't forget to give us a copy of your license before we leave."

"Sir, may I ask one question?" Glenn asked Matt.

Matt nodded. "Go ahead."

Glenn looked angrily at Randy. "Is throwing her in the dumpster to die what you meant by taking care of her?" He turned on his heel and left the hall.

"Damn good question; I have the same one." Matt's hand fisted at his side.

"I didn't throw her in the dumpster. I walked my friend back to his home. When I got back to the clinic, she was gone."

"He walked his friend back home. Now isn't that nice of him, Matt? A girl lies dying, and he walks his friend home. The doctor had told him to get her to the hospital quickly, and he leaves her. Hell, you both make me sick. How long did you leave her alone and who did you pay to get rid of her?" Taylor's scowl deepened.

"We should take them in for questioning. There's more to this story than these folks are telling us. These two are either soft in the head or hiding something. I'm betting it's the second one." Matt looked at Taylor. "You want to bring them into Blue Cove? It's closer."

"Sounds good to me. Larissa was found there." Taylor stood and motioned them to move.

Matt found Jessie and Frank, and they walked together toward the car. "We're taking them in for questioning. I'm not sure how long this will take, but you two might have to have dinner without me, tonight."

"Of course, this comes first." Frank put Radar in his crate. "What's your take on them so far?"

"I'm not sure they actually murdered Larissa. Her dad was shaken. They are at the very least guilty of neglect, and I know they are hiding something. Maybe time at the station or in a jail cell might loosen one or both of their tongues." Matt started the car. "Lab results should be back soon, and the DNA should tell us more."

"I don't get it." Jessie frowned. "How could her dad let this happen to her? I want to know why."

"You and me both, sweetheart." Matt made eye contact with her in the rearview mirror.

"Jessie talked to Mrs. Young." Frank fiddled with his seat belt which had pulled too tight when the car stopped.

"Her name is Rose. If you're feeling like I am after talking to her, then you're angry."

"Damn right I am." Matt turned onto the highway and headed back to Blue Cove. "I want to hear about your conversation with Mrs. Young."

"She was afraid to be seen talking to me." Jessie told him about their conversation.

"Why a woman would put up with all the crap, I don't understand." Matt frowned.

"An abused woman believes there's no way out for her. Olivia left a few times, but he would always find her." Jessie spoke up from the backseat. "Roger beat her to make her afraid to try and leave him the next time. He would always promise never to hit her again, and when he did, it was always her fault. Often a woman has no resources to leave or start over again. She is trapped, afraid, and feels helpless." Jessie paused. "I saw it with Sally. When you're told often enough how stupid you are, you tend to believe it after a while. I'm not sure if that's the case here, though."

"Why?" Matt glanced at her in the rearview mirror.

"I can't put my finger on it, but something seemed a little off to me about Rose Young. Her tears didn't move me, and I didn't feel sorry for her at all, which is not like me. It could be I was too angry to get a good read on her."

"At least Olivia and Sally are safe for now. But I can't promise that their husbands won't go after them. I've seen it happen too many times." Matt called Kenny on his radio and told him he was bringing in two suspects.

"All I know is as I watched the people while we were waiting for you, I could see those folks need help. It will take some counseling to get them out from under the control of the leaders of their movement." Frank shook his head. "I wish people would stop to think before they leap into something. When a faction takes away a person's individuality, their ability to question, and their will to make decisions for themselves, warning sirens should go off everywhere."

"I guess the need to belong to something and be surrounded by people who care is a greater tug than the red flags, no matter how bizarre it may seem." Jessie wrinkled her nose. "Their dresses were a turnoff for me. I'm too fashion conscious. I'm not nearly as much a fashionista as Katie is, but at least I want to dress as if I live in this century."

"This has been a strange day all the way around." Matt slowed down as he approached the turnoff to Blue Cove. "Radar did a damn fine job again. I appreciate you coming, Frank. His track will help us build the story of what happened. If the stains on the tomb come back here with Larissa's DNA, we will have another piece of the puzzle. She was at the campsite, too, and the sample I found should be the proof. All thanks to your dog."

"He did well and still amazes me." Frank's lips curved into a smile.

"Jess, I'll get out here. Frank can take you home and then meet you later at the Inn. I'll try to get there if I can." Matt parked outside of the station and opened her door. "I'll see you later, sweetheart, or I'll call you and let you know what I've learned. Why don't you sit up front?" He gave her a quick kiss and was gone.

Chapter 27

Jessie made her way to the Inn. Yoshi, Katie's gardener, had been working on the grounds when the weather permitted, getting it ready for spring. Soon the garden would be filled with colorful flowers and fragrant aromas. Reading a few books in the garden was on the top of her warm weather to-do list. Jessie walked up the steps to the back porch and stopped. She loved this place. Her life had changed since she had moved into her cottage. Part of the reason was standing inside: her friend. Being near Katie again was fun. Meeting Matt had been the best. Falling in love with him, well, it didn't get any better. She had learned a few things about herself along the way, too. She was much stronger than she had thought. Seeing ghosts had never been on her radar in New York, but Blue Cove reminded her that she could stand on her own two feet. Or maybe swing up into a tree, if need be, and then jump on the shooter below at the perfect moment to save the man she loved. She could stand up to a dirty cop or shoot a hitman if she had to. Life here was at times challenging, but it wasn't dull, for sure.

Jessie heard the car before it came into view. She couldn't see who it was, but she knew the occupant was trouble. The man got out of his car. Bruce. She should have known.

He waved as he approached her. "Hello, Jessie."

His smooth voice had the same effect on her as nails on a chalkboard. "Where's my wife?" He walked up the stairs, getting close enough to make eye contact with her.

She refused to be intimidated. "Sally's not here, Bruce." What had Sally ever seen in him? "To tell you the truth I have no idea where she is." Jessie looked him directly in the eyes until he glanced away.

"Geez, Jessie, you're smart enough to know you shouldn't mess with me." He glared at her. "This is what comes from being top in your class. You're a liar. I don't believe you." He gritted his teeth.

"I don't care whether you believe me or not. Sally is not here." She took a step back from him.

"You can't hide my damn wife from me. I'm Sally's husband, and I know my rights." He grabbed her arm, squeezing and wringing it.

Jessie slapped his hand away. "You gave those rights away when you started abusing her."

"Hear me well, you bitch," he snarled. "I will hound you, follow you, and be your worst nightmare until you tell me where my wife is." He reached for her arm again.

Jessie moved faster. She grabbed his arm and pinned it behind his back. Then she shoved him against the outside wall and tightened her hold on his arm, pulling it back and up far enough that he yelped. Whew, she had done it the way she had learned in class, and it worked. "As far as I can see you have two choices. Although, the first one no longer exists because you threatened me. You could have asked about your wife, and when you learned she wasn't here you could have gotten in your car and driven away. No name calling or threats. But no, you had to be a bad boy. Jail is the next stop for you." Jessie yelled through the open back door, "Katie, if you're in there, call the cops. Bruce decided to pay us a visit."

Tom flew through the screen door. "I'll take over now, Jessie. Nice job, by the way." He smiled at her, then patted Bruce down and found his gun. "I'd say he came looking for trouble." Tom handed Jessie the gun.

"What's going on?" Katie opened the screen and peeked out.

"Our old friend Bruce stopped by for a visit. He decided to threaten me and got himself in a bit of a jam with Tom." Jessie reached for her phone.

Tom put the cuffs on Bruce. "Call the police, and we'll let them deal with him."

"Hi, Kenny, this is Jessie. We need an officer at the Inn." She proceeded to tell him what was going on. When Jessie disconnected, she saw Katie standing in front of Bruce.

"Who do you think you are, Bruce Kingman?" Katie got in his face. "You're on my property, and you dare to threaten my friend. We saw the pictures of what you did to Sally—who is another friend, by the way." Her pointed finger was poking his chest. "Sally's not here. She's safe and away from you. Darn, you. *We* can't even know where she is, and that makes me mad." Katie glared at him.

"You can't keep my wife from me. I know my rights," Bruce yelled and then started hurling expletives at them.

"No sir, you don't." Tom led him over to a chair to sit down. "I happen to know there's a restraining order. Your only right is to leave her the hell alone."

Kip and Gary arrived and took him into custody. "We'll be back to check out his car." They led him, swearing and glaring, to their cruiser.

Jessie glanced at Tom. "I doubt they'll be able to keep him long, but it might buy us some time."

"No doubt his high-priced lawyer will get him out, but only after Matt scares him out of Blue Cove." Tom opened the door for Katie and Jessie. "Nice move, pinning him against the wall. Where did you learn that maneuver?"

"I've been taking classes. When Bruce grabbed my arm, it hurt, and I didn't want him to punch me. I acted to protect myself." Jessie rubbed her wrist where a bruise was starting to form.

"You did it perfectly. I couldn't have done it better myself." Tom smiled at her. "Matt would have been proud to see you in action."

"It's amazing what healthy fear and a little knowledge can do to motivate you."

"Bruce won't give up without a fight. He'll keep looking for his wife. He's angry right now. I imagine he'll try something stupid and wind up in jail. Hopefully, he'll stop before he goes to prison or kills her."

"I hope so. I can see what Sally has been up against." Jessie shuddered. "He wasn't happy with me if the anger in his eyes was any indication."

"I'm sure he wasn't. It's all about control and intimidation for an abuser."

"Jessie?" Katie was spooning the vegetables into a bowl. "Could you take this out to the buffet table for me?" Katie pointed to a large bowl of salad on the counter.

"At your service." Jessie reached for the salad and took it to the dining room. She helped Katie take the remaining dishes of food to the table. Frank sat beside her during dinner. He got into a conversation with Tom, which gave Jessie time to watch her friend. Katie's glances never strayed far from Tom. Something was definitely going on with those two. Katie had the glow of a woman enjoying a nice flirtation. The next few months could prove interesting. Jessie smiled. She was happy for her friend and could hardly wait to hear from Katie's lips what she was feeling.

Katie leaned across the table. "What has you smiling?" she whispered.

"Nothing, in particular, I'm happy to be among my friends." Jessie's smile broadened when Matt slipped into the empty chair beside her, brushing up against her shoulder as he did.

He grinned at her. "I've heard quite the story about you. Is it true you apprehended Bruce with a twist of his arm?" He winked. "It seems Gary and Kip are impressed after hearing about it from Tom." Matt leaned closer to her. "Bruce wasn't happy about your arm-hold, though. You might have made him your enemy."

"Is that right? He'll have to take a number and get in line." Jessie rolled her eyes. "I seem to have a knack for making the fellas mad." Her eyes crinkled at the corners.

Chapter 28

"This was a fun evening." Matt walked Jessie back to her cottage. "I'll fill you in on what's going on with Larissa's case as soon as I get the information I'm waiting on."

"Thanks." She stopped at her door.

"Bruce is cooling his heels in a jail cell until his lawyer gets here in the morning. I hope it'll put enough fear in him to give up on finding Sally, but I'm not holding out much hope. He's one angry man."

"Should I be worried?" Jessie's brows rose.

"Cautious, yes, but I think he'll leave you alone. You embarrassed him by getting the best of him and not being intimidated by his bluster. If my hunch plays out, Bruce will leave town. He might make some harassing phone calls, though."

"At least I can always hang up."

"Exactly." He reached around her to unlock the door. "Just when I think you couldn't do anything to surprise me, you do something I wasn't counting on. Jess, you blow my mind, sweetheart." He leaned close and kissed her. "I'm yours for a little while." He opened the door for her.

"Did you notice the glances our friends were giving each other? Katie may be falling for Tom. Your friend had better not hurt her."

"I could say the same thing to you. Tom is close to

falling himself, and Katie is flighty compared to Tom." He caressed her cheek. "I know the vulnerable feeling of falling."

"Is that right?" She tilted her head back, her lips parted.

"Yeah, sweetheart." He leaned closer still. "Don't break my heart."

"I wouldn't think of it." She tugged his head toward her and kissed him.

"I'm happy to hear it." He took a deep breath. His heart was racing. It was his turn to kiss her. Every other coherent thought left Matt's mind. She felt right in his arms—a perfect fit. He tightened his hold, drawing her closer. He should leave, but his body had a mind of its own.

She put her hand on his chest and pulled back. "Matt, is Frank waiting?"

"Nope," he mumbled as he nibbled on her ear. "He's on his way back to my place and a lounge chair if I know him."

"He does love your chair." She took his hand and pulled him toward the couch. "For the record, I'm not sold on the whole Katie and Tom thing yet."

"I know, I'm not either." He sat, pulling her into his lap. "My mind is on other things right now." His finger traced her bottom lip. "I've got you right where I want you."

****

Jessie got into bed and was reaching for her book when her phone rang. "I didn't expect you to call tonight. Did you have a chance to read the chapters?"

"I'm on my way to your place to talk."

"I'll be waiting." Jessie slipped out of bed. She put

on her robe and went to the living room to turn on the back porch light. Peeking out the window, she opened the door as soon as Katie got there. "I thought you'd be too busy with guests—Tom—to want to talk tonight."

"You understand me so well, Jessie. It's precisely because of Tom I needed to talk to you. Listen to me. I don't ask you often about men; it's usually the other way around." Katie leaned back in the chair and closed her eyes. "How do you know if it's love? The give up your freedom marrying kind of love? I mean, look at the mess Sally got into."

"I'm not sure how to answer you. I know how I feel when I'm with Matt, and how I feel when we're apart. You know me, though, I take things slow and easy—that's who I am. I'm feeling him out and trying him on for size to see if we mesh," Jessie added. "Once you know your heart, you are ready. The need to be with them has to be stronger than the desire to be free."

"How about you, Jessie, are you there?" Katie fussed with the throw on the arm of the chair.

"I'm closer now than I've ever been and get nearer to the tipping point all the time."

"Wow, I never thought I'd hear you say it." Katie's jaw dropped open.

"Well, don't tell anyone because I would like to tell Matt at the right time when I'm ready."

"I would never tell him; he needs to hear it from you." Katie stood. "Thanks, friend, you helped. I think I'll try to get to know Tom before I jump, which isn't my normal way of doing things. Seeing Bruce tonight reminded me to be cautious. Plus, I took a leap with Jeremy only to find out we didn't mesh. We had nothing in common. Tom and I seem to hit it off. Tom makes me feel special like no one else has. He doesn't berate me but likes my crazy personality, which is a plus. And if I'm totally honest, there is someone else whom I still think about—but he's not interested in me, so I have to move on, right? I need to take it slow. There will be no blind leaps, only a conscious jump when I'm ready." Katie hugged Jessie when she stood.

"Who?" Jessie was surprised to hear Katie's confession.

Katie shook her head. "It will remain a secret because it's not going to happen." She walked to the door. "Now, I'm going home to get into bed and call you. Let's keep our tradition."

"Sounds perfect to me." Jessie followed her to the door and locked it when she left. She took a glass of water to her room and waited for Katie's call. Who was the mystery man? Jessie had an idea. Then the phone rang and the next hour was filled with their discussion, arguments, and laughter. This was a tradition their daughters could continue someday, if and when they both had little girls. They had to. Jessie reached over to turn off the light. Yes, they had to have little girls who would be best friends, also.

Jessie woke suddenly and found Larissa sitting in her room. She yawned and sat up. The clock said one-thirty. "What are you doing here?"

Larissa began to move about the room. Fascinated, Jessie saw her comb and brush set lift off her dresser and suspend in mid-air. The pages of the book on her nightstand flipped back and forth rapidly.

"I hope you're enjoying yourself," she mumbled, while the chair moved slowly across the room to the opposite corner. A blanket at the foot of the bed was folded and placed neatly over the back of the chair. Next, a picture floated by Jessie, nearly smacking her in the head and was placed where the picture of Sadie had hung. Sadie's picture found its home where the other one had been.

"I'll try to find out how your daughter is doing and who will adopt her. Is that what's troubling you?" Jessie saw Larissa stop and sit in the chair. She must have struck a chord. "She is such a beautiful baby. Would you like me to take a picture of her? I'll try to get a photo to show you. I'm sorry I didn't think of it before." It was possible Matt had one in the police file. Jessie hoped so. "Are you staying here tonight?" Jessie didn't expect an answer.

She didn't get one. Larissa watched her. Jessie closed her eyes and tried to turn off her thoughts. A quick peek a few minutes later found Larissa still sitting there. Jessie rolled over. She was too sleepy to care. She snuggled down under her covers, plumping the pillow under her head. Larissa was forgotten for the moment, and Jessie slept.

The sunlight coming through the slits in the blinds and the sound of the alarm stirred her. Rubbing the sleep from her eyes, she sat on the edge of the bed and stretched. A frown replaced a smile as her eyes processed the room. Larissa was missing along with several other items. Jessie went in search of a missing chair, the picture of Sadie, and a large vase of flowers. She found them in the living room only after she'd tripped, catching her foot on a chair that hadn't been there the night before. Jessie threw up her hands. The next several minutes were spent tidying the mess Larissa had left her. This case had better be solved soon. Jessie's chin rose. Larissa was becoming a challenge. How was it even possible to win a fight with a ghost? Matt would get a kick out it, but it was starting to bug her.

Chapter 29

Matt smiled and chuckled at every word she was telling him. "I don't know what to say to you. I've never run into a problem quite like this before in my line of work." He glanced around the store. "Is she here now?"

"No, I haven't seen her this morning, which is strange, and my store was fine when I came in. I hope she won't be coming to my house every night." She waved at Molly, who was coming through the door.

"I have a total mystery going on over there." Molly pointed to the open door. "A lot of stuff was moved in the night. Chairs, paintings, even coffee mugs." Molly frowned at Matt who was laughing. "I don't think it's funny. We either have a prowler or an extremely strong mouse."

"I'll leave Jessie to explain it to you when she can." He grinned.

"I'll be back later to talk, Jessie. I can't wait to hear why this is funny to him, and he's not writing up a report." Molly went back to wait on her customers.

"How am I going to explain Larissa to her?" She frowned at him which made him laugh harder. "You seem to be in a mighty happy mood this morning. Your laughing could be considered to be annoying by some."

"Am I bothering you, sweetheart?" He traced the line of her jaw with his finger.

"I might consider it a tad bothersome." Her eyes sparkled.

"Only a little? I might have to work on it to improve," he said in a husky whisper, leaning closer to her. "I tried calling you last night, but you must have been talking." He brushed her hair away from her face.

"Katie was in a talkative mood." Her breath caught, and she stepped back, hitting the table.

"Careful, sweetheart." He caught her around the waist to steady her. "I've got you."

"You sure do." She blushed. "Are you having fun?"

"Who me? Yes." He gave her a wry grin. He kissed her until she was kissing him back. "I like this campaign of mine. I'm enjoying myself a hundred percent." He tugged her with him toward the door. "I need to get to work. We'll talk tonight at dinner."

She was fanning her face. "Before you leave I wanted to ask you if you have a photo of the baby in your case file that you could copy for me. Larissa needs to see her daughter."

"I have a few photos which the nurses at the hospital gave me. I'll be right back." He went out to his car and came back in carrying a large envelope. "If this will calm your ghost, I'm happy to do my part."

Jessie looked at the photo. "Isn't she the sweetest baby ever? I'm in love."

"I know the feeling." He pulled her into his side. "I hope Larissa stays out of trouble. Would you mind recording your talk with Molly? I want to hear it." He chuckled as she stood with him by the door.

"I'd call that annoying." She pinched his arm.

"Happy to do my part. See you later." He turned

before he walked out the door and kissed her again. "Have a good day."

"You too." It was time to get to work.

****

Matt walked into the station, and Dylan was waiting. "We got the word; Kingman's lawyer is coming with his bail money."

"Okay. Take Bruce to the interrogation room, and I'll be right there. I want to say a few things before his lawyer gets here." Matt walked down the hall.

"My lawyer is on his way; I told you I'd get out of here," Bruce bragged to Matt as he walked in. "You've got nothing to hold me on."

"You were arrested on menacing and assault charges. Those charges stand, and you'll have to appear in court.You don't have to say anything without your lawyer present, but if you waive the right, it's up to you."

"I'm not talking." Bruce folded his arms across his chest.

"Good, because what I want you to do is listen. You've threatened a few folks in my town. One of those was your wife, and you were stupid cnough to leave those threats on her phone. If I were you, I'd give up trying to find Sally, wait for the divorce to be over, and go on with your life. I doubt you're going to do it, though. You aren't smart enough to leave well enough alone."

"Look here, I'm nobody's dummy," he snarled. "I want my wife back."

"The thing is, she doesn't want *you*. She's tired of being knocked around and battered by you. If any harm comes to Sally, you're number one on the suspect list. I have a copy of the restraining order, which you've already seen." Matt waved the copy in front of him. "By law, this document tells you the only right you have is to stay away from her. You were already breaking the law by harassing her, as well as by following her here. I know you were served with divorce papers, and since you live in a no-fault state you can contest it, but the divorce will happen. She wants it, and your marriage will be dissolved by the date listed on the papers. Do you understand so far?" Matt waited for him to nod. "What you need is an anger management class. You're too angry, Bruce. You have to get hold of yourself before you do something stupid, ruin your life, and wind up in prison or worse. I've talked to the judge, who has agreed to this as a possible course of action instead of jail time. I'll explain it to your lawyer when he gets here. While you're waiting, I suggest that you think about what I'm about to offer you. In layman's terms, because of your clean record until the restraining order, if you agree to go to anger management class, do community service, and go back home to cool your heels for a couple of months under check-in supervision, you can walk out of here. If you don't agree to those terms, you'll stick around for sentencing. I'd take it if I were you."

Bruce glared at him. "I'm not saying anything without talking to my lawyer first."

"That's fine. There is one more thing I want to discuss with you." Matt leaned toward Bruce. "Keep your damn hands off Jessie and Katie. Neither one of them knows where Sally is. We did that to protect them and your wife from you. Jessie can take care of herself, as you found out, but I won't let citizens be harassed.

Basically, Bruce, I want you out of Blue Cove, and I don't want to see you here ever again." Matt read an incoming text. "Your attorney has arrived. I'll talk to him about the charges you're facing and the bargain we're offering. He will advise you. Have a nice day, Mr. Kingman." Matt walked out of the room.

Matt talked with Bruce's attorney about what was being offered to his client as a way to avoid jail time. His attorney encouraged Bruce to take it, and he agreed. Matt handed the attorney the paperwork.

"This must be signed by the teacher of the class he attends, his supervisor, and has to be sent back to this office by the date listed here or he'll be found in contempt, and a warrant will be issued." Bruce walked out of his office.

"Do you think he'll take your advice?" Dylan asked.

"I have no clue if he listened or which way he'll go. I hope for Sally's sake he'll go home and behave himself. I hope the reality of the law and possible jail time will put the brakes on him. At least Bruce knows he can't beat his wife, intimidate other citizens, and assault anyone under the guise of his rights."

The rest of the afternoon was spent with Deputy Taylor questioning Phillips and Young. Their attorney was a young man from the compound. Matt fished for information and got little or nothing. The session was going nowhere, and as long as the two men were together, they wouldn't talk. Matt talked with Taylor, and they decided to let them go. Separate appointments were set for each of them to come back in for questioning. What they needed now was a break.

The two men walked out of the station with their

attorney. There was more to their story, and Matt wanted to get to the bottom of it. The group's existence was a mystery. Very few of the people around them knew who they were. He frowned. Mrs. Albright and the ladies in her group were close to being ruled out. Matt had no firm suspects in Larissa's murder.

"Hey, Matt, I hate to interrupt your thoughts, but Dave Lewis wants you to call when you get a chance." Gary stood in the doorway. "I was given this note to pass on to you." He handed Matt a sealed envelope.

"Thanks, Gary, I'll get on it." He grabbed the phone and made his call. No answer, so he left a message asking Dave to return his call. Then he took the letter opener and sliced open the envelope.

Sir,

I would like to speak to you privately without my attorney present if that is possible. I will find a reason for leaving the compound and be here tomorrow morning as early as eight. I need to get some things off my chest.

Marvin Young

Matt smiled as he left the office. Was this the possible break he was looking for? Marvin Young might be ready to talk.

Chapter 30

Jessie was waiting for Matt. This was one of the best times of the day, and it had been a quiet day. Larissa hadn't come back. All Jessie had to deal with were her customers and an explanation to Molly about Larissa. Bless Matt's heart. It had been an uncomfortable conversation, and Molly was still giving her strange looks. Jessie hoped Molly would keep it to herself, or she could kiss her business goodbye. Darn Matt. She didn't want to be the "strange" lady in town. Jessie locked the front door.

"Please tell me what I saw." Molly came running through the doors her eyes as large as saucers.

"Whoa, slow down. What did you say?" Jessie put up her hand.

"I thought you were weird, but I *saw* her. She's sitting in a chair in Joe's, looking out the window. Why can I see her?"

Jessie went to look, and sure enough, Larissa was sitting there staring out the window. "I have no idea. No one has been able to see her so far, but me. She must have wanted you to."

"I don't like it. Look—my hand is still shaking, and the hair is standing up on my neck. Will the ghost hurt me, do you think?" Molly stumbled into a chair.

"No, I don't believe she would. Larissa is young. Here, let me try something to get her over here." Jessie went to the counter and reached for the envelope with the photos of the baby in it. "Larissa," she called. "I have a picture of your sweet baby girl for you to see." Jessie felt the cool rush of air and knew her ghost was standing near her. She placed the photo on the counter.

Molly took a peek. "She's a beautiful baby. Would you look at all her hair." Molly rubbed her arms. "She's here, isn't she?"

Jessie nodded. "She's a sweet baby girl." She felt the tears come as she watched Larissa gaze at her daughter's photo. With a sad expression, Larissa went to resume her watch in the chair at the front of Jessie's store. Jessie placed the photo on the book table for her to see.

"Please don't tell anyone I could see her," Molly pleaded.

"I won't tell anyone on you if you won't tell on me." Jessie smiled at her. "It's our secret."

"No offense, but I hope she stays in your store tonight. It took me a while to straighten out the mess she made over there." Molly pointed to Joe's.

"I'm not offended, although I can't guarantee that she'll stay here. She's been wandering more. She might be restless. She's watching for her murderer. At least that's what I think. Our biggest hope to putting an end to her visits is to solve the case so she can rest in peace." Jessie crossed her fingers.

"I should finish closing." Molly walked to the open doors. "Your secret is safe with me." Molly closed the doors between the businesses.

Jessie noticed how pensive Larissa was. It was best to leave her in a quiet mood for the evening. She could always try her luck with some questions tomorrow.

Jessie went out to meet Matt when he parked in front of the store. Molly's secret was safe with her. Jessie wouldn't even tell Matt.

"Hi, sweetheart, how was your day?" Matt held her free hand while she locked the door.

"It was quiet and slightly uncomfortable thanks to you." She glared at him and ruined it with a smile.

"Moi?" He pointed at himself and grinned.

"Yes, you had to know Molly would ask about your statement that I would explain who had rearranged Joe's. She still doesn't know what to think of me." She frowned. "I like to keep this part of my life quiet. The fewer people who know, the better."

"Was Molly okay with it?"

"Do you remember how you were when you first found out? She took it about the same way." Jessie smiled. "I'll survive. Where are we going for dinner?"

"Is Angelo's all right?"

She nodded, buttoning her coat. The air was brisk but not too cold. "We can walk, and I can get my car afterward."

"You seeing all this stuff has become commonplace to me. Especially since I've gotten to know you." Matt slowed his pace to match hers.

"Are you saying I appear normal enough, even in spite of all the strange baggage, that you aren't worried about it anymore?"

"Yeah, something like that." He grinned.

"I get it. I'm not shocked by seeing ghosts and hearing voices anymore. I'm not sure what that says about me. Although, Larissa has been somewhat of a challenge." Jessie walked through the door Matt was holding open. "Maybe now that I'm getting used to life being this way, it will all disappear."

"Do you think it works that way?" Matt gave her a doubtful glance.

"No, probably not, but I can hope, can't I?" She followed the hostess to the table.

"It hasn't been too bad, has it? I mean, we've solved some big cases, and we met, which is the highlight of my life to this point."

"Subtract the bombs, bullets, voodoo, and rearrangement of my store, and I've taken things well, all things considered." Jessie ordered spaghetti and meatballs. "Finding Abigail, Adriana, and of course, Larissa's sweet baby girl are the pluses to it all."

Matt told her about Bruce and what had happened to him. "My hope is he'll do what he committed to do and move on with his life when the divorce is final. But I don't know."

"It's hard to tell about people. Bruce was a great guy in school. He was popular, the head of the student body, and always at the top of the class in grade point average. Straight As, all the years I knew him."

"Was it his dreams or his parents'? That's a lot to live up to when you're a teenage boy." Matt shook his head. "The energy level in our house made my parents sign us up for every sports program available. They kept us running full speed, hoping that we'd be too tired to move by the time we got home." Matt smiled at the memory. "It didn't work. We still found time to drive them nuts."

"Bruce wanted to be the best at everything he tried, and so did Sally. She competed with me even when there was no competition. I can imagine how their marriage went with both of them wanting to be number one." Jessie thanked the waiter when he placed her salad in front of her.

"Obviously, it didn't." Matt reached for a piece of garlic bread.

"The question becomes when does dreaming for the best for your kids become pushing and driving them?" She sipped her wine. "How do you know where and when to stop?"

"Communication. My parents found out Jason liked music and not sports and enrolled him in guitar lessons. He was happy to never play football or any other sport again. My oldest brother loved photography. They bought him a camera, and he's doing what he loves to this day. None of us are married yet, which makes my parents worry that they'll never be grandparents."

"I can't remember my mom ever pushing me to be anything, but my father always wanted me to be able to stand on my own two feet. He'd seen too many women left to raise kids on their own with no money. I can't fault him for it, only the way he pushed me back then was hard to take at the time." She flipped her hair over her shoulder. "I guess I can see his point and thank him for it. I did give him a few gray hairs over the years."

"I know we gave my parents their fair share. Three boys only a few years apart in one household can be a handful for any woman." Matt took her hand. "Not to change the subject but Larissa's father asked to come talk to me tomorrow without his lawyer. He said he had some things to get off his chest. I hope this will give us a break in the case."

"Do you think he murdered his daughter?" Jessie leaned close to him and asked it softly.

"No, I don't. Phillips might have had a part in it, but I still believe there is more to it. I keep wondering who the father of the baby is. Does he live in the compound, or did she meet him when she ran away? Why hasn't he shown up to claim the child? It makes me wonder if he might have murdered her."

"A twist I didn't consider. Did you test the baby's DNA?" Jessie rummaged through her purse for her notebook.

"Yes, the father is always a possible suspect in a murder case."

"Will Roger have to face abuse charges?" she asked the first question on her list. Jessie took a bite of her spaghetti.

"Of course, Olivia's parents have hired an attorney and are ready to press charges. Because she was underage, he will face extra charges." Matt took a swig of his beer.

"I'm glad. I hope Roger goes to jail. He'd do it again in a heartbeat." Jessie frowned.

"Have you seen Roger around?" Matt asked her.

"Not since the time I told you about when Larissa hurled the dictionary at him."

"If you do see him in town, call us right away."

"I will. Roger is not a nice man, and I would rather not deal with him alone."

The air was colder when they left the restaurant. Jessie pulled her collar up around her neck. Matt walked her to her car and kissed her goodbye. "I always look forward to our time together." He kissed her again. "Keep your eyes open, sweetheart. We're at the point in the case when things can start happening fast."

"I will."

"I love you, Jess."

"I love you too, Matt." She started her car and drove home.

****

After discussing Corrine's book with Katie, she promised Katie to check with Matt about dinner. Tom had decided to stay the whole week. Jessie shut off her light and burrowed under the warm blanket. Laying her head back on the pillow, she closed her eyes. Her body was tired, but her mind was wide awake. Katie, Tom, and who? Jessie sighed. Her eyes popped open. What had Matt meant about keeping her eyes open? Was he concerned about Bruce and not telling her? No, he would have said to watch for Bruce. She closed her eyes again. Her thoughts drifted to the overwhelming sadness on Larissa's face when she had looked at her baby's photo earlier. Larissa had wanted her baby. Abruptly the picture changed, and Jessie struggled to sit up. Larissa was running through the trees with two men in pursuit. Holding her stomach, panting for air, she ran toward the crypt with the men not far behind. Larissa crept into the dark, musty place, cowering down behind the tomb, terror filling her eyes. How she hated this place. Memories flooded Larissa's mind, and Jessie could see them. Nights spent alone in the darkness with only the dead and a male figure who loomed over her. Jessie saw the pleasure he got from abusing her. "*Mama,*" Larissa cried. "*Please, I don't want to die alone.*" Jessie saw another figure and how he had risked being caught to bring her food. Jessie wept as the man held Larissa, and they cried together. Pain flooded Jessie with each of Larissa's memories. Shush. She held her breath. They were coming closer. The rusty gate creaked when it was pushed open. *"Please don't let them come,"* Larissa whispered under her breath. She held perfectly still, trying not to make a sound. They were inside the tomb, and light from their flashlights bounced around the walls. It was over. They had found her. She wept, and Jessie cried with her. One of the men pulled a knife from his boot, and she knew now that at least two men had helped to murder Larissa.

Tears streamed down Jessie's cheeks. Mr. Young had tried to help his daughter. Matt needed to know that more than physical beatings were going on. Someone at the compound could be a sexual predator. She reached for her phone and then stopped herself. It was late. She could tell Matt in the morning.

Chapter 31

Early the next morning Matt met Mr. Young at the police station. "Would you like some coffee?" he asked. Young glanced behind him as if he feared a tail.

"Thanks, I could use some. I'm a bit nervous, but I need to do this." Young put some cream and sugar in his coffee.

"Let's go to my office. We won't be interrupted there." Matt led the way and sat at his desk. He motioned for Young to be seated. Young's foot tapped the floor, and his hands trembled.

"Thank you for seeing me, sir. My name is Marvin Young." He extended his hand, which Matt shook. "No one calls me by my first name at the compound, but I like to hear it every now and then. It reminds me of who I once was." His dark brown eyes looked troubled. His hair, streaked with gray, was getting thin on top.

"I'm Matt Parker. I need to get some formalities out of the way. If you'll sign here, this simply says you've waived your right to have an attorney present." Matt handed him a pen and waited for him sign the form. "You can begin when you're ready. I will be recording our conversation." Matt placed a small recorder on his desk.

"I figured you would." He cleared his throat. "I'm sure you're wondering how I got to this place. I guess in some ways, I am, too."

Matt nodded. "Several questions have come to mind." Matt noticed the janitor cleaning the hall. He'd been working there a couple of weeks, and Matt had just learned his name. He thought it best to close his door.

"I'll try not to take up too much of your time. I suppose the best place to start is at the beginning." He slumped forward in his chair. "Several years ago, when Larissa was a toddler, I witnessed a horrific mass shooting at my place of work. There were several fatalities and injuries. I should have been among them. I came face to face with one of the shooters, but his gun jammed, and I escaped. I can see him in my mind to this day. Phillips and Crawford worked in the same building for other companies. They both saw the other shooter running through the hall and spraying folks with bullets. They survived with minor injuries. It was a high-profile case involving some powerful people. A corporate espionage revenge shooting is what the DA told me. Several of the witnesses said there were three shooters, but only two were ever identified. The government placed us in the witness protection program. I was the only one who saw the first shooter; Randy and Doc saw the other one. After we had testified in court and the men were convicted, we all went our separate ways with new names, social security numbers, and identities." He took a sip of his coffee. "My real name was Marvin Denton. When you look me up online, you'll read about the trial and my sudden death afterward, which was staged."

"I thought you were hiding something." Matt tapped his pencil on his notepad.

"I still look over my shoulder, worried they will

find me and murder my family. They threatened my life on several occasions, including in the courtroom. It made for a dramatic trial and many sleepless nights for my Rose. When Larissa was beaten and dropped at the gate, I feared they had found us. It was a sick, helpless feeling."

"Why?" Matt studied the man across from him.

"They had promised to find me, no matter how long it took. I received a note a few weeks ago saying they had my daughter, and they would dump her broken body outside my gate. I called my contact in the program, and the detective said he hadn't heard of any movement. He didn't think it was a remnant of the trial, but he'd check into it and get back to me. As of yet, I haven't heard from him."

"Who do you think might have killed her?" Matt rested his elbow on his desk.

"I don't know." His face was haggard. "It has to be someone who knows my past, someone close to me or someone at the compound."

"How did you come to live with this group?" Matt jotted notes.

"In the beginning, I wandered from job to job and town to town. I was easily spooked and afraid to put down roots. I was sure they could trace us and put a hit on us. I didn't have a home phone or cell. I wanted to keep my family safe, you understand. Randy and Doc, the other two witnesses, went different ways, but we managed to stay in touch. The DA caught up to me several months later and told me my father had died. He had left me the land here as my inheritance. I never got to see him through the whole process. They were afraid my parents' lives would be in jeopardy." Marvin stared out the window. "I lost some things I can never get back."

"No wonder you wanted to be off the grid. You didn't want to be found." Matt drank his coffee.

"I moved my family here and was joined by Phillips, Crawford, and their families. All except for Randy's oldest son, Randy Junior, or RJ, as they called him. He moved to another city. Out of necessity, we lived a secluded existence. We grew our own food, generated our own electricity, and lived a simple life. I was never a religious man, but Phillips was. He wanted to add the element of faith and recruit carefully through word of mouth for others to join us in our community. It was my land, and so they voted me the leader. We voted to have the Bible be our final guide in all we did. The more people who joined, the more complicated it became. The word tyrannical comes to mind. I'm a weak man." He looked down, shoulders hunched. "I should have confronted what I saw over the years, but I did nothing. Maybe if I had, my daughter would still be alive, and my wife wouldn't hate me."

"What do you mean?" Matt's eyes narrowed.

"It's not that I believe any of my friends murdered Larissa, but the unyielding rules we developed left my creative, free-spirited daughter no room. She had to rebel. I couldn't live by them; how could I expect her to?" Tears welled up in his eyes.

Matt let him talk for a while. A better picture had emerged in Matt's mind by the time Marvin was done with his story. Matt was sure that he had never beaten his daughter or wife, but someone had. Young had never taken a stand against Randy's version of the physical discipline. "Spare the rod and the spoil the child" was Randy's motto. He had quoted it several times when Matt had questioned him about his discipline methods. Marvin would live with the guilt the rest of his life.

Matt looked through his recent calls and saw Jessie's name. He reached for his phone and called her. "I saw you called. What's up?" he asked when she answered.

"Katie wants us to go for drinks and appetizers at Liam's and Connor's pub tonight. Will it work for you? We're talking corned beef and cabbage plus live Irish music," she told him to sway his decision.

"I can swing it. Frank left town this morning but will come back if we need him. Why Liam's place?"

"It's their Grand Opening week, and they've saved us a table."

"Okay, sounds good. I wouldn't mind a little Irish food and music."

"I did want to talk to you about something else. Not over the phone, though. Do you want me to pick you up from work so we can talk?" Jessie asked.

"I'll have one of the guys drop me off at the store, and we'll ride together. See you later, Jess."

"Okay."

If she didn't want to talk over the phone, something was bothering her. With her, it usually meant something significant. Another lead in the case maybe. Matt's phone buzzed.

"Chief, Lewis on line one."

"Thanks, Kenny." Matt answered the line.

"Matt, I have some interesting test results." The coroner's gravelly voice came over the phone. "Can you drop by sometime today?"

"I'll be there soon. What are we looking at?"

"It could be helpful, or it might throw a monkey wrench into the whole case. How does that sound?"

Matt rubbed his temples. "I don't like the monkey wrench idea. I'll be by soon." Damn, what he didn't need was a new question.

****

Matt left Lewis' office shaking his head. He had several new questions and no answers. There was DNA under Larissa's nails, but it wasn't a match to any they had in the system, though Dave's assistant was still running checks. The peculiar thing was that there were two types of DNA found under her nails. They were still waiting on the DNA from the baby. The killer could be the father. Matt pulled up in front of Jessie's store and smiled. His car naturally went there when he was out. He liked dropping in on her.

He walked in the door and stood quietly while she waited on a customer. "Hi." He smiled as she approached. "It looks like you're busy. I was hoping you would have a few minutes to talk."

"Go over to Joe's and have one of Molly's wonderful creations. I shouldn't be too long." She smiled at him.

"Do you want something?"

"Iced tea would be nice." She followed him to the open doors. "I'll see you in a few."

"I'll bring it back here and wait. I need to go over this case."

"Be my guest. My chairs are here for you to relax and enjoy. Remember not to sit in that one." Jessie pointed Larissa's chair. "It's out of order."

Matt brought over two glasses of tea and a chicken

salad sandwich. He sat where he could watch Jessie at work. She was ringing up a customer. Matt took a bite of his sandwich. The man she was waiting on seemed vaguely familiar to Matt. Where had he seen him before? Nervous type. The guy bounced from foot to foot and kept glancing his way.

"Finally, a break." She sat in the chair beside him.

"Do you know the name of the man who just left?"

"No. Why?" She took a sip of her tea.

"Did he pay with a card?"

"No, cash. What's up?" She tilted her head to look at him.

"He looks familiar, and I was trying to figure out why." Matt took a sip of his tea. "You wanted to tell me something."

"Yes. Last night I had a vision of Larissa." She explained to Matt what she had seen. "There were at least two who were involved in the murder for sure."

"Did you see who they were?" Matt popped a chip into his mouth.

"No, that would be too easy, but through her memories, I saw some of what has happened to her. Her father tried to help her and was the one to release her, so she could flee." Jessie paused. "Larissa was not only beaten, but I think a man may have molested her when she was alone at the crypt. The father of the baby could be one of the men who tortured her or one of the men at the compound. My bet there is still someone whom we know nothing about yet."

"Interesting. That could account for the extra DNA we found on Larissa." Matt took a bite of his sandwich.

"Did Dave find a match?" Jessie stood when the bell above the door rang. "I'll be back."

"The answer is no, but he's still looking through the database of info." Matt stood and wrapped up what was left of his meal. He reached for his tea. "I'll leave you to your work and see you later. Is the pub still on for tonight?"

"Yes." She went to help her customer find a book. "See you soon."

****

Matt drove back to the station with more questions than answers. Jessie's information added another aspect to consider. He needed to talk to Marvin again.

Before Matt walked into the station, he called Marvin on the special number he had given him.

"Mr. Young, Chief Parker here. Can you talk now or is it possible for you to come in before Randy's scheduled appointment tomorrow?"

"I can talk."

"Is it possible someone in the compound molested your daughter?"

"A few weeks ago I would have told you absolutely not, but I'm not sure now. Larissa told me about things done to her the last time we were together. They were horrible things, and I should have confronted the leaders then. Instead, I set her free and told her to leave the compound."

"You need to bring your wife and come in and talk. I want to find out all the information I can before any other young women are hurt. If Randy and Glenn were in the witness protection program, then their real names would be different, too."

"Yes." Marvin told Matt the two names. "As you can see we only changed our last names. We'll meet you at the station in the morning. There is something else." Marvin paused. "Randy has been odd lately and so has Amos, another leader. Randy spends a lot of time arguing on the phone with someone. I have no idea who."

"Thank you. We'll leave Randy and Glenn's names as they are for our purposes, but I want to look into their backgrounds. I'll see you in the morning."

Matt sent an email off to Jeremy to do a background check on the two names Young had given him.

Jeremy called within the hour. "Marvin Young was correct about Marvin Denton being officially dead. I found the information when I did his background check. His story is true."

"Thanks, Jeremy, send me the link. I would like to read it."

"Will do. Talk to you later, when I get the information you asked for."

Dylan knocked on his open door. "Are you busy tonight or would you like to have a beer and play some darts?"

"Jessie and I are headed to Liam's place. They're having the grand opening this week. You should come with us. There'll be beer and darts along with some great Irish food and music."

"It sounds like it might be fun." Dylan tilted his head. "Who all is going besides Jessie?"

"Tom and Katie will be there, too. Liam saved a table for us. You may as well come along."

"Tom is still in town? I thought he was only here for the weekend." Dylan leaned against the frame of the door.

"He stayed so he could go tonight. He has a thing

for Katie." Matt closed the file on his desk.

"Do you think it's serious between her and Tom?" Dylan pushed away from the wall.

"They're figuring it out." Matt drew circles on his notepad.

"Unlike you and Jessie, they don't seem to fit together." Dylan folded his arms.

"You could be right, I'm sure they'll figure it out in time. Katie knew Jeremy wasn't a match for her."

"Katie has changed, don't you think?"

"I guess, I haven't thought much about it." Matt stood. "Do you want to go with us tonight?"

"I'll think about it." Dylan turned to leave. "Did you still need a ride?"

"Are you ready to leave?" Matt grabbed the file on his desk and shoved it his briefcase.

"Yep. I'll shut my office and be right back." Dylan nodded at the janitor outside Matt's door.

Matt's phone buzzed. "I need to take this."

"Sir, you have a call on line two, an Officer Brinks from Harrisville."

"Thanks, Kenny." Matt pushed line two. "This is Chief Parker."

"I'm Officer Brinks with the Harrisville PD. We wanted to let you know that Bruce Kingman attacked his estranged wife this morning when she was leaving the shelter for an appointment. He is in jail. He has several charges against him now including assault with a deadly weapon and attempted murder. Kingman shot her."

Matt swore under his breath. "Is Mrs. Kingman all right?"

"She's in surgery now. The doctor said she should

pull through."

"Thank you, Brinks, I'll tell her friends." Matt hung up the phone. He met Dylan at the officer's entrance.

"What's up?" Dylan pushed the station door open as they walked out.

"Sally Kingman was shot by her husband." Matt frowned.

"Hell, is she going to be okay?" Dylan stopped.

Matt told Dylan what the Harrisville officer had told him. "I'll have to tell Jessie and Katie tonight. She wanted them to know."

Dylan pulled into the space in front of Jessie's store. "Matt, save me a place at the table. I'll be there in a bit."

Chapter 32

"Hi, sweetheart, how was your day?" Matt walked through the door Jessie was holding open.

"Okay, but I'm glad it's over." She closed and locked the door and turned the sign around.

"I asked Dylan to come tonight. Is that all right?" Matt shut off the front lights.

"Of course. Dylan is always welcome." Jessie finished her closing routine and was ready to leave.

"I figured as much, but it never hurts to ask." Matt made sure the back door was locked as they walked out. "I got a call from an officer in Harrisville before I left the station." Matt held the car door open for her.

"What did he want?" She latched her seat belt and turned to look at him.

"Bruce found out where Sally was and shot her. Her case is no longer in my hands."

Jessie's face paled. "Is she going to be okay?"

"Yes. When I talked to the hospital, they told me Sally was out of surgery and resting." Matt told her all he knew. "She wanted to make sure I told Katie and you."

"I don't understand what happens to people to make them angry enough to kill their spouses. Why don't they walk away, divorce them, start over, or whatever?"

"I've asked the same questions more than a few

times. I can't say I've gotten a good answer from anyone to date."

"Katie and I will have to drive over to see her." She frowned. "I'm not sure when we can get there."

"It will have to be in the near future. As soon as it's possible, the authorities want to move Sally out of the area for her safety." Matt started the car and pulled onto Main Street. "I forgot to mention that Frank is on his way back to town. He'll be here later tonight. I want to go to the compound again after I talk to Marvin and Rose tomorrow."

"It's probably a good idea. The group sticks close together and will cover for one another." Jessie frowned. "I can't figure out, for the life of me, why Rose didn't put up a fight for her daughter and her niece."

"I can't either. How could a mother not fight for her daughter?" Matt's moved into the turn lane.

"What about her father? You've met Mr. Young. Does he seem that bad to you?"

"He doesn't, but I'm not seeing him in his role as an elder among the group either."

"True, I suppose you're right. Anyone can put on an act for a while. Eventually, the real person will surface. Pressure has a tendency to bring it out."

"That's the exact reason we are going to the compound again. It's time to apply pressure to our friends and see what boils over." Matt glanced at her. "I keep thinking about what Taylor said the other day. Who knew we were running that night?"

"I forgot he had mentioned it. That might be the person we are missing." She sounded excited.

Matt pulled into space in the parking lot for the

Seaside Village. "They got an ideal spot for their business venture."

"I agree. Liam's business should get a lot of tourist traffic. It's a great location. The back has a deck with outdoor seating and a panoramic view of the waterfront. I sat out there the other day and watched the boats coming and going. You can't ask for more." Jessie grabbed his hand as they walked to the pub.

"I feel the same way about you. I love it when you grab my hand." He smiled at her and squeezed hers.

"I'll let Katie know about Sally. I can't believe Bruce found her so quickly."

"He probably had help. Maybe a private investigator tailing her or something." Matt held the door to the pub open.

Liam walked over to them. "I'm so glad you came." He gave Jessie a kiss on the cheek. "How's my girl tonight?"

"I'm fine. I hope you have room for another at our table. Dylan is coming, too. Wow, your place is packed." She followed Liam to the table.

"I know. It's off to a good start." He was beaming. Connor was talking to Katie and turned around to give Jessie a hug.

Jessie pulled Katie aside and told her about Sally. "We should call the hospital to see if she can talk or at least see how she's doing."

"I agree. I can't believe that snake got to Sally. Boy, would I like to have a few minutes alone with Bruce. I'd like to do some major damage to him and his big ego." Katie sat down beside Tom. She told him about Sally.

Jessie was in the perfect spot to watch her friend all

evening. Tom and Katie seem to get on very well, but no spark ever seemed to flare between them. Of course, they were still feeling out their relationship.

When Dylan arrived, he sat next to Matt. "Did you hear anything else about Sally?" Dylan glanced at Katie.

"Only what I heard earlier," Matt answered.

As the evening progressed, Dylan's eyes kept glancing Katie's way when he thought no one was watching. Jessie would have been happy to point out to Dylan that he was too late. He had done nothing the whole time Katie had liked him, not to mention the fact that Tom was in her life now. Too bad so sad, Dylan. It would have been easy to tell him right this moment if Katie wasn't also sending longing glances Dylan's way. Jessie smiled. Her hand tapped on the table to the rhythm of the Irish song playing.

"What are you smiling about?" Matt whispered in her ear.

"I figured out something important about my friend."

"I wonder what that might be." Matt grinned.

"Oh, a little something. It's not important." Her hand touched his.

"I think it's very important. We can't let our two friends go through their life wondering if they had missed their one true love now, can we? Not when we're so happy."

Her mouth dropped open. "How did you know?" she asked Matt softly.

"It's my power of observation, and those two are not good at hiding it. It's plain to see how our friends feel about each other. It took Tom being interested in

Katie to move Dylan off the sidelines."

"I'm not sure if he's off the sidelines yet." Jessie glanced at Dylan, who was talking to a cute waitress. Katie was glaring at her.

"I'd say he's contemplating the idea. It ought to be fun to watch."

"We might have to meddle a little, or they'll never see each other. You know, throw them together more often. Are you in?" She fluttered her lashes at him.

"Sounds devious, but I'm in." He winked at her.

She rested her head on his shoulder. "We make a good team."

"The best." He brushed his lips across her cheek. "Tom leaves tomorrow. I think we should make our move then." He cocked his head.

"I like your style, Mr. Parker."

"What are you two whispering about? You look like you're conspiring." Katie watched them closely.

"You might say that." He nodded his head. "But I'll never tell."

Jessie knew Katie would hound them to know and was grateful when Liam stopped by the table. "Your place is great, Liam." She grabbed the chance to change the subject.

"Thanks, it was one of the better ideas Connor and I've had. I've decided to take a few risks to make a few of my dreams come true. I'm here to enjoy it because of you." Liam patted Jessie's shoulder. "If ever this guy doesn't treat you right and you need a replacement, you know where to find me." Liam winked at her as he walked away from the table.

Jessie clasped Matt's hand and leaned close to him. "You're safe."

"I know." He smiled at her.

Before the group went their separate ways, Jessie and Katie managed to talk to Sally for a few minutes while the nurse held the phone up to her ear. The nurse had reassured them that Sally was progressing quite nicely.

"She sounds good, considering everything she's been through." Katie turned around to face Jessie.

"Domestic violence is all about control, and Sally defied him. It took guts for her to do it." Jessie smiled at her friend. "It will be good to visit with her. She'll need us to be there for her until at least after the trial."

"She can count on me for sure." Katie checked her phone. "Will Saturday work for you?"

"It should be fine. I'll go to the store on Saturday and get things ready for Audrey, and then I'll swing by and pick you up." Jessie gave Katie a quick squeeze.

"Perfect. Tom leaves tomorrow morning. It's been fun having him here, but I'm not jumping, remember?" Katie expelled her breath. "We'll see. I'm relieved he's leaving for now. I feel stressed trying to keep him entertained. It's like when I wear a pair of killer heels to look great, I'm always glad to kick them off and be comfortable. I can go back to being me."

"You're smart about not jumping. I'm sure you'll know when you should take the next step, if at all." Jessie shifted her weight to her other leg. Katie had told her a lot about her feelings with that statement.

Katie glanced toward where Tom, Matt, and Dylan stood. "I'm surprised he came tonight."

"Who?" Jessie managed to keep a straight face.

"Dylan. I haven't seen him in a while." Katie frowned when she looked at him.

"Matt asked him to come along; I hope you don't mind."

"Of course not. Only, it seems I'm like a plague to Dylan, and he avoids any place where I am. I'm a little surprised, is all."

"Maybe he didn't know you'd be here." Jessie didn't point out to her friend that Dylan had been at the Inn several times in the last few weeks. It was to her advantage to let Katie believe Dylan wasn't interested in her for a few more days. Jessie planned—oblivious to Katie's tapping foot, her surroundings, and the person in the car outside who watched her while making plans of his own.

Chapter 33

Jessie was up early. Something was bothering her, but she had no clue what it was. She walked into the kitchen and took a bowl from the cabinet. All she wanted this morning was a bowl of Chocolate Crispies with milk. Not a nutritional breakfast for sure, but the cereal had been her favorite since she was a kid. From the moment she'd discovered the milk turned to chocolate milk when she poured it over the cereal, it was her go-to comfort food. Some things from childhood were worth hanging on to. This was one of them, as far as she was concerned. She had a second bowl and enjoyed it as much as the first.

Jessie put on her jacket and grabbed her purse and keys. She picked up her badge and stuck it in her pocket. Why? There was no need for it, but she wanted it—just in case. She took one last look in the mirror to make sure everything was in place. Once in the car, she honked and waved on her way past the Inn. Tradition felt right this morning. Katie knew she'd be back to pick her up in a little while. Jessie pulled over before the turn onto the highway and grabbed her phone out of her purse, texting a reminder to Matt that she'd see him later when she got back from Harrisville. She asked him to check in on Audrey later and stuck her phone in her jacket pocket.

When Jessie pulled into her parking space at the

store, she noticed Rose at the back door. "I didn't expect to see you this morning. I thought you were meeting with Chief Parker." Jessie stepped out of her car, leaving her purse on the seat.

"I wanted to talk to you first." Rose was leaning against the door, blocking Jessie's way in. "I need help before he kills me."

"Who is going to kill you?" Jessie stood near her car.

"My husband. He hurt my little girl." Rose held her side, swaying and steadying herself against the door.

What was up? A warning alarm went off in Jessie's mind. Something wasn't right. "Are you saying that Marvin is the one who hurt Larissa?" Jessie saw Larissa's expression as she saw her mother. There was no love lost there. "Are you okay?" Jessie asked Rose when she swayed again. She stepped toward her with caution. Rose suddenly slumped to the ground. Jessie scanned the area. No one was around. She stepped closer, reaching her hand down to check on Rose. Rose grabbed her, yanking her off balance. Jessie had no time to react to the hand that shoved a reeking cloth over her nose and mouth. She tried in vain to pull it from her face, slapping and kicking, until she sagged, feeling her limbs go weak, and then it was dark.

****

"My wife said she would meet me here. I wonder where she is." Marvin Young looked at his watch again.

"We'll wait a few more minutes." Matt frowned. His gut told him something wasn't right. "I'll be right back. I need to check on something." Matt charged down the hall to Dylan's office.

"What's up, Chief?" Dylan looked up from his

desk.

"I want you to fill in on this interview with Mr. and Mrs. Young. His wife hasn't shown up yet, which has me concerned. I have a list of questions on the inside of the file. Something isn't jiving, and I need to go check on Jessie."

"I can interview him." Dylan stood.

"Hold him here and keep him talking." Matt's phone rang. "Calm down, Katie, I can't understand you. Don't worry. I'll go check it out. I'm sure she got stuck at the store."

"What was that all about?" Dylan asked the minute Matt stopped talking.

"Jessie was supposed to pick up Katie. They were heading to Harrisville to visit Sally this morning. Jessie hasn't shown yet, which isn't like her, and she's not answering her phone. Katie is sure something is wrong. It's not like Jessie to be late without letting Katie know."

Kenny came rushing down the hall. "Matt, you need to get over to Jessie's store. Audrey said it's an emergency."

"Go, Matt. I'll start the interview for you. I'll hold him until you get back." Dylan nudged him toward the door.

"Thanks." Matt raced to his car. She had to be okay. His heart was racing as he turned on the lights and siren.

****

The first thing Matt saw when he arrived at the store was Audrey and Molly in tears. His mind started to race. "Ladies, what's going on?"

"Jessie's gone." Audrey managed to say through

her sobs.

"What do you mean gone?" His eyes narrowed, his expression grim.

"Her car is out back, I found her keys on the ground, and her purse is still in the car." Audrey led the way. "This is how I found it." She sniffed.

Jessie's car door was still standing open, and her purse was sitting on the seat looking undisturbed. Robbery wasn't the obvious motive. He sorted through the bag, taking out her wallet. The wallet still had cash and credit cards in plain view. The keys were on the ground near the back door. Matt noticed marks on the ground, indicating some kind of scuffle. He squatted to get a better look. He needed to get Frank and Radar over there fast. He placed the call to Kenny and told him to get the investigative team to Idle Time Books ASAP. Frank was the next person he called. Matt paced as he waited for the others to arrive. He couldn't lose her. A sick feeling swirled around his insides. His fist curled and uncurled at his side. He had to hold it together. If he fell apart, he wouldn't be able to help her, and he had to find her. He couldn't think of any other outcome.

His phone rang. "Matt, Kenny told me what's going on. I had Kip take over the interview."

"How's it going there?" Matt took a deep breath.

"We wrapped up the preliminary questions. Young's wife hasn't shown yet, and he's upset about it."

"I doubt she'll be coming." Matt swiped at the moisture in his eyes. "Jessie has been abducted."

"Damn, Matt, Kenny didn't tell me that."

"You need to get Marvin to talk. His wife might

have something to do with it, but there are others. I'm sure of it. Tell me anything he says. Call Katie, and tell her what happened."

"I will. Matt, are you going to be okay? I can come and take over for you."

"Hell no, I'm not okay." He drew a shuddering breath. "But I have to get it together fast. I have a case to solve."

"I'll get Kip to finish the interview. I'm coming. We've been friends too long for me not to be there with you."

"Thanks, man, I could use you here. Frank is on his way. I asked him to come back to do the compound today. Thank God, I did. I know how crucial it is for the search to have the dog tracking as soon as possible."

"I'll be there right away."

Matt tried to pull himself together. Jessie needed him to be a cop right now, and he would do his job. Damn, he hated feeling so helpless. He turned back to Audrey. "Audrey, let's close the store today. The police will be working the scene, and I don't want anything compromised."

"Fine, I don't think I could work anyway." Audrey reached for a tissue. "Jessie never even made it in to open the safe…" The next words caught in her throat.

Frank got Radar out of his crate as soon as he arrived. "You tell me what to do, and I'll do it."

Matt nodded. "Did any of you see her cell phone?" Matt searched her purse and car looking under the seats. It wasn't there. Was it possible she had it on her? Matt's next call was to Jeremy. He explained what had happened. "Could you check to see if you can pick up the GPS on her phone? Jessie might have grabbed it; at least I hope she has it."

"If she has it, I'll track it. We can pinpoint the area if she has it and they don't find it on her. Let's hope she has it on silent, so it doesn't ring and give it away. I'll call you with anything I find." Jeremy paused. "She'll be okay, Matt. Jessie is resourceful; she'll find the way to tell us where she's at."

"I know you're right. If there's a way, she'll find it." Matt ended his call. "Jessie, talk to me," he whispered. Matt became aware of the small group gathered in her store. Katie was standing next to Molly, and Reba and Dylan were watching him. It didn't take long for news to travel in a small town or for friends to gather around for support.

"Chief, I think you need to hear what Reba has to say." Dylan walked Reba over to where Matt stood.

"She's strong, son. You've taught her well. They surprised our dear girl, but she'll find a way out of this. I can feel it inside of me. She's no pushover." Reba patted his hand. "It's that darn man in the motorhome. He's one of them, I'm sure. I saw him racing out of town earlier when I went to the market. He was in a big hurry, but he's not the surprise. Jessie was aware of him and watched out for him. The person who trapped her had to be someone she wouldn't suspect. There's someone else, too. I don't want to worry you, but I want to let you know what you're facing. Each of them is capable of murder and culpable in one already."

Matt thanked her, and his mind went into overdrive. Matt had seen Roger's work first hand with Olivia. Rose could be involved, but who was the other person or persons? They needed to get to work.

"Frank, let's start the track," he said tightly. "This

sweater was in her car. I've seen her wear it." Matt looked at Dylan. "Follow us in the car. I'm not sure how far we may have to go."

Frank put Radar's line on. He knelt beside him with the scent article in his hand. "Let's find her, fella. Let's find our girl."

Radar put his nose to the ground and followed her scent. He stopped by her car, near the back door of the store, pulled Frank around the side of Joe's Coffee Shop, and out onto Main Street. Matt noticed several footprints beside the coffee shop. Radar veered to the left on Main and headed out of town. He continued on, tracking hard, for several blocks. The dog stopped where the road into Blue Cove connected with the turn onto the highway, and he veered to the left again. At least Matt knew the direction they had taken out of town.

"We need to go back to the compound, but I want to be careful not to tip them off."

"Do you think they took her there?" Dylan turned to talk to Matt.

"No, but I'm curious whether Radar can pick up anything there. Jessie said something to me the other day about how those folks would cover for each other and hide those whom they knew."

"How about the crypt?" Frank asked.

"I can't imagine they'd go there right away, but I wouldn't be surprised if they end up back there in the next few days. We'll be watching."

"Do you want to go to the compound now?" Dylan asked.

"No, let's go to the store and get Frank's car. You need to go back to the station and get the search warrant. It's in the file. Talk with Kip while you're there, and see if he's learned anything from Marvin. In the meantime, I want to think about what our next move should be."

"You have to take me with you." Katie grabbed Matt's hand. "She's my friend, and I can't take this not knowing."

"You know I can't do that, Katie." Matt turned to Dylan. "Keep her informed." He drove away.

Chapter 34

Jessie massaged her forehead. It hurt like blazes. The constant motion was making her sick. Where was she? She could hear men talking through the fog. Who were they? She didn't want to move; it made her head hurt worse. The store was the last thing she could remember. She winced when they hit a bump in the road. Why couldn't she remember? Her eyes shut. She had made it to the store, but then what happened? *Think, Jessie*. Rose was waiting for her. She remembered that much. It didn't seem right. It was Rose who had pulled her to the ground, and then it all went dark. What could she do to make the pounding in her head stop? What had been on that rag?

"How much of that stuff did Rose give our lady friend?" a man's voice asked. "She's been out for a while. Is she moving? I hope Rose didn't kill her. No more body dumping for me."

"I can't see her moving. I'll check," a familiar voice said.

Jessie heard steps. She lay still. The wind from his breath fluttered across her face as he bent over her. His hand was touching her mouth. It repulsed her. *Don't move, don't you dare move, Jessie.* He yanked her hair and pinched her arm. It took everything she had not to make a sound and to remain limp and unresisting. His face was so close to hers that his breath was making her nauseous.

"She's breathing. I can feel the air coming from her mouth. But she's pale and as still as death." He bent closer. "She's out cold. I should knock her out again myself when she wakes up for helping my wife get away from me."

"Leave her be. The longer she sleeps, the easier it is for us. She's not our problem. We did our part. The others will take care of her."

"You've got that right." The man's weight lifted off the bed.

"Get back up here and sit down. It's about to get bumpy."

"I would still like to pop her one. I get angry every time I think of her helping Olivia." His shoes clunked as he walked away.

"We're going to do it like we've been told. We have to do it the way the leaders tell us to this time. We messed up, and the next time it could get us killed."

Each bump in the road made the pounding in her head worse. *Think, Jessie.* She carefully pulled her phone from her coat. It was on silent. She hadn't turned it on this morning, thankfully. Katie must have called several times by now. Where could she hide it? Matt would notice that her phone wasn't among the things she'd left. *Please let him notice.* Jeremy could follow the GPS on her phone to locate her position as long as the battery didn't die. Maybe she should shut it off. First, what she needed was something for her head. Once the darn fog lifted, maybe she could think of a coherent plan. She would fight back, but for now, she would rest her head and save her strength. Her eyes closed again.

****

"I refuse to run off half-cocked. It won't bring Jessie back." Matt frowned.

"Tell us what you want to do." Dylan stood beside him.

"I want to question Marvin. His wife has to be in on this. He has to know something he's not telling us." Matt got into the car where Frank and Radar were waiting. Matt drove back to the station and went straight to the interrogation room. Kip was interviewing Young. Matt looked over the file as Kip asked Marvin a couple more questions. Then it was Matt's turn. "What aren't you telling us about your wife? You had to know that she wasn't getting along with Larissa."

"I knew, but I had no idea how bad it was until recently when Rose told me I was enabling our daughter's sin." He hung his head. "I had talked to Rose on more than one occasion about not believing the way the group did. I'd had enough of the junk, but Rose embraced the whole idea and told me she'd divorce me if I ever gave up my place as the leader." He raised his head, his expression bleak. "I don't know how we lost the simplicity we started with."

"What was the turning point?" Matt asked.

"I wish I knew for sure. It seemed in each new situation someone called for some new crazy rule to control the followers we had. Rose was constantly worried about our position in the group. She fretted over how others would look at us if our daughter kept coming around."

"What about you? Were you afraid of losing power?" Matt straddled the chair.

"Truthfully, I no longer cared. I was done with all

of their rules. Before Larissa showed up that night, I had told Rose I was ready to find our daughter and leave. She fought with me, saying it was our land and our home. She told me she wouldn't go with me, but I was still ready to give it up—and her, if necessary—to save my daughter. Rose knew I was serious. She left the house crying. I have no idea where she went." He buried his face in his hands. "Oh, God, I can't believe...I didn't think she meant it."

"What?" Matt's fist pounded the table.

"She said if I tried to resign she'd kill our daughter. I thought she was upset. I never thought she'd do it." Marvin bowed his head.

Matt looked grim. "Do you know how many times I've heard those exact words uttered?" Matt ground his teeth. "People don't usually talk about killing someone unless they've actually thought about it." He paused. "Someone in your compound is the father of Larissa's baby, and there is a cover-up going on. Are you involved, Marvin?"

"I'm not. I've done some stupid things, but I would never hurt my daughter." He started to cry. "If I knew who the father was, I'd give you the name."

"Could Rose be involved in the murder of your daughter?"

"I know Larissa was scared of her mama. Olivia, my niece, was, too. I was the one who tore the compound apart asking questions until I found where they hid Larissa. I helped her get away. I was livid when I found that Larissa was alone in the crypt. It was the first time I ever really got angry with my wife." His hands covered his face, and he sobbed.

Matt handed him the box of tissues. "Continue

when you're ready. She led us to believe that it was you doing the abusing, and the women were subservient to the men. Even Olivia thought it was you."

"Among the teachings of the group that's true, but I never treated Rose that way or Larissa either. I never taught it, but I didn't stop the others from teaching it either." He slumped forward in his chair. "Have you ever been disgusted with yourself, Officer? Right now, I can't tolerate myself." He swiped at the tears in his eyes. "The night Larissa was in the clinic, she begged me not to go get her mother or to leave her alone. I was so spineless, I let Randy talk me into leaving her. How could I have left my daughter's side when she was hurting so bad?" Marvin hung his head. "No matter what, I'll always blame myself for Larissa's death. I should have been aware of what was happening in my own family. I sure as hell should have called the ambulance and never left her side."

"Yes, you should have," Matt said harshly, "but now you have a chance to do it right. Another young woman's life is in danger. Your wife is involved. Can you think of anyone in your group who might have wanted your daughter dead?" Matt studied the man sitting across from him. "Think, man, time is of the essence."

Marvin shook his head. "I don't know. It's hard to imagine anyone you know doing such a despicable act, but then I guess anyone is capable."

"I'm asking again, who was the father of Larissa's baby?"

"I wish I knew. At first, I thought the father was one of the young bucks at the compound, but she swore it wasn't. She wouldn't tell me who it was, either." He scowled. "Come to think of it, Rose was in the room when I asked her. Larissa refused to answer any more of my questions. Rose kept calling her rebellious and quoting scriptures at her. I got nowhere, and Rose screamed terrible things at her. She called her a Jezebel and worse. It makes me sick to think about it now."

What was wrong with this man to stand by and let this happen to his daughter? Matt stood up abruptly. "I'm going to the compound, and you're going with me. On the way there, I want you to think of anything, no matter how insignificant it seems that Larissa, Rose, or anyone else might have told you." Matt stared down at him. "What you say can't save your daughter, but it could save another woman's life." Matt took him by the arm—not very gently—and walked with Marvin out of the station. Matt paused as his phone rang. "Go ahead and get in the car. I need to take this call."

"Matt, this is Jeremy. She has her phone with her. I was able to follow their movement for a while, and then the signal went out. It could be they are out of her carrier's coverage area, or her phone died. I doubt it's her battery, though. Jessie is a creature of habit. She charges the battery every night, so it shouldn't be dead yet. It's too early in the day. I'll keep tabs on it and let you know if it pops back up on the screen. Has anything else come up?"

"No, not yet." He clenched his jaw. "We're on our way to the Young's compound to see what else the dog can come up with. Roger is one of the abductors. I've seen Roger's handiwork up close and personal, and I hope Jessie's training kicks in before he can hurt her."

"I'll call you if I get a location at any point. I found some information on Randy and Crawford, which I'll send to your email. You'll find it interesting."

"Thanks, Jeremy." Matt got in the car and started it. He had to find her fast. Roger was a ticking time bomb. Anything could set him off.

****

Jessie awakened with a start when one of the men grabbed her hands and feet trying to bind them together. She started kicking. "Where am I?" He held her hands together behind her back and tied them tight. At least her headache was better. How would she get out of this mess? She had to fight.

"Roger, get in here. I need you. Hold her legs so I can tie her feet."

"You want me to knock her out?" Roger's hand fisted.

"No, hold her feet and keep her still, so I can tie them." His weight settled on the back of her legs.

"Please, where am I?" She bucked, trying to throw him off.

Roger pressed harder and backhanded her across the face. "Hold still, or I'll knock you out." He slapped her again.

She knew he would, too. What could she do? Her head was reeling from the blow. *Think Jessie, what did you learn*? So far, none of her classes had taught her how to get free if she found herself tied up. Was there a class for that? Matt would know. She put up a fight. The longer she was in captivity, the less likely she was to survive. She had to get free. She wiggled and kicked, but they still tied her feet together. Panting, Jessie watched Roger walk away. If looks could kill, she would be dead.

"Don't worry your pretty little head about

anything." The other man bent closer to her and whispered, "You're safe, and I'll do my best to keep you that way. I won't let Roger hit you anymore if I can stop him. I'm sorry we have to keep you tied up, but those were our orders. They don't want you to get away. That should hold you good and tight." He patted her back as he stood.

"Who are they? I have the right to know." Jessie glared at the man.

"I can't give you any information. You'll have to trust me, I guess."

"Let's get going. We need to meet the others," Roger said. "We'll chain the door on the outside so she can't get out."

"She'll never get free. We tied her up tight." The man followed Roger out of the motorhome bedroom.

They were leaving her. Jessie listened. The engine of a car started, which had to mean they'd been at this site before. Maybe it was where one of them lived. This couldn't be good. She had no time to lose. Jessie got to work trying to free her hands. She tugged the rope until it rubbed her skin raw. It wasn't working as she had seen in the movies. Tears welled up in her eyes. What good was it, if she couldn't get her hands free? She had a phone in her pocket, but no way to call. Darn. She cried and tried again. Frustrated by how inept she felt, she stopped and tried to move her fingers and loosen the ropes. If only she could sit up, maybe she could get a better angle. Turning over was easy enough, but maneuvering herself into a sitting position was almost a joke. Jessie scooted up the bed until she reached the corner of the table beside the mattress. She rubbed the rope back and forth across the corner hoping to weaken it. It was hopeless. Tears streamed down her cheeks. "Don't you dare give up, Jessica Lynn!" That's when Jessie saw her. Larissa was watching her every move, standing at the end of the bed. "At least I'm not alone. Too bad you can't untie a knot." She had to hurry. She had no idea how close they were or when they would be back.

Jessie rubbed the ropes harder with renewed energy. "Is this what they did to you?" Jessie wiggled one of her hands free. "Look." She held up a free hand and went to work releasing the rope wrapped around the wrist of her other hand. *Hurry, hurry*! It was getting dark. The rope gave way. She stuffed the piece of rope in her pocket. Her feet were next, and reaching them wasn't as easy. Another moment in life when she wished she were shorter, like Katie. Her long legs made it hard to reach her ankles. Would her head ever stop spinning? If she leaned over any farther, she would fall on her head. Jessie stifled the nervous giggle in her throat. She would rather take her chances out in the dark night than in this small space with the two men. She eased herself to her feet and then squatted to get closer to her feet. It took a few minutes, but with a few tugs more, she was free.

Jessie searched the cabinets in the motorhome's kitchen area for things to take. She pulled a flashlight out of the overhead cabinet above the seat. She flicked it on, and there was light. The batteries were working. Moving to another cabinet, she found some crackers, granola bars, and a plastic grocery bag to carry her stash. Opening the refrigerator, she found bottled water. Roger had indeed chained the door. She tried it first, which left only the emergency exit window. Every motorhome had one. Jessie grabbed the blanket off the foot of the bed before she left. Reading the instructions on the window, she pushed on it. It opened, and she scrambled out letting herself slide to the ground. "Come on, Larissa. I'm out of here." Jessie had no idea where she was. Her phone was still charged but had no service. Turning on the flashlight, she moved its light around the area. A dirt road was to the right of the motor home. Roger must have camped here before. In every direction, there were trees and more trees. If luck were on her side, she'd make it through the night. *Stay near the road, but out of sight*, she told herself. She knew Matt was looking for her, and more would be by morning.

Chapter 35

Matt had spent most of the afternoon following Radar from house to house. None of the people they were looking for were at the houses Radar had indicated on. No one seemed to know where the occupants were or when they would be back. Matt took a sweater that belonged to Rose from among her things. He knew the routine for a track now. He also knew that every moment counted when it came to Jessie's life. Rose was involved. Matt knew it. Dylan stood with him the entire day, and Matt was thankful he was there. He asked pertinent questions and kept Matt's mind sharp.

"I'd like to see if the dog could lead us to Rose, but it's getting dark. We'll have to wait until morning." He handed the sweater to Frank. "Marvin, I'm leaving you here. I don't want to alert Rose to anything, in case she returns. I want you to call me if your wife or any of the other folks come back. I won't be far away and can make it back in no time. Can I trust you?" he asked wearily.

"Yes, sir, you can." Marvin met his eyes. "I'm not going anywhere. I want to find out what happened to my daughter, too."

"We can try to track now if you want," Frank spoke up. "Radar has worked tracks at night, but we don't know the general area to begin looking, which makes it harder." Frank pulled on the leash to keep the dog close.

"We'll wait. Dylan and I are going do some surveillance tonight. Take Radar back to my place and get yourself some dinner. I have a hunch. I may be off base, but I want to check it out." Matt and Frank walked to the car. He reminded Mr. Young once again not to go anywhere, that they weren't through questioning him, and to be sure to call if his wife showed. "I'll see you later, Frank." He gave Radar a pat. "If I need you, I'll call you back. In the meantime, get some rest." Matt stepped back as Frank let Radar into his crate. "You'll both need to be fresh tomorrow. We need to find Jessie."

Mr. Young had told Matt about another way to get to the crypt. They could drive there, and it required almost no walking. There was a place where they could park in the trees and watch the area.

"Are you okay?" Dylan fastened his seat belt.

"I've been better." Matt frowned. "I want to find her tonight. I hate all the waiting."

"Jessie's resourceful. She already has a plan, you can count on it. I wouldn't doubt she's already given her abductors fits." Dylan started the car.

"You're probably right, but I keep thinking about what they might have done to her." His fist curled. "Jessie wouldn't go down without a fight, and the scene didn't look as if there had been much of a scuffle."

"They used a drug; I'm sure of it. Whoever it was took Jessie by surprise, but they won't be able to do it a second time. I've seen her in action, and she's strong. She'll be okay." His phone rang, and Dylan looked at his caller ID. "Katie. She's called several times. I should call her back. I know she's worried." Dylan pulled over to the side of the road.

"Go ahead. Our phones will have to remain on silent for a while, so call Katie before we get any closer." Matt leaned his head against the window as Dylan talked and closed his eyes. *Jessie, I know you heard Abigail's thoughts so I hope you can hear mine. I'm looking for you, sweetheart. Don't give up. Keep fighting. I'm coming for you. If I have to tear these woods apart, I'll find you.*

****

Jessie moved far enough away from the RV to hide in the bushes but remained close enough to hear when and if they came back. She had no idea where she was and where to go from here. She turned the flashlight on to make sure of her footing and found a fallen tree to sit on. It was cold, dark, and the trees rustled in the breeze, heightening her fears. The woods could be dangerous at night. She began to weigh out the pros and cons of moving farther away. Roger and the man knew the area better than she did. They could come looking for her. On the other hand, Matt could be looking for her, too, and he might find the motorhome first. *Please let him be the one to find me.* She looked up at the starry sky. Her mind told her to keep moving, but her body didn't want to go another step. The chilly air cut through her jacket, sending shivers down her spine. Happy she had grabbed the blanket even though it was a pain to carry, she wrapped herself in it. Her teeth at least stopped chattering. If she didn't make a plan soon, she might turn into a Popsicle before long. *"Don't give up; keep fighting, I'm coming for you."* Matt was in her head. He must be thinking of her. She forced herself to stand but didn't move. What direction should she go? Thoughts rushed in and out of her mind as the sounds of the night seemed to scream through the trees. Remember this moment, Jessie, and you'll not go camping alone in the woods. *If you get through this night in one piece, a well-deserved trip to the city is your reward, along with a new outfit or better yet, a scone of your choosing from Java Joe's Coffee Shop.* Jessie frowned. What really made her mad was that Rose had lied to her. Where had her usual warning been? Not working this time, obviously. Boy, would she like to get her hands on Rose! Anger was good. It helped push the fear into the far corners of her mind. She sat down again.

How long had she leaned against the old tree? She didn't know, but she heard the sound of a vehicle approaching. She scurried into the brush. They couldn't see her, but she wanted to watch them. The car kept on going. Darn. She relaxed against the tree trunk again. If she had known someone else would pass this way, she could have flagged the car down and asked for help.

Jessie saw the lights of another car and then heard it pull in close. The engine stopped. It was Roger and the other man. She strained to listen to what they were saying.

"Well, that didn't go well." The other man opened the door. "We're supposed to deliver her dead."

"Hell, I'm done doing their dirty work," Roger said loudly. "Larissa was enough. I may beat my wife, but I won't kill a stranger. I wouldn't mind slugging her, though. She did help my wife leave me. I'm in trouble because of her."

"You're in trouble but not because of her."

"Damn, Adam, I came here to have a new life. You're the one who told me it was a great place to live.

I thought for a while it might be, but now I want out. They can kill her if they want her dead. I'm going to get in my motorhome with her in it and keep driving." His voice was getting louder.

"Don't even think of it. You're still married, and the cops are already looking for us. We need to turn the woman loose. Kidnapping carries heavy charges if they catch us. Besides, you heard Randy. Your wife's parents have filed charges against you. You'll serve time for slapping her around."

"I heard him, but I'm not sure if he's telling the truth or manipulating us. He's damn good at it when he wants a favor. I've fallen for the whole guilt trip before and played his stupid game to clean up their mess. Now they want us to take care of it again. They don't want to dirty their hands. Nothing is worth murder not even for them. They're power-crazy nuts. I'm done." Roger swore. "How did it go so wrong? Olivia and I were happy enough in the beginning."

"You were new and naïve like me in the beginning. Olivia saw things we didn't and began to ask them about their practices. She saw how the women were treated. Larissa told me about it, too, but I didn't believe her. In fact, I liked it until I saw it from her perspective. The leaders don't like to have their authority questioned. Olivia was young and didn't understand all the rules. She wanted her parents at the wedding. What's wrong with that? Even I couldn't understand their reasoning. Everything was wrong from the start, and you know it." He said a few other things that Jessie couldn't hear. "You should never have hit Olivia, Roger."

"I know that now, but Randy told me it was my job

to keep her in line. A man is supposed to rule his household. He's the head of the home. I never meant to hurt her, though. After a while, it got easy to blame her for everything and use my fists. I saw my dad do it often enough, and my mom never left. I'll never get to see her or my kid. What a mess I've made."

"Your dad and Randy were both wrong, but it's too late with Olivia. Even I know that beating a woman is wrong. You need help, Roger," Adam spoke sternly. "Rose has changed everything since she got involved."

"It's true about Rose, but there's someone else behind this, too. Randy has been strange and so has Doc. All I can say is I'm not killing the woman. If you want to, you can," Roger yelled out. "I don't give a damn what they say. I'm not going to do it. I may be a lot of things, but I'm no murderer."

"I don't want to kill her, either. I don't have the stomach for it. I say we drive away. Leave the motorhome because they'll be looking for it." Adam paused. "You know, I loved Larissa."

"If you loved Larissa why in the hell did you throw her in the dumpster?"

"I was scared, and I thought she was dead already. Randy said the cops would blame me if I didn't do what he said."

"Some great new life we made for ourselves. It's a hell of a mess! Should we untie her?" Roger asked.

"No. We can take the chain off the door, though. Maybe the woman will get free on her own. We need time to make a clean getaway."

"I have one question, Adam. Why didn't you stop them from hurting Larissa if you cared?"

"Rose wouldn't let me near her. A leader guarded

Larissa around the clock. Marvin set her free, but they had the power to get to her. In freeing her, Marvin sent her to her death. Although, they would have killed her anyway to cover things up. Larissa knew too much."

"This is depressing. I don't want to talk about it anymore. I'm leaving. Are you coming?" Roger opened the car door.

"I'm coming." The other man removed the chain from the door of the RV. He got back in the car, and the doors slammed.

Jessie heard the engine start, and they were gone. What had she heard? Rose was obviously up to her eyeballs in the mess, but who were the men they were talking about? Now she knew who had thrown Larissa in the trash. Adam and Roger. Matt would have to sort it out. For tonight, she could remain here safely and try to find her way back in the morning. It was cold out, but she'd rather take her chances outside than to have them come back for something. She would stay where she was. A few minutes later, she was glad she had, as headlights once more flooded the motorhome. They were back. They went inside and flipped on the lights.

"Hell, she got free. Now I know we have to get out of here." Roger's voice carried to where she hid. "She had to be good to get those ropes off."

With the lights streaming from the windows, Jessie could make out the first few letters of the license plate. The two men carried out a couple of bags. They'd left the car doors open, and Roger set a gun on the dash of the car. Adam carried out a six-pack of beer and a bag of chips. They both went back inside. Jessie threw off the blanket, and keeping low to the ground, ran silently to the car. She grabbed the gun and the keys that were still in the ignition. Perfect. She made her way to the front of the RV and waited for one of them to come out. One of the men shut off the lights in the back bedroom. Roger stepped out the door alone. He carried a bag to the car and turned back to the motorhome.

"Where'd you put the keys, Adam? I need to open the trunk."

"They're in the ignition," Adam yelled out.

"No, they aren't. Flip on the damn outside light so I can see. You must have dropped them."

"I never took them out of the ignition."

Roger dropped the bag and ransacked the car. "What the hell is going on?" His voice took on a nervous edge. "I know I set my gun there a minute ago."

"Calm down, let's look again." Adam stood beside Roger with their backs to Jessie.

"Are you looking for something, boys?" Jessie held the keys up for them to see. They turned to see a gun pointed at them.

Roger started for her. "We can take her. There are two of us."

Jessie shot near his feet, and Roger stopped in his tracks. "There may be two of you, but this makes it possible for me to drop at least one of you. Is that how you want to play?" She stared at them. "Which one?"

"What do you want?" Roger muttered a few curses.

"You should never call the lady with the gun names, Roger. It's not nice, and I'm already angry about the headache your drug gave me. I also don't appreciate the way you yanked my hair and hit me either."

"Tell us what you want us to do." Adam didn't

move.

"I'd be happy to. You fellas overlooked a couple important facts when you took me this morning. You weren't paying attention to your job. I had a phone on me, and the police are able to trace our location even as we stand here. You also missed this bright shiny object." She held up her police badge for them to see. Jessie grabbed the piece of rope from her pocket and tossed it to Adam. "Slow and easy, Adam, I want you to tie Roger's hands nice and tight behind his back. If he fights you, I'll be happy to shoot him." She kept the gun aimed at them. "In case you're wondering, I do know how to use this, and I'm a pretty good shot."

"Now what?" Adam asked after he'd tied Roger's hands.

"We're going to get into the car and take a little drive. I know a man who would love to meet you. He'll be happy to hear everything I heard tonight."

Chapter 36

Matt's phone sounded a call as they got close to the turnoff for the crypt. His heart leaped as the screen lit. "Jess," he gasped. "Are you okay, sweetheart?"

"I'm better now that I've heard your voice. I'm bringing you a present, two of our suspects."

"Where are you?"

"Near the turnoff to the State Park. We're on our way back to Blue Cove. You'll be able to get some valuable information from these two."

"I'll send Kip out to escort you into town in case they try something funny. We'll be right behind you, sweetheart."

"They should behave themselves. I have a gun pointed at both of their backs, and you know me. I shot a notorious hitman; I'm capable of shooting them if I need to. I do appreciate your care and concern."

"Keep talking, Jess, you're doing fine. I'm sure Jeremy has zeroed in on your location by now. I'm going to call him and send a police escort for you. Love you, Jess. I want to hear the story, all of it."

"Of course, you will. I have some complaining and whining to do. Oh, and, Matt?"

"Yes."

"I love you, too."

"I'm happy to hear it, sweetheart." He grinned. "What kind of vehicle are you in?" His smile broadened when she asked Adam. He was going to have to work on the makes and models of cars with her.

Matt hung up and answered Jeremy's call. "Did you pick up her phone signal?"

"Sure did," Jeremy replied. He gave Matt the location and miles out of Blue Cove.

"We talked a few minutes ago. I can't wait to hear how Jessie did it. Her captors became her captives."

"You'll have to fill me in once you have the whole story. It sounds interesting." Jeremy chuckled.

"I will. Right now I want to call for backup to escort our suspects into town." Matt hung up and called the station. A car was on the way. His fingers tapped on the armrest. His girl never ceased to amaze him.

****

Jessie was happy to see the police cruiser when it passed them, turned around, and followed close behind them. When their car went by another cruiser at the side of the road, the first car got in front of them and the second pulled in behind them. "I bet you boys never thought you would have your own personal police escort. Chief Parker is the best."

"I bet you're his gal. Am I right?" Adam looked at her in the mirror.

She nodded at him. "When you're right, you're right."

"Of all the dumb luck." Roger shook his head. "And I was dumb enough to hit her," he mumbled under his breath.

"He doesn't like it when I get hurt." She enjoyed rubbing it in. "Of course, I'll have to tell him. I hope that you didn't bruise me. It was too dark for me to get a close look at my face."

277

"Can I ask you something?" Adam met her eyes in the mirror.

"Sure." She saw him frown.

"Are you the same lady I read about who helped save those kids and shot the hitman who was at the hospital to kill the chief?"

Jessie smiled to herself. "Yes, I am."

"Damn, I was afraid you'd say that. Roger, we're in big trouble."

"It sure as hell looks that way." Roger's head slumped forward.

Jessie let out a sigh of relief when they pulled into the police station, but she kept the gun trained on the men in the front seat.

"We'll take over from here, Jessie." Kip cuffed Adam, and Gary took hold of Roger's arm after he'd cuffed him and led them into the station to book them.

Taking a deep breath of the chilly night air, she leaned her hip against the car door and waited for the one person she wanted to see. A car flew into the parking lot with lights on. It was him. Her hand went to her heart. He jumped out as soon as the car came to a stop. Wow, he was a handsome sight. As he raced toward her, Jessie's pulse quickened. He opened his arms, and she ran into their circle. Two strong arms closed around her holding her tight, and she cried.

"It's okay, sweetheart." He gently stroked the side of her face. He whispered into her ear and nibbled on it at the same time. "I'm never letting you out of my sight again, love."

"Of course, you will. You can't watch me twenty-four seven. You'd never get anything done that way."

"You want to bet? I'm good at multitasking." He

kissed her cheek. "I have a feeling watching you is going to be my full-time job. Not that I'm complaining. I like looking at you."

"You're sweet." Her breath caught in her throat when she tilted her head back and saw the look in his eyes.

"Damn, Jess, there's nothing sweet about it. I've aged ten years today. I want you where I can see you."

"Dylan," Jessie called out. "You need to take him inside to calm down." She smiled and patted his hand.

"Not without you, love. I'm not going anywhere without you. Besides, you have a story to tell me. Something tells me it's a doozy." He put an arm around her shoulder and drew her into his side.

"I'm with you all the way." She drew his head down and kissed him.

"You two need to take this inside. You wouldn't want to attract a crowd," Dylan teased them. He gave Matt a pat on the back. "I told you she could take care of herself. I, for one, can't wait to hear this story. I've been around for the rest of them and this one ought to be equally good."

Jessie sat down in the waiting room while Matt went to check on the suspects. He came back within a few minutes. "Go into my office. Call Frank and tell him you're okay and call Katie, too, while you're at it. I'm going to sit in on the interrogation for a while. It seems they waived their rights and are in a talkative mood. I'll be back to question you. Don't you go anywhere." He shook a finger at her. "I'll be back."

"Who me?" She pointed at herself. "No car." She shrugged. "I'm staying right here where you can keep an eye on me while I keep mine on you." She gave him a flirtatious smile and sauntered back to his office.

Jessie called Katie. They laughed and cried together. Frank told her he was happy that she was safe. Reba had known all along that she'd be okay. Sadie was happy to hear from her and glad to know she was all right after the fact. It was comforting to have people around her who cared. The only one left to talk to now was Matt. She was tired and wanted to go home. She waited; she wandered into the officers' dining area to get some water and a candy bar from the vending machine. She went back to Matt's office and waited some more.

"Those two are singing their heads off." Matt's voice startled her. "You must be tired." He softened his voice.

"I am." She yawned and realized she had dozed off in his chair. "It's hard to believe it's only been a day. It seems so much longer."

"Tell me your story so you can get some rest. You're not going home, though, until Rose and the others are in jail." He sat on the edge of his desk close to her. "Kip drove your car here. It's parked outside, and your purse is locked up in evidence. You can get them before you leave." He laced his fingers through hers. "As soon as Dylan gets here, you can begin." Their eyes met and locked on each other. "I was worried, Jess."

"I know. I was, too."

"I'm here." Dylan smiled and sat down beside her.

Jessie began her story. "I knew something wasn't right when I saw Rose standing at the back door." Jessie sighed. "I'm a softy. I missed the warnings going off in my head."

"What happened next?" Dylan asked.

Jessie told them what happened when she woke up and Roger was there to check on her. "I don't like that man." She scowled. "He's a bully. A lot like Randy in that regard."

Matt pushed her hair behind her ear and traced the edges of the bruise on her cheek. "How did you come by this?"

"Roger felt like he needed to hit me to make me hold still. You know, Matt, I don't think he likes me. He blames me for Olivia getting away. He mentioned it to me a few times."

Matt's lips thinned, and the lines on his forehead stood out. His hand curled into a fist and then relaxed. "I knew I didn't like Roger after seeing his handiwork on Olivia. Does it hurt?" He turned her face toward the light to take a closer look.

"It did when he hit me."

"How did you get away?" Dylan sat forward in his chair.

"They said they had to go and meet the others and left. I began to work on loosening the ropes. It didn't go well. Which reminds me, Matt, do they have a class to teach you how to get out of ropes? It seems like something I might need to know."

He shook his head and grinned. "You might need to ask the teacher in your self-defense class."

"My wrists are still sore from rubbing the rope back and forth."

Matt lifted her hand and frowned when he saw the red marks.

"You know it doesn't work like I've seen them do on TV." Jessie glared at Dylan when he laughed.

"I'm sure it doesn't." Matt gently massaged her wrists.

His tenderness was her undoing. "I wanted to give up, but that's when I saw her." Tears welled up in Jessie's eyes as she talked.

"Who did you see?" Matt handed her a tissue.

"Larissa. Knowing I wasn't alone seemed to help. I gave myself a pep talk and got to work." Jessie went on to tell them about how she untied the ropes.

"Jessie, I'm sure you've had more experience than any of your teachers have with breaking out of captivity. You might need to teach the classes on how to escape unusual and sticky situations." Dylan smiled at her.

"I wonder if Larissa helped me get my hands free or if I did it on my own. I guess it doesn't matter." Jessie rubbed the back of her neck and continued.

"Taking the blanket and flashlight was smart, and staying close but hidden was even smarter. I'm proud of you, Jess. You could have gotten lost out there. There's nothing wrong with your survival instinct."

She could feel a blush tint her face. Matt's words of praise made her feel warm and happy inside. She went on to tell him about how she acquired the gun, and how she managed to turn the tables on Roger and Adam.

"Well, I'll be heading out. I told you she was resourceful, Matt," Dylan spoke as he left Matt's office.

"Yep, you did." He turned her hand over in his. "You know, Jess, Roger was ordered to kill you. They are supposed to get back with their contact when they finish the job. We are trying to convince the two of them to work with us. After a night behind bars, my gut tells me they'll be willing to consider it." Matt glanced at her. "If and when we set up the meeting, you'll be a part of it. You earned the right to, and I think you have some unfinished business with Rose."

"I wouldn't mind being a part of bringing her to justice. I know Larissa suffered. So did Olivia. I don't think Rose did, though. She's devious, but I could be wrong."

"For now, Kip is driving you to your house to pick up what you need and then on to my house. Frank is waiting and said he'd have supper ready for you. Until we catch all the suspects, I'm keeping my eye on you." Matt stood.

"What about my car?"

"I'll drive it to my house, so you have it, but you won't be going anywhere without a police escort."

She nodded, not really minding at all. "Does that mean to see Sally, too?"

"Yes, for now. Once we know we have everyone who was involved, you'll be free again."

"Stuck with you and the other hunky cops? I can think of a lot worse fates." She smiled at him and walked out of his office before him.

Chapter 37

Matt's head was spinning after he left the interrogation room. What a mess. It hadn't taken Matt long to figure out that Adam was a follower. He was a soft-hearted fellow whom the leadership of the group exploited because of his willingness to do good for others. Phillips had manipulated him. Roger's upbringing, on the other hand, had hardened him. He was quick to lash out in anger. Matt was convinced that the group's leaders had handpicked both of them to do their dirty work. They were involved in what had happened to Larissa, and they were complicit in her murder, but their leaders had influenced them. Matt would let them sit in jail to think about what he had told them. They had agreed to waive the rights to have an attorney present before answering questions. If they worked with the police, the judge might go easier on them.

Matt read his notes, going over the conversations in his mind again. Adam had moved to the compound several years ago with his family. He'd loved it until a few months ago. He had invited Roger to come join him. Roger had fallen all over himself apologizing for hitting Jessie.

"How do you think it went?" Dylan interrupted his thoughts.

"We are no closer to knowing the name of

Larissa's killer than when we started." Matt sat back to rub his eyes. "Those two are clueless. I'm getting a better picture of the group, though, and it's not pretty. I can't believe they've operated under the radar this long."

"It's as Adam told us; they rarely came to town. If they went at all, it was to Rocky Pointe or Harrisville to pick up supplies. They had their own doctor to treat them. No one would have seen the bruises on the kids or women to be able to report the abuse to the police."

"The thing that bothers me the most is that some of those people got into this mess honestly, looking for a better and simpler life. They aren't guilty of the murder, but you know their lives and faith will be shattered."

"What's next on the agenda?" Dylan looked at his incoming text with a smile, a sheepish look on his face.

"Katie, I presume?" Matt grinned at him when he nodded.

"She wants me to take her to see Sally Mansfield tomorrow. They refuse to call her by her married name anymore. Of course, Jessie will want to come, too."

"Jessie isn't going anywhere without me," Matt said flatly, "It's too fresh in my mind still."

"Yeah, I saw the way you two looked at each other." Dylan smirked. "It's only a matter of time until you're married with kids crawling all over you."

"I wouldn't mind." Matt laughed. "I have a goal in mind, and I've been bringing Jess around to my way of thinking slow and easy for the last couple of months. I admit the last few cases have made me rethink the whole idea. Slow isn't working for me anymore." Matt opened the door and walked out of the station with Dylan right behind him.

"I've been thinking about asking Katie on a date," Dylan said after a moment. "Watching you and Jessie has made me realize that I need someone in my life, too."

Matt shook Dylan's hand. "I'm glad to hear it. She's a great girl."

"A date, I'm not talking marriage. Even the idea scares me." He made a face. "I'm not sure I'd be any good at it."

"I'll tell you what scares me worse is thinking of my life without Jessie in it." Matt shook his head. "I've had several chances to consider that bleak picture. Marriage seems like a piece of cake in comparison."

"I get it. Seeing Katie with Tom the other day had the same effect on me as walking miles with a rock in my shoe. I didn't like the feeling. But marriage is a long way off for me."

"We'll see about that." Matt chuckled. "Maybe we should go to Harrisville together tomorrow."

"I'll send you a text later to tell you the time." Dylan stopped at Jessie's car.

"I'm going to let Jessie help in this case. She's earned the right, and I know she's itching to get at Rose."

"We'll talk later," Dylan called over his shoulder.

****

Matt parked Jessie's car and walked into his house. "I thought you'd be in bed, Frank." Matt sat on the couch.

"I wasn't tired. I took a nap earlier, and now I'm up." He grinned, making the lines around his eyes crinkle. "This chair is comfortable. I sat in it when I first got back and promptly fell asleep. I'm hoping that if I sit here long enough, it will do the trick again."

"Is Jessie asleep?"

"Yes." He nodded. "She ate dinner and went right to bed. I haven't heard a peep out of her all evening." Frank muted the sound on the TV. "How did it go with the suspects?"

"I didn't learn much about the murder. Neither man knew much. Oblivious or they're damn good at faking it, but I learned a lot about the group they are with."

"I've always known these groups exist, but you don't usually hear about them unless something goes wrong. I remember hearing about a group where the leaders beat the pastor's son, trying to save him. He died, and they were convicted of murder." Frank frowned.

Matt shook his head. "I guess they're out there, but at least they're not the norm."

"If you're hungry I can heat up the leftovers. It was pretty good if I do say so myself." Frank stood.

"Sounds good. I'll wash up and be right back." Matt walked down the hall.

Matt paused outside the bedroom door to listen. All was quiet. He opened it and slipped in quietly. His breath caught in his throat. She lay curled up on her side, and her hair fell across her cheek. Jessie was safe. He exhaled a deep breath. He had lived a lifetime in one day, today. How much risk could one person take before their luck runs out? She had asked him that once. Matt wasn't sure. As much as she involved her life in the lives of others, he was afraid she would test the answer to that question to the max.

No other woman had ever done this to him before. Jessie made him feel vulnerable yet secure at the same time. She loved him. He stood gazing at her. She told him in a hundred different ways. Her glances sent heat to his core, the way she touched him when she didn't realize she was doing it, and the way she walked straight into his arms after a hard experience told him she trusted him. Emotions and feelings had never been easy for him to put into words. The word love hardly seemed to convey what he wanted to say and how he felt, but it would have to do for now. "Jess," he whispered, "love, you're in for all the charm I can muster. I want you where I can keep an eye on you from now on." He watched her stir and turn over. Matt stood there for another moment and then walked out of the room.

Chapter 38

Early the next morning, the two couples were on their way to Harrisville. Jessie could see Dylan watching Katie in the rearview mirror. She loved how the two of them were sneaking looks at each other when they thought no one was looking. Katie would be engaged to Dylan and married before her at this rate.

Frank had opted to stay behind at Matt's place. Radar needed to be fresh for his next track, which would be soon. Matt seemed relaxed. Dylan was driving, and Matt was lost in thought. At least Jessie thought he was. He had been so sweet to her this morning. He had made her coffee, asked her a dozen times if she was all right, and touched the bruise on her cheek tenderly more than once. She worried about him. His job was stressful enough without adding her baggage to the cquation.

"Jessie, I hope you're not in one of your quiet, pensive moods. We have a long drive, and I'm in a mood to talk."

"Talk away." Jessie turned to Katie.

"Sally is happy we're coming." Katie pushed her hair behind her ears. "She wants to hear about your ordeal from you in person. I'm telling you, Jessie, you have to stop all this nonsense. It's too hard for everybody."

"You make it sound like it's something I can

control." Jessie glared at her. "I didn't ask to be abducted you know."

"Well, I think it's possible for you to do something about it. You should quit being helpful. People would ignore you then as they do me. You don't see me asking questions or writing stories and upsetting everyone around me." Katie's hands moved with each word.

"True, but it's not your job to ask questions unless it's of me." Jessie paused. "You could be right about not getting involved, but I'll never know for sure. I'm not even going to try to find out. I have to ask questions; it's what I do. I can't imagine saying or doing nothing in the face of injustice; it's not how I'm wired." Jessie tilted her head when she spoke.

"I, for one, am tired of my best friend being shot at and me, too, if I'm with her." Katie turned her head to hide her smile. "You must see the effect you have on people."

"Katie, it's a good thing Jess likes you." Matt turned around to look at her, shaking his head.

"She knows I'm teasing her, although I do worry about her and would like it if her life was as boring as mine. Or maybe I'm jealous because she is always saving someone from something." Katie couldn't stop the laugh from coming. "Plus, I'll always owe her big time for saving my brother's life."

"I'm going to hold you to it, trust me." Jessie patted Katie's arm.

****

"I hate hospitals," Katie said when they walked out of Sally's room. "They're depressing and in desperate need of an interior decorator."

"It's not a hotel, Katie." Jessie sighed.

"I know. I'm not dumb, you know. People would get better faster in nicer surroundings is all. I mean, don't you think these places are a little depressing?"

Jessie put her arm around Katie. "Yes, especially when our friend is in the room. Sally looks good, considering all she's been through."

"I thought she looked awful." Katie frowned. "We'll cheer her up, though, once she moves to Blue Cove."

"*If* she moves there. Right now, she needs to spend time with her parents. She still has recovery, therapy, and a trial to get through." Jessie frowned. "I hope Bruce spends a long time in prison for what he did to her. Statistics say he won't, but I'm still hoping."

"You're turning Sally into an activist for women. Did you hear how she was talking?" Katie grinned. "She sounds like you."

"I heard." Jessie smiled. "It was life's circumstances which turned her into one, not me."

"Next thing you know she'll be in Blue Cove working as an undercover detective like you."

"More like a reluctant one." Jessie laughed. "I hope seeing a ghost isn't contagious."

"I suppose she'll be okay. I would find it hard to trust a man again. Bruce really messed her up." Katie smiled at a child who toddled by.

"Every woman needs to know how to defend herself." Jessie saw Katie roll her eyes. "I know I'm on my soapbox again, but I don't care. This subject is too important to ignore. Women are often the victims of crime. Men are naturally stronger, so we have to be smarter, that's all there is to it."

Katie picked up a magazine and began to thumb

through it. Jessie kept glancing out the window and watching for the car. Matt had an appointment with the Harrisville police. He had to deliver the warrant from his department with the charges against Bruce Kingman, and he wanted to see how the case was progressing. Jessie was interested, too. She had penned several notes while talking with Sally and felt one of her articles coming on.

"They're here." Jessie stood, slinging her purse over her shoulder.

"Good, I'm hungry." Katie followed her out to the waiting car.

They stopped at a restaurant a couple of the locals had said was the best in town. The conversation was fun but watching Katie and Dylan trying to hide their feelings was the best part of all.

Chapter 39

Matt and Frank dropped Jessie off at the store on Monday morning. "See you after work, sweetheart. Have a good day." Matt opened the car door for her.

"Thanks, you too. I hope Roger and Adam are willing to deal." She unlocked the door.

"Me, too. One of your bodyguards will be out of uniform, but keeping an eye on you and your store. I don't trust Rose or the others. They may be feeling desperate about now. They can't be too happy Roger hasn't gotten back to them yet."

"No, I don't imagine they are."

"We'll keep you safe."

"I have no doubt about it." Jessie scrunched up her face.

Matt lifted her chin. "Why the strange look?"

"I admit my self-esteem has taken a major hit as of late. With all the people who've wanted to kill me or have me murdered, I can't help but wonder what that says about me as a person."

"From my point of view, I'd say you're almost perfect." He gave her a quick kiss. "We'll see you after five unless something happens before then."

"Before I forget to tell you, Pastor Kevin called on Friday to tell me the classes on domestic violence will be this fall. He has rounded up some great speakers. We both thought it would be good if Sally could share her experience, and she agreed to it if it's safe for her to come here by then."

"It should be." He waved before getting in the car. "I love you." He mouthed the words.

Jessie smiled and watched him drive away. "First things first." She sighed and put the chair back where it belonged. Then she straightened the book table and the counter. When she opened the doors to Joe's, Molly ran over and gave her a big hug.

"I'm so glad you're safe. Audrey and I were so scared for you. Your purse was in the car, your keys on the ground, and there was no sign of you. I want to hear all about it." She darted toward the doorway to the coffee shop. "I'll be back with coffee, a scone, and I'm ready to listen. I'd better make it two cups of coffee and two scones because Reba is here."

"Sounds good." Jessie watched Reba park her car in front of the store and went to open the door.

"Good morning, dear." Reba paused in the doorway to hug her tight. "I've come to hear about your ordeal. Other than the bruise on your cheek, you don't look any worse for wear."

"Thank you. I'm doing well." Jessie followed Reba into the store. "This case is strange and getting more so all the time."

"I knew it would be. You'll find out a few more strange details before it's all over." Reba shifted her purse to her other arm.

"Howdy, Reba. I came bearing goodies so we can listen to her story." Molly carried in a tray with coffee and a plate of fresh scones, and they sat at the table in the center of the store.

Jessie told them about the abduction. She loved

their expressions when she told them how she'd gotten free. "They're in jail, and Matt is hoping they'll work with him to help catch the others."

"They will, dear." Reba took a sip of her coffee. "How is your store ghost doing?" She lowered her voice.

"She's still moving things around. I forgot to tell you that she was with me in the RV. When I saw her, I felt a renewed energy to try working on the ropes again. I'm not sure what to think about her being there. Did I get my hands free on my own or did she help me? I'm still wondering."

"A little of both, I suppose." Reba patted Jessie's hand.

"You mean Reba knows about you know who?" Molly pointed at the chair.

"Yes. Reba is the person in the know about these things. If you have any questions, she's the one to ask." Jessie smiled at Molly's expression. "We don't tell many people about what we see or hear. Others wouldn't understand, so it's our little mystery. I can't say we even understand. Do we?" Jessie glanced at Reba.

"No, it's more like we make the best of our situation."

"You don't need to worry about us telling anyone, Molly. Your secret is safe with us." Jessie took a bite of her scone.

"I take it you've seen Larissa, too." Reba patted Molly's hand.

"Yes, after she rearranged the coffee shop. I thought we'd been vandalized." Molly smiled. "Matt laughed and told me to ask Jessie all about it after he left. When Jessie told me, I thought she was kidding, but later I saw Larissa sitting at the table by the window." Molly glanced at the empty chair by the window. "Speaking of the coffee shop, you are looking at the new owner. Our loan is approved, and we close at the end of the month."

"That's wonderful, dear." Reba smiled. "You'll be such great neighbors for Jessie."

"Molly, I'm so excited for you." Jessie clapped her hands. "I'll be a faithful customer."

"You can count on me, too. I do like my hot tea and occasional coffee and of course, a lovely English scone."

"I'm glad you're here to celebrate it with us, friend. I still shake when I think about your abduction." Molly hugged Jessie again. "I guess as the new owner that I had better get back to work taking care of my investment." She picked up the tray and took it with her.

"I want these books." Reba handed Jessie a paper with the titles written on it.

Jessie went to get the books from the shelves and took them to the counter. "I know you'll enjoy this author. Who doesn't love to read a good book?"

"I know I do." Reba leaned close to her. There were customers in the store. "Be careful of the one with a shadow in his past. He's more dangerous than the others are and has destroyed many lives. It may all come out now or come around another time."

"I'm not sure what you mean." Jessie frowned.

"Some of those involved you've seen. One is out front but is still unknown to you and to the others. A man's secrets can be dangerous. Don't trust anyone in the group." Reba patted her hand. "It'll work out; I'm sure. How's your friend Katie?"

Jessie shivered. She wished Reba's warnings didn't always sound so dire. "She's good, and I think she's falling in love."

"With our own handsome Dylan Mitchel, I do believe. I've seen the way she's looked at him since she moved here. I'd say she's been in love with him for a while, even though she has checked out several men since. Dylan, on the other hand, has been dragging his feet. He was interested, but it took him a while to realize that he wanted to do something about it. Leave it to another man to show interest, and suddenly the chase is on." Reba nodded her head with a smile on her face. "I told you she would have an adventure of her own."

"Yes, you did. You blow my mind with what you know." Jessie shook her head. "I'm having fun watching them. When she's happy, so am I."

"You're a good friend, Jessie dear." Reba smiled at her. "Ah, love, what's not to like about people falling in love? It's almost springtime, the flowers will be blooming soon, and love is in the air." Reba closed her wallet and put it back in her purse. "We need a wedding to celebrate. It's a joy watching you young folks. You waste so much time before you give in. Life is too short to waste any moment you can spend loving someone. We all do it, though. I did, too." She smiled. "We can't make it too easy for our men, now can we?"

"You're something, Reba. You deliver a warning and then make me laugh with your next statement." Jessie heard the bell above the door.

"Such is life—the good times mixed with the bad." The corners of her mouth turned down. "Well, I'm off.

Keep your eyes open for the bad one in the shadows. Dear Jessie, buy a new dress." Reba handed her an envelope with money in it. "I can see the no in your eyes, but yes, you *will* take it. I insist. Matt needs to see you looking all spiffy for him."

Jessie walked her to the door and gave her a hug on her way out. "Thank you."

"You know you're like a daughter to me." Reba dabbed at her eyes.

Jessie wiped the tears in her own eyes and waved as Reba drove away. "May I help you?" She turned and approached the attractive woman at the book table.

"Yes, you may." The woman turned around to face her. "I wanted to thank you for saving my daughter's life. I'm Olivia's mother. I believe she would be dead, had it not been for you."

"I was happy to do what I could." Jessie hid her surprise. "I'm glad I could be there for her."

"I'd like to give you back the money you gave her."

"No, it's not necessary." She shook her head. "I wanted Olivia to have the money. She needed help, and I'd like to believe someone would do the same for me."

"Had you not assisted her and then got that nice Officer Parker involved her story would have ended differently. I believe Roger would have killed her if he had found her first." The woman sat down in the chair and rummaged through her purse for a tissue.

"I thought the same thing at the time. Does Chief Parker know you are in town?" Jessie sat across from her.

"I'm supposed to meet with him at ten-thirty. He told me Roger was in jail along with another young man. I hope he stays there for a long time." She wiped at the tears running down her cheeks. "He confirmed what Olivia told me, that my beautiful niece Larissa is dead."

"Had you seen her much?" Jessie saw Larissa standing behind her aunt.

"No, not in quite a few years. My sister did send me pictures of her up to a few years ago when everything suddenly stopped." She frowned. "I always blamed it on Marvin. After what Olivia told me, now I'm not sure anymore. I think my sister is more complicit than she leads people to believe."

"I met your sister Rose. We had quite a run-in this past week." Jessie explained what had happened to her.

"I can't believe my sister would do some of the things I've heard about. The group Rose is messed up with sounds perfectly horrible. Rose was shy and quiet growing up." Her eyes flashed. "I get angry when I think of her not letting my own daughter call me to tell me she was alive. She let me worry all that time. I thought Olivia was dead." She frowned. "Olivia might have been alive, but she was living in hell. I would have done anything to get her and my niece out of there, had I known."

"Is Olivia here?"

"No, I wouldn't let her come." She shook her head. "I didn't know where Roger was, and I didn't want to risk it. We had the marriage annulled. I have a few things I want to say to my sister about what she let happen to my daughter and to my niece." Larissa swayed back and forth behind the chair. "My sister is guilty of something. I have a feeling she may be a bigger part of the problem. I'm going to find out, and I won't leave until I do." She got abruptly to her feet. "I'll stop in to see you before I leave, and I will always be grateful for how you helped my little girl."

"Please stop by anytime." Jessie walked her to the door. "I only wish I could have done more."

Chapter 40

The court-appointed lawyer counseled Adam and Roger to do whatever they could to cooperate with the police. In the end, they were convinced it would help their cause before the judge. Roger was facing several charges in the abuse case regarding Olivia. A Florida judge had issued a restraining order against him. He wasn't to attempt to see Olivia or contact her in any way, including by social media or phone. Matt set it up for Roger to call Randy while they monitored the call.

"Sir, this is Roger."

"What took you so long to call? We've been waiting." Randy sounded angry.

"We had a bit of trouble with the woman, but we got it done." Roger paced.

"Glad to hear it. Of course, we'll have to see for ourselves."

"I understand. Where do you want us to meet you and when?" Roger asked.

"At the crypt, at midnight. Make sure you're not being followed."

"We'll be there," Roger told him.

"How's Adam doing? If he starts talking, you might have to kill him, too."

"He's fine. Adam's the one who pulled the trigger." Roger crossed his fingers at the lie.

"Looks like maybe we can count on him after all."

There was a pause, and then Randy spoke again. "There will be something for you both for a job well done. Don't be late."

"We won't."

"He's one cold fish." Deputy Taylor had listened in. He had the warrant to arrest Randy for child abuse. The county had established credible evidence and built a solid case against him. Olivia's testimony had helped. "All of the leaders have some explaining to do about how the children were treated in the compound."

"You can add conspiracy to commit murder to those charges." Matt added a few notes in his notebook. "I talked to Marvin Young this morning. He hasn't seen his wife since the night she walked out. I don't know whether he's innocent or he's playing us like Rose did. I also talked to the detective in charge of the witness protection program, and he told me that from his dealings with Marvin, he felt Young was a nice guy. Randy's personality was more volatile, and he put up a fight about entering the protection program. The detective knew less about Glenn Crawford. He was a quiet man, had a large family practice, and was by all counts brilliant and well-respected. Randy seems to be the obvious choice, but I'm not buying the idea that he murdered Larissa. The evidence isn't adding up for me yet on him. He's involved, but I'm not convinced he beat her. This may have to play out more yet."

Matt met with the deputies from the county and the officers from his unit who would be involved in the operation. He wanted them on the site long before midnight. They would place a mannequin in a body bag in the trunk of Adam's car to buy them a little time. It was a solid plan. They had enough law enforcement, a fake body, and Roger was wearing a wire. He wanted all officers in protective vests, as well as Jessie. There was always the possibility of something going wrong. It came with the territory. Radar was the safety net if something went haywire. He could track them if they bolted.

Matt grabbed a cup of coffee and headed to his office, where he called Jessie. "Hi, sweetheart, how's your day going?"

"An early bus tour stopped at the coffee shop, which is always great for my sales. Olivia's mother came into the store earlier, also. She said she was going to meet you at ten-thirty. She's not happy with her sister."

"No, she let me know that on the phone more than once." He nodded. "I'm waiting for her now."

"Reba was also here. She had one of her famous warnings for me."

"What did she say?"

"The most dangerous person to be aware of is someone we can't see—someone in the shadows."

"I've been thinking the same thing all morning. It's not the obvious one. Who are we looking for?"

"Good question and I hope Larissa is going to help us answer it. I'm asking her to ride along tonight. Who knows if she will?"

"Roger made contact with Randy, and they're supposed to meet at midnight." Matt told her about the plans they had made. "You'll need to wear a vest. You know the routine."

"I'm beginning to."

"I'll be there at five with your vest. We'll swing by to pick up Frank and Radar. Are you feeling okay with all of this?"

"I'll be ready. I want to help Larissa find some peace." Jessie's voice was firm. "What happened to her shouldn't happen to anyone. From everything I've heard, the elders treated her unfairly from the beginning. She was supposed to be an example that the other kids could look up to. That's a lot of pressure to put on a young woman. I want Rose to own up to what she allowed her beautiful daughter to go through. I'm hopeful she'll spend time behind bars for what she did."

"She will. We have enough evidence already to press charges. I need to run, Jess; my ten-thirty is here."

****

"Good morning. Please be seated." Matt pointed to the chair in front of his desk as the slender woman entered his office. Olivia got her looks from her mother. She was an attractive woman with a nice smile. He could see Olivia in her mannerisms.

"I'm Kathryn, Olivia's mother." She sat, crossing her legs at the ankles.

"It's nice to meet you." Matt sat when she did.

"My husband and I are grateful for all you did to get my daughter home to us. She means the world to us. We had lost hope of ever seeing her alive again. Her call that morning was an answer to my prayers."

"Jessie helped the most." Matt opened the file on his desk.

"I know she did, and thankfully she had the presence of mind to get you involved." She pulled a piece of paper out of her purse. "I may or may not see my sister, but I want some answers. Here is a list of questions. If you get the chance to ask them for me, I would be thankful."

Matt took the piece of paper from her. "I'll be happy to ask her when we bring her in for questioning." He placed the list in the open file. "How is Olivia doing?"

"From the day she arrived home, we've watched her withdraw into herself. Guilt and nightmares plague her. We found a counselor who specializes in deprogramming escapees from cultic and violent groups. It's only the beginning for her. He calls it exit counseling. That group messed with her thinking something awful. Her counselor told us our happy young daughter is only a shadow of her former self. It will take time for her to come around—if she ever does. Add domestic violence to the equation, and you have scars, both physical and emotional. It won't be easy for her to trust a man again. Her greatest fear right now is of being a single mother." Her voice caught. "We have our work cut out for us, but we also have her." She drew a shuddering breath.

"That's a big deal, and she has you to help her recover. Her testimony will help those kids who are still in the compound. I hope she can see how important that is." Matt glanced at the file on his desk. "How long will you be in the area?"

"I'll stay until tomorrow or the next day. As I told you earlier, I went to the compound hoping to see Rose. Marvin told me she had been gone for several days, and he didn't know where she was. I'm angry with my sister. Marvin was nice enough and tried to answer all the questions he could. I'm not pleased with him either, though." She let out an angry breath. "He's too passive, but at least he acknowledged it."

"How can we help you?"

"I guess what I want is for you not to forget Olivia and us." She raised beseeching eyes to his face. "When you get answers will you please pass them on to us?"

"I'll tell you what I can." He nodded. "The rest you'll learn during the trial."

"I want to see my sister caught and made to answer for her part in this. I appreciate you giving my daughter back to me." She stood.

Matt stood, and she shook his hand. "I'll let you know when Rose is in custody."

"Thank you." She walked out of his office.

****

Jessie's day was done. She put the money in the safe, closed the doors into the coffee shop with a wave to Molly, and cleared the counter off. She locked the front door when the final customer left. Strange, the man sitting in Joe's looked familiar. "Larissa, I need your help. I want you to come with us tonight. You'll have to point out the ones who hurt you. I'm not sure if we have it right, and we need you." She felt a chilly wind swirl around her.

She finished her closing routine and grabbed a small stack of books off the counter. She wanted to add them to the book table. Shutting off the lights, she went out to meet Matt, who was standing in front of the store.

"Hi, sweetheart." He opened the car door for her. "How was your day?"

"Okay." She sounded preoccupied.

"Is something bothering you?" Matt waited for her to get in the car.

"I hope Larissa can help point out her killer. Her case isn't as simple as Sally and Olivia's were. Anyone in the group could have hurt her." She slipped into the front seat.

Matt closed her door. "True, but I'm betting on someone in the leadership."

"I'm sure you're probably right, but who?" She frowned with concentration.

"That's the big question." Matt closed the car door. "They'll cover for each other which will make it harder."

"Harder isn't good." She latched her seat belt.

"No, not good, but with a little luck we might be able to get them to turn on each other." He let out a gusty breath.

Jessie studied Matt. He was quiet. "I'd like to see them fighting among themselves. How do we make it happen?"

"When the time is right, we'll pit them against each other." He stared out the windshield. "Adam and Roger are our one link to draw them out, and we'll have a surprise or two ready."

Chapter 41

Matt spent time on a conference call with Deputy Taylor and Agent Kimble. They designed the plan to keep Adam and Roger as safe as possible. Kimble made it clear what they needed to do. An hour later, it was time to roll.

"Radar might have his work cut out for him tonight. These folks could scatter in different directions. I'm not sure how many will show." Matt turned onto the highway out of town.

"He's ready. Will we be walking into the area?" Frank asked.

"Marvin told me another way to get there. We will have less walking and a place to hide the cars. Dylan checked it out earlier." Matt glanced at Dylan. "How was it?"

"It's easier than the trailhead, that's for sure." He paused to look at an incoming text. "It's a bumpy road in spots, but this vehicle will make it with no problem." Dylan turned around in his seat. "Do you two have enough leg room back there?"

"I do. How about you, Jessie?" Frank asked.

"I'm fine. Was the text from Katie?" She'd noticed Dylan's smile. He nodded. She leaned close to him. "Be kind to my friend. You have the power to break her heart."

"I want to win her heart," he murmured. "Not

break it."

The closer they got to the area, the more uneasy Jessie's insides were. Her nerves were dancing all over each other. Jessie knew something was off but had no idea what. It was still a few hours before the scheduled meeting time, and yet panic was rising inside of her. Why? Reba's warning to her about the man in the shadows wasn't sitting well. It could be the man in the coffee shop. He hadn't been in the shadows. Had he? Her mind raced from thought to thought.

When they arrived on site, Matt set up a command center. As officers checked in, Matt gave them their assignments. Jessie loved watching how efficient he was with his men. They all knew what he expected of them. She should feel secure. He was great at his job and would do everything to keep her safe, but still, she paced. Jessie understood her part—he had told her several times. Larissa was making her nervous. She was one of the unknown factors. Larissa wasn't easy to gauge. Jessie had no idea what she would do, but she was sure it would be unusual.

She made herself comfortable in the place Matt had assigned to her. The sky was already dark, and the stars seemed to be out in the millions without the city lights to distract from the view. The crescent moon nestled among the stars, looking right at home. Jessie took a deep breath trying to still her racing heart, her eyes focused on the heavens. Despite everything, it was a beautiful night.

"Are you okay? You've been quiet all evening." Matt crouched down beside her.

"I'm not sure. Reba's words keep ringing in my head, and I don't know what to do about them."

"Don't trust anyone in their group. Even if they seem normal, don't believe anything you hear or see. Go with your instincts. They haven't led you astray yet." He put a hand on her arm. "I can take you out of this if you want."

"No, it's not that." She shook her head. "I'm not sure what it is. I may be overreacting." Jessie grabbed his hand. She didn't want him to worry about her on top of everything else.

"Jess, sweetheart, you know I've come to trust your premonitions or whatever they are. If you're concerned or edgy, it's for a darn good reason. Let's break it down and analyze it." His thumb stroked the palm of her hand. "What is the flash point?"

"Well, seeing a man in Joe's and the fact he was familiar, didn't help. Larissa is agitated, and I never know what she's going to do."

"Back up, you didn't tell me about a man." Matt frowned.

"Sorry, it must have slipped my mind." Jessie tried to pull her hand away.

"Did you see him at the compound?"

"I have no idea where I saw him. It could have been the store." She was irritated.

"We'll forget the man for now. Tell me about Larissa." He held on to her hand.

"Yes. I've seen Larissa a few times. All I know is something isn't quite right."

"Matt, you'd better take a look. We didn't factor this into our plans." Dylan came on the radio.

Matt stood. His head jerked around when he heard the squeak of the gate. "What the hell?" A large group wearing hooded robes emerged from the trees, making their way to the crypt. One by one, they filed through the door out of sight. A murmuring chant filled the night.

"What should we do?" Deputy Taylor's voice came across the radio.

"Nothing. We watch for now. I don't want to give away our positions. For all we know, this could be a trap." Matt watched the last of the gathering group file in. They had to be in the secret room below. No way all those folks could fit inside the tomb area.

"Larissa is there with them." Jessie focused on her darting form as she wove in and out of the group. Jessie couldn't tell if Larissa recognized anyone, but she was moving from person to person until she disappeared inside.

"This might account for my uneasiness." Jessie scowled.

"Matt, those are men in the robes. They are too large for women. I also heard someone who passed near me say that the government was trying to seize their lands and way of life. They were going to have to take a stand this time. They weren't going to hide anymore."

"Dylan, stay close by. I'm going to check and see if Marvin is around." Matt called Marvin, and he answered right away. "Does your group ever meet at the tomb?"

"Yes, once a month. Why?"

"Are they there tonight?"

"They shouldn't be, but I wouldn't know. I have stayed to myself since Rose left."

"What do they do?"

"It's a secret society for the men. There are ceremonial symbols, and they do some chants. I did them, but didn't put much stock in it." Marvin gave him more details.

"Why the robes?" Matt's hand fisted at his side.

"The robes are part of the secret order the men's group belongs to. It's no big deal, really. Like a fraternity."

"Tell me, does this fraternity carry weapons?"

"Knives, swords, and whips all are used in the ceremonies. They are ancient rituals that seem to please those involved."

"Do you have permission to use the crypt?" Matt paced.

"We never got permission. A couple of the men stumbled on the crypt, and it seemed like the perfect spot for the ceremonies. They thought the atmosphere enhanced the ritual. We tried not to disturb anything because a coven meets there, also."

Matt listened as Marvin told him more about the group and their secret rituals. "Those were the symbols carved on your daughter's body, weren't they?"

"Yes." Marvin's voice quivered. "The odd thing is that this isn't a night for them to meet there. This is usually the coven's night. They come around ten or eleven if they show up. We are never there on the same night."

"Oh, hell, we have a situation here." Matt hung up. "I'll be back, Jess."

She watched Matt walk away. He wasn't happy about the conversation. His facial expression had changed from calm to thunderous in a few moments of time. The plans were probably about to change again. Matt ordered them to stay in place while a small group of officers took up positions surrounding the crypt.

When Jessie had envisioned the night, it was not like this.

Chapter 42

The longer the evening wore on, the more restless Jessie became. The night was quiet, but the atmosphere was charged. The people they wanted weren't in the group in the crypt—Jessie guessed that they were there only to distract them. She was sure of it, and Matt needed to know. Where was Matt? Jessie couldn't see him. *What was that*? She strained to hear what sounded like women's voices singing. Jessie's jaw dropped open. A group of women came dancing and swaying into view. No wonder Matt was angry. Dylan went to talk to them. At the same precise moment, the door to the crypt opened up, and the men began flooding out. Officers flew out of their hiding places with guns drawn and confusion ensued. Jessie didn't know what to watch first. The women from the coven were yelling at the men. The police were commanding the men to remove their robes and were checking them for weapons. The men were not cooperating.

A sudden chill raced down her spine. Behind her! When she turned to look, Jessie found a gun pointed at her. Not again. "Matt," she yelled out.

The man grabbed her, slapping his hand across her mouth. "You're coming with me. If you know what's good for you, you'll keep your mouth shut."

She could feel the gun barrel against her back. "Where are you taking me?"

"You'll find out soon enough. You've caused us enough trouble." He shoved her in the back.

"What did I do? I don't even know any of you." Jessie turned to glance at him. Larissa was darting around him.

"Right. Don't give me your crap. You messed with Roger's wife and believed her lies. You got the cops involved. You wrote about Larissa and told lies about our group. You have to pay, and we have ways of protecting our own. Besides, you made our Rose cry."

Jessie remembered him. "You're willing to add murder to your group rituals? Some religion."

"No one's been murdered yet. Quit your yapping or I'll be tempted to shut you up myself."

"You know that's what your leaders are going to do to me." Jessie stumbled and fell to her knees when he shoved her again. "You'll be an accessory to murder."

"Keep moving." He poked her with the gun again.

Jessie's mind raced. Where was he taking her? She had to do something. *Think, Jessie*. She tripped over a tree root and fell forward, pitching into the darkness. She thrust her hand out to keep from smashing her face into the tree trunk coming at her. The pain shot all the way up her arm to her shoulder.

****

Something wasn't right. After the dust had settled, and they had sorted through everyone at the crypt, Matt didn't see any of the key players. Damn, this had been a trap. Matt remembered Jessie. Racing toward where he told her to wait, he called her name, but there was no answer. Her sweater was lying on the ground. "Dylan, they have Jessie," Matt shouted out. "This whole mess was to get her. Watch these two." Matt pointed at Adam and Roger. He barked orders as he went. "Frank, get Radar ready. We have to find her. They'll kill her." He threw Jessie's sweater to Frank.

Frank put the line on Radar. He placed the sweater in front of the dog's nose. "Let's find Jessie, Radar. Find her, boy." Radar went first, to where Matt had told her to wait and then went through the trees, pulling hard as he followed her scent.

"I can't believe I didn't consider this possibility. All the people showing up took me by complete surprise."

"There was no way you could have known." Kip stepped over a tree limb on the ground.

"You have to think of every scenario. There are risks in every situation no matter how well you plan. I was worried about an ambush of Roger and Adam, but I should have known it was Jessie they wanted all along." Matt hoped the guard dog at the compound was locked in for the night.

"He's working it. They definitely came through here." Frank pointed ahead. Radar pulled hard, and Frank was jogging to stay with him. Kip and Matt were having a hard time keeping pace with him. Radar took them to the back fence of the compound. "They have to have her somewhere in here."

"How do we get in undetected?" Kip looked at the fence, checking for a loose area where they could get Radar through. Finding a section, he kicked it, and it gave way. He held it down with his foot while the others climbed over. The dog continued tracking across the compound. He came to the building Matt remembered as the clinic and stopped. The lights were on.

Motioning for the others to stay out of sight Matt looked through an open window. Jessie was sitting on an examination table. She was pale. The voices inside drifted out to him.

"Rose, what do you want me to do with her?" Matt couldn't see the speaker's face.

"You know what. It doesn't have to be messy." Her voice was hard. "Use a drug; there are enough of them here." Rose followed Crawford to the locked cabinet to get the syringe. Doc filled it from a small vile, his hands shaking as he did.

"The woods are crawling with cops." Randy walked into the room. "We need to get it done and get her out of here."

"I'm sorry to have to do this. It won't cause you any pain. I promise." Crawford stepped toward her. "Hold her down." Randy grabbed her legs, and the big man held her arms.

"Is that what you said to Larissa?" Jessie frowned at him as the men moved toward her. "You're not sorry, none of you are." Jessie glanced around the room, leveling her stare at each person for a moment. "Did you drug her and then beat her too? She's here you know. All of you are guilty of hurting her some way, and one of you could be the father of her baby." Jessie glared at each of the men. "You are all sick. Most of all I blame you." Jessie motioned at Rose. "You're her mother." Jessie winced when Rose slapped her across the face.

"Get it over with," Rose yelled at Crawford. She never saw the large book coming. The medical volume nailed her in the head. "Which one of you did that?"

Rose glared at the three men as she rubbed the knot.

The big man let go of Jessie's arms and backed away. Fear written on his face, he shook his head.

"You see her, don't you?" Jessie looked at him. "It's Larissa's way of letting you know she's here. If I were you, I'd be afraid. She doesn't look too happy to me." Jessie watched Rose scan the room, and her face paled.

"Shut up." Rose slapped Jessie again. She screamed and slapped at the air above her head. "Stop doing that." She eyed Jessie with suspicion.

"I'm telling you, it isn't me. Larissa isn't happy with any of you." Jessie frowned at her. "You could have put a stop to what was happening to her, but you were jealous of your own daughter, weren't you? She was young, pretty, and above all, free from the rigid rules you chose to live by. She was everything you used to be."

Rose raised her hand to hit Jessie again. "Not this time," Jessie shouted. She drew back her good arm and slugged Rose in the face, stunning her. Rose's head flew back from the force causing her to stumble off balance. Randy let go of Jessie to catch Rose, barely grabbing her before she hit the ground. Matt rubbed his eyes and looked again. "That's my girl." Matt's body tensed as Crawford lunged at her. The needle in Crawford's shaking hand moved back and forth. He didn't want to startle him. It was too close to her artery. Damn. Matt had no idea where he might stick it. He started to move, but Kimble told him to stay put. It had to play out.

Jessie slapped at Doc's hand, sending the needle spinning to the ground. Matt saw Jessie grimace and hold her arm as if in pain. Rose dove for the needle, but it suddenly flew across the room, narrowly missing Randy's face as it passed and stuck on the wall. They were all stunned. Matt looked from face to face. That's when he saw a dark figure creeping out of the back room.

"I'll take your gun, Amos." He stuck his gun in the big man's back and grabbed the rifle from his hands.

"RJ, I told you to stay away." Randy's cheeks puffed out in anger.

"I don't have to listen to you anymore." RJ smirked. "The truth is I've wanted to see you for a while now, Daddy Dearest. I arranged this little gathering in your honor. I have some memories I want your friends to hear about the kind of father you were. All of you including you"—he pointed at Crawford— "sit down where I can see you."

It was then that Matt noticed Marvin standing in the open door with a gun. What the hell was going on? Matt remained glued to the spot with Kimble's hand holding him back. He motioned to the officers arriving on scene to take up spots around the building exits and to wait for his signal.

"I bet you fine upstanding religious folks didn't know you've harbored a murderer in your midst. That's right." He pointed the gun at his dad. "Not only does this fine man like to quote scripture while he hits his wife and children, but he's no better than the devil himself."

"Shut up, RJ." Randy hurled expletives at his son.

"Nice greeting, old man, but you're not going to shut me up this time. You can't threaten me. I'm the one with the gun." He shifted it back and forth. "I've stored all these things I've wanted to say to you for a long time, and you're going to listen. I know your darkest secrets, and these fine folks have a right to know." He smirked. "Although, trying to kill the kind bookstore lady tells me they aren't so nice either."

"I said shut up, RJ." Randy stood and took a step. The sound of the gun blasted the room, and Randy went twisting and screaming to the ground. "You shot me. I can't believe you shot me." He cursed.

"No one move. You hear me?" He waved the gun again. "I hope he bleeds to death. The next one who moves can join my father. I have something to say to my old man, and you're my witnesses. You have forced me to do your dirty work for years. It took me a while, but I figured out you were the third shooter in the massacre. You convinced them the person got away. You sure did." RJ had a wild look in his eyes. "I went back to our old house and found where you buried the blood-spattered clothes you were wearing. I handed them over to the police. They should be here soon. You've always been a sick bastard." Randy was pale and moaning. "I won't let you die. Quit your whining. That's more than I can say you did for all those people you shot. For what? How much did they pay you to destroy all those families? I want you to spend your life in prison and after that in hell." He shook his head and moved the Glock back and forth between his hands. "You're not such a big man now, you lying SOB. You quoted scripture in church, beat us if we didn't obey you, and murdered innocent people who simply went to work. You make me sick. All of you are no better than him." He shook his head, pacing in front of them. "Marvin, you can come in now. I can see you there.

I've said what I wanted to say. It's your turn."

"I should kill all of you for what you did to my little girl." He kept the gun on them. "You are a sick woman, Rose. I would have never believed you were capable of what I just heard." He sobbed. "Baby girl, if you're here like this young lady said you are, your papa is sorry I didn't believe you."

"She knows," Jessie said softly.

"You're a weak man; you always were." Rose faced Marvin, her eyes narrowed. "These men gave you a chance to be something great and your daughter was ruining it. I couldn't stand by and let her destroy it with her sinful actions." Larissa whirled around her.

"You hypocrite! You don't believe murder is sinful?" His hand began to shake, and anger flashed across his face.

"I said the same thing to my dad," RJ snarled. "You didn't think I was smart enough, did you, old man? Well, look who's on the floor now. Agent Kimble, if you can hear me, he's all yours."

Rose's face paled. "Get her away from me." She screamed and closed her eyes.

Matt could see RJ getting more agitated, and Marvin was no better. He motioned for his officers to move. They raced through the doors. Matt stood next to Marvin. "I know you want to pull the trigger," Matt said, "but I can't let you throw your life away. Give me the gun." Marvin kept his eyes fixed on Rose, his finger on the trigger. "She's not worth it, man." He slowly stretched out a hand, closed it over the barrel of the gun, and eased it out of his hand.

"You too, son, your father will go to prison for what he's done. I heard it all, every word," Agent

Kimble said as he took his gun.

Frank held on to Radar who was growling at Randy. "Sit, boy, sit. You know a bad guy when you see him." He patted his head.

Matt turned the gun on the group in the room. "You have the right to remain silent and refuse to answer questions. Anything you say may be used against you in a court of law." Matt recited the Miranda warning in a cold monotone. "Do you understand your rights?" He told them to sit and went to stand next to Jessie.

"How did you find me?" She gazed into Matt's eyes.

"Radar tracked you here." His finger traced the curve of her cheek, and his eyes went to her right arm, which she cradled against her. It was swollen and turning dark at the wrist. "How did you hurt your arm? Was it one of these folks who hurt you?" Matt motioned to where they were sitting.

She shook her head. "He shoved me a few times." She pointed to a man sitting in the corner next to Doc. "I actually tripped over a root and hit a tree. The tree fared better than I did." She smiled at him.

"Did you stick your hand out to take the impact?" He grimaced when she nodded. "We need ice." Marvin showed him an icemaker in the next room. Matt put the ice in a bag. "Let's put this on your wrist. It's swollen. We need to have a doctor take a look at it."

Radar nudged her leg, and she patted his head. "Frank, maybe you should move here. He could keep track of me twenty-four seven."

"I know where I saw him before." Jessie pointed at RJ. "He was in my store the day you asked me if I knew his name."

"I know." Matt nodded. "And he's the new janitor at the police station. I'll tell you more about him later."

Kimble took charge of Randy, and as soon as Dylan and Deputy Taylor arrived, Matt let them take over his part. The suspects were cuffed. Crawford rendered aid until the ambulance could get there for Randy. "I'm taking her to the ER to have this arm looked at," he told Dylan. "I'll be in to question them after you book them." Matt saluted Kimble.

"I was notified that the FBI would take him." Taylor pointed at Randy. "I can see everything is under control. It seems child abuse is a small part of his now lengthy rap sheet."

"What do you want Gary to do with all of the people at the tomb?" Dylan asked Matt. He was on the phone with Gary.

"Tell him to release all of them except for Roger and Adam. They have to face charges yet. The women are free to go home. Get the names of all the men and send them home. Make sure they know they are to be at the dining hall tomorrow at noon."

"Here are the keys to the car." Dylan tossed them to Matt. "Kip can take me back to town."

****

Matt helped her into the car, taking care not to bump her arm. He latched the seat belt for her and was careful when he closed the door. "Jess, sweetheart, you deliberately goaded them. Did you want them to kill you?" Matt turned toward her as soon as he shut the car door. He frowned. "You take too many chances. I'm going to be old before my time from worrying about you." Matt scowled, and Frank snickered.

"I wanted them to turn on each other. Larissa was in the room, and she was protecting me. I wanted them to know she was there, especially Rose. Besides, it's your fault. You told me to stay put, and then you went off and forgot I was there." Jessie frowned and Frank laughed.

"You two sound like you're married." Frank grinned. "You did forget her, Matt, but it was a strange night so it could have happened to anyone."

"See, I told you," she muttered under her breath.

"You do take a lot of chances, Jess, but you also have a strange knack for solving cases with a group of unusual friends. Your ghost can sure throw a book. She has a wicked pitch and punches." Frank laughed again. He chuckled off and on the whole way back to town.

"She's not my ghost, at least I hope not permanently."

Matt pulled into a parking space near the emergency room entrance. "Do you want to come in with us, Frank?"

"No, I'll stay in the car with the dog."

"This might take a while." Matt opened the car door. "Are you sure you want to wait?"

"Yeah." Frank nodded. "I might need to take Radar out for a walk."

Matt handed Frank the keys. "It might get cold, or you might want to go get something to drink." Matt walked Jessie into the room and signed her in at the desk. He waited with her until the nurse called her back into the examining area, and then Matt went out to check on Frank.

He found Frank dozing in the passenger seat. "How's the dog?"

"He's fine." Frank yawned. "I took him for a short walk, and he's done for the night."

"Do you need anything?" Matt asked him.

"No, but can I give you a piece of advice?" He looked over at Matt.

"Advise away." Matt smiled at him.

"You'd better marry her," he said soberly. "At the rate she's going, she won't last long."

"You're telling me." Matt scowled.

"Don't ask her tonight, though; she might be miffed at you."

"You think?" Matt ran his hand through his hair.

Frank grinned. "You're fun to watch. I know why people get married. Love is too exhausting when you're single and courting one another."

"Are you cold? You can turn the heat on if you need to." Matt changed the subject.

"No, I'm fine." Frank's eyes crinkled at the corners.

"If you don't mind, I'll call the station while we're waiting." Matt pulled his phone from his pocket.

"Call away. I might take myself a nap." Frank leaned his head back and closed his eyes.

Matt made the call. "Is everyone back, Gary?"

"The suspects are all locked up tight for the night. The woman hasn't stopped talking since she got here."

"I'll be there soon." He glanced at his phone as a text came in from Jessie. "Jessie has finished, it looks like." Matt walked back into the hospital. He listened as the nurse gave her instructions.

"What did the doctor say?"

"I fractured my forearm and jammed my wrist and a couple of fingers. Do you want to sign my cast?" Her arm was in a sling, and she waved it at him. "You should be nice to me and stop frowning. I hurt." She sighed. "I can't even say it was done taking down a bad guy. No, not me. I had to take on a tree."

"Jess, I'm sorry I forgot you." He held her good hand.

"I was teasing. I know you had your hands full. It was a strange night. I get mad every time I think of those folks." She let him open the door for her.

"Is it broken?" Frank asked.

She nodded. "The doctor said it isn't a bad break, but still, I did a number on it."

"You can stay at my house with us tonight," Matt said. "We'll get you home tomorrow sometime."

Matt dropped them off at the house and went back to the station. It was going to be a long night.

Chapter 43

Jessie didn't see Matt much over the next several days. She saw a lot of Dylan and Katie, though. Katie was constantly fussing over her. Jessie had to eat at the Inn every night after work. Dylan was always there, and the two of them walked her home. Katie was head over heels in love with Dylan. Jessie could see it—her friend was radiant. She had never seen Katie like this with any man for longer than a few days. It had been there in Katie's eyes from the first day Jessie had moved to Blue Cove. Dylan was the one for Katie, and Jessie was happy he had come to realize it.

"Jessie, are you up?" Katie was tapping at the door.

"What are you doing up so late?" Jessie opened the door.

"I had to see you and tell you in person." She held up her left hand, and there was a sparkling diamond ring on it. "He asked me to marry him. I've never been this happy in my life."

"Oh, Katie, your ring is beautiful." Jessie reached for her hand to take a closer look. The white gold band had a gorgeous compass point solitaire diamond that sparkled in the light.

"He picked it out himself and surprised me." Katie glanced at the ring on her hand.

"I'm so happy for you." They cried, laughed, and hugged. "Whew, he moves fast."

"Dylan told me when he figured it out there was no reason to wait. Tom's interest in me made him realize someone could come along and snatch me away, and he'd better get with it."

"It doesn't surprise me." Jessie smiled at her. "I've watched him looking at you."

Katie told her about his proposal with all the details. "It was so romantic." She sighed.

"It's nice to know Dylan can be romantic." Jessie grinned.

"We don't have a date yet, but you will be my maid of honor. Please say you will."

"You know I will. I'd be honored." Jessie looked again at the beautiful diamond.

"We always planned and dreamed about our wedding day. Do you remember?"

"Of course, I do. We'll have to drag out all our old planning books and see how much our ideas have changed since then. If I remember, your groom-to-be always had dark hair and mine was always blond." Jessie's eyes lit. "I couldn't imagine being with anyone else but my dark-haired hunky cop with the amazing blue eyes. You got the blond." Jessie smiled at her.

"Jessie, I'm so happy I could burst with the pleasure of it. I've loved him from the first minute I laid eyes on him. I scared him off—you know how I can be—but he came around."

"He sure did. I'm happy for you." Jessie listened as Katie talked for the next hour. She heard every detail of the many wonderful qualities of Dylan.

"I want Sally in the wedding, too. We will have to wait for a while until she can be with us. I think my mother will go crazy over this. She's wanted me to get married for so long." Katie stood. "I need to get back to the Inn. You are the first one I've told."

"I'm so glad you did. My two special friends are getting married. How cool is that!" Jessie hugged Katie again and walked her to the door. It was perfect.

"I'll call you when the guests are settled. We have another chapter to talk over." She waved as she walked back to the Inn.

While she waited for Katie to call, Jessie found her wedding planning book. She laughed as she looked at the pictures and her plans. Katie was a part of her fondest memories growing up, and she couldn't be happier for her friend. Jessie tried to picture Katie as a wife and mother. Egad, a mother. *Please, one thing at a time*, she chided herself. It was enough to think of Katie as engaged, for now.

****

Matt called Jessie several times, and her line was busy. It was late, but Matt wanted to talk to her. Watching the slow-moving hands of the clock, he tried once again. Finally. "Hi, sweetheart. You've been a busy girl tonight."

"Katie and I were chatting about the book we're reading. Of course, we paused every now and then to talk about the extraordinary qualities of her brand new fiancé."

"The station is abuzz with it. The guys are all razzing Dylan. I hope it settles down soon. We'll see."

"It won't." She laughed. "Dylan made up his mind so quickly. It's mind blowing."

"I'd tell you what they're saying, but guys aren't always couth if you know what I mean. Sometimes I feel sorry for the ladies who work around the lot of us."

"I've had my share of experience with the banter. Liam and Connor were my first introduction. The men in the news business were not much different. I did go in and out of the police precinct, too. Trust me, I understand." She paused. "You've been busy, yourself. You haven't had time to sign my cast yet."

"You know how I get when I'm closing up a case." He sighed. "You'll have to testify at the trials."

"You're the best at what you do, and I'll be ready; I've testified at a few trials since I've been here." She sighed.

"You always do a good job, too." He took a deep breath. "Jess, I need your perspective. I want to talk to you."

"Talk away."

"I would rather talk in person if that's okay with you. When do you get off work tomorrow?"

"You never have to ask, of course. You can come tomorrow or anytime you want to. Audrey is working at the store all day tomorrow. It's the first Saturday I've had off in a while. I'm looking forward to it. I heard it's supposed to be a beautiful day."

"I have a meeting in the morning with Dave Lewis. The DNA is back, and we will soon know for sure who the father is and who had the most reason to kill Larissa." Matt picked up the remote, turned on the TV, and muted it.

"I'll wait, but I'm pretty sure I already know."

"You'll find out if you're right tomorrow." He turned to the sports channel to watch the scores on the bottom.

"Did Frank get off okay?" He heard her yawn.

"He did. I miss that big drooling dog of his. Radar

is easy to have around. He sleeps most of the time, but when he works, he's one of the best I've ever seen." Matt leaned back in his recliner. "With Rose in jail, has Larissa left your store?"

"No, she's still rearranging things. I wonder if she's there to stay." He heard her yawn again.

"I'm not sure what to say about that. I guess you'll know soon enough. You need to get some sleep. I love you, Jess, and sweet dreams."

"I love you, too. See you tomorrow."

Chapter 44

Jessie slept in later than usual. After breakfast, she grabbed her tote bag to carry her book, her tablet, phone, and a few other essentials for the morning. Putting on her floppy hat and shades, she planned to stroll to her favorite place, the Inn's private beach area. This time of year, very few people used it. Stepping out the cottage door, she inhaled. Spring was in the air; the tulips and daffodils were pushing up in front of the cottage and all over the garden. Soon the irises would be out in force. A simple short walk and a few stairs brought her to a front row seat to the beauty of the cove.

Jessie paused at the top of the hill before walking down the steps. The cove had taken on its deep blue hue. Sailboats dotted the water. The ocean had a way of calming the turmoil within her. Standing here, she could forget the troubles of the past few weeks and relish the sea's constancy. Making her way down to the beach, she stretched out on an oversized chaise longue and smiled. Katie had remarked when she bought them that two people could fit on them. She had proclaimed them as romantic.

Jessie's thoughts found their way to the paper. One after the other, the waves lapped the shoreline as she filled the pages. It was her secret for now, but her book was taking shape. The heroine was a young, exciting version of her Grandma Sadie, and the hero was similar to her Grandpa Max. Of course, it was fiction, but she saw them in every word she wrote. Truth be told, she saw a little of herself, too. She gazed out to sea at a sailboat gliding by. She inhaled the wonderful sea air. This is what she had envisioned when she first moved to Blue Cove; sitting on the beach and writing words at a rapid pace, lost in the moment.

****

Matt knocked on her door, but she didn't answer. As if drawn, he made his way to the top of the small hill. His breath caught in his throat. She was a part of the beauty in front of him. Taking the steps, he moved toward her. On the last stair, he stopped and waited until she turned when she sensed him there. Her smile invited him. "I didn't want to interrupt you."

"You could never intrude." She closed her notebook and shoved it clumsily into the tote. "Darn this cast, it always gets in the way."

"You were lost to the world. What are you writing?" He moved closer.

"My thoughts." She smiled at him and patted the area beside her for him to sit down. "What did you want to talk to me about?"

"Does this still hurt?" He touched her cast gently.

She shook her head. "An ache or twinge every once in a while, but it itches under this thing." She tapped it. "Still, I can use my hand with no problem." She wiggled her fingers for him to see.

"I find it hard in this setting to think of the case at all. Seeing you here like this reminds me of why I love living in Blue Cove."

"I was thinking the same thing myself, earlier. It's

beautiful, the day is perfect, and you complete the picture." She scooted over to make room for him next to her.

"Whom do I have to thank for this wonderful contraption?" He took her hand in his as he stretched out.

"I believe you'll have to thank Katie. She bought them oversized because they were romantic."

"I agree, but it makes it a lot harder to concentrate on why I came here."

"How about if I move and sit on the end?" She gave him a mischievous grin.

"Don't you dare move! I've got you right where I want you." Their eyes met. He placed his hand on each side of her face and kissed her. "I've wanted to do that since I saw you from the hill." He smiled when she sighed. "Now, we can begin." He found himself moving to the edge of the chaise. He needed distance, or he'd never get through this.

She fluttered her lashes at him. "Is it getting too hot for you?" She drew her legs up to give him more room.

"You could say that." He turned his head to look at her.

"Where shall we start?" She smiled at him.

"During the interrogation, Rose fell apart. She told us everything. It was Marvin's land. What Marvin had told us was all true. He had invited the Phillips and the Crawford family to come and live with them. It was Randy's idea to make it a religious group and open it to others. Somewhere along the line, the power and control went to their heads. They lost sight of all that made them good as a group in the beginning." He turned toward her. "Of course, no one knew of Randy's past. Randy, as you heard, was one angry man and hiding a lot. He was a hardnosed disciplinarian but was trying not to do anything that would draw attention to himself." Matt shook his head. "It's all beginning to come out in the press now. I doubt he ever thought RJ would have the nerve to stand up to his bullying."

"I've been wondering how RJ came to work at the station."

"With Agent Kimble and the DA's knowledge, RJ called his father. Kimble had arranged for him to work for us. It was hush-hush from the beginning. Only I knew about it at the station. The DA notified Marvin the night we went to the crypt. He played along to help us set the trap. We had to make it look as real as possible. They didn't want anything accidently leaked. They had been looking for the third gunman for a while."

"You mean it was all an act that day in my store when you asked who RJ was."

Matt grinned. "I did a damn good job." Matt looked away. "It didn't all go according to the plan because Larissa's death and the involvement of the others added an element of surprise. No one, including Marvin, had a clue how deep Rose's involvement in Larissa's death was. We all thought it was Randy. In truth, it was Rose who was the driving force behind the strange rules and actions of the members."

"RJ was the familiar man in Joe's that day. What will happen to him? He did shoot his father after all." Jessie pushed a stray hair behind her ear.

"He'll be able to plead to a lesser offense for helping to bring his father to justice." Matt ran his hand through his hair. "He played most of his part well until his anger got the best of him." Matt paused, glancing at the waves lapping the shore. "In the beginning, RJ had to convince his father he wanted to be a part of the movement. His father never let up on him. Randy encouraged him to spy on us while he worked at the station. RJ was the one who told Randy we would be jogging that night."

"We could have been killed." Jessie shook her head.

"Roger set the ambush. Phillips did his best to fuel his anger and to manipulate Roger. It wasn't too hard. He was mad at Olivia, and he didn't trust you. He got close to hitting us."

"Too close for comfort if you ask me." Jessie adjusted her hat. "Who was the man that snatched me from the crypt?"

"Amos Phillips was the culprit. He is a widower and Randy's brother. I couldn't see the resemblance until after I had heard they were brothers. Amos was infatuated with Rose, and he would have done anything for her. Let's just say Rose used him on many occasions, including hurting her daughter."

"That's sick." Jessie scowled. "How's Marvin handling all of this?"

"Right now, he can't believe he put his family in jeopardy by allowing Randy to come to the compound. He's angry with himself for not figuring it out earlier and protecting his daughter. He still finds it hard to believe Rose was involved in her murder."

"I had a feeling Rose was the main person behind Larissa's murder. As sick as this may sound, I believe she was jealous of her daughter." Jessie touched his hand. "Do you think they would have really killed me?"

"Yes, the drug in the syringe was lethal. We had it tested." Matt frowned. "I was watching and ready to move regardless of what Kimble said to do, but Crawford's shaky hand and its nearness to your neck made it tricky at best. Thankfully, RJ showed up, and you knocked the needle out of the doc's hand."

"You wouldn't have let anything happen to me." She turned her head away from him and smiled. "Unless of course, you forgot about me."

"Will you ever let me live it down?" Matt sighed heavily. "Frank told the guys at work, and they razz me all the time."

"Sorry. You did eventually remember me and come to my rescue."

"Some rescue. I got there in time to hear you goading them into hitting you. Jess, when I think of all that could have happened to you…"

She grabbed his hand and stroked the palm of his hand with her thumb. "But it didn't happen. I'm here and safe. It's all good."

"Who do you think is the father of the baby?" Matt asked her.

"At first, I thought it was Glenn's baby. I thought he was a predator, but the baby is Adam's child. They were young and hiding the fact they were in love. I don't believe Adam knew she was pregnant with his baby, which makes what he did to her the saddest part of this case." She glanced at the water lapping the shore.

"You're right. Rose convinced Adam that Larissa had a boyfriend in town and that he was the father. I would have never guessed Adam either." He shook his head. "Adam was devastated when he found out. He'll never forgive himself or Rose." Matt's voice was gruff. "Rose was angry at Adam for getting near Larissa. She was angrier with Larissa for being an embarrassment to her family. Let me tell you, the whole damn thing was sordid. Their actions tore several lives apart in their group. Most of the folks were sincere. I doubt they'll trust so easily again."

"Who murdered Larissa?" Jessie asked.

"Marvin had found Larissa once and set her free. He didn't know they had caught her again and kept her at the crypt. This is where it gets twisted. It began with the idea of delivering Larissa from her sinful life and ended with an exorcism that went wrong. Rose was furious with Larissa; she knew Larissa was pregnant with Adam's baby. That's why Larissa was kept at the tomb and guarded by Amos. Rose could see their position in the group slipping away. She asked Doc, Amos, and Randy to help her save her child. It started with scripture, but Larissa refused to cooperate. It escalated into beating her. Larissa was hurt but got away. Rose sent Amos and Roger after her. Roger was anxious to do his part. It was his idea to carve the symbols in her skin to make it look like some odd cult murder. But they refused to kill her and dumped her at the gate of the compound instead. They both got carried away in their attempt to subdue her."

"How nice of them," she said sarcastically. "I'm telling you, women never fare well in domestic violence or abuse."

"Roger is sadistic, and one angry young man. He had grown up seeing his dad hit his mother over the years. Phillips encouraged him to beat his wife to keep her in submission. Something Roger had often heard when he was young. He was surprised Olivia had defied him. Even though he was angry, he admired her courage. He never saw his mother stand up for herself." Matt frowned. "I find it strange that men who know nothing about the Bible know and can quote the scripture about wives being in submission to their husbands. Jess, Larissa suffered something terrible." His hand fisted in hers. "I get so angry about what they did to her in the guise of helping her."

"I doubt that they know the rest of that scripture, though," she said softly, "which says to love your wife." Jessie shook her head. "I'm grateful that Olivia got away."

"All thanks to you. I can't figure out for the life of me what makes a group like this tick. Amos and Roger were the ones who dumped her at the gate. The doctor had wanted to help her that night and felt deep remorse for his part in all of it. Randy kept them from calling the ambulance by saying that they could drive her there quicker. He led Marvin to believe the past had caught up with him. Randy had already convinced Adam and Roger they had to dump her or Adam would be blamed. Why they dumped her at the church, I will never know. Maybe in their warped minds, there was some kind of symbolism there. Too bad they didn't dump her at the hospital."

"What about all the men who showed up at the crypt that night?"

"They were all pawns in the game of the leaders." Matt leaned back against her legs.

"I hope the articles I wrote will make people think before they hit or manipulate a woman or child. Most of all, I hope it will help someone to find the courage to leave like Olivia and Sally did, before it's too late." She toyed with his hair. "What about the baby?"

"Marvin requested that Olivia and her mother be considered as parents for the child. That way he could be a part of his granddaughter's life. The details are being worked out now."

"Wonderful." Jessie clapped her hands.

"Marvin will be on probation and do community service for a long time for his part in this fiasco. Roger and Adam will go to prison along with their leaders."

"As they should." She touched his hand.

Matt laced his fingers through hers. "Here's the thing, Jess. I was worried about you out there. This whole coming to see you and having to leave you to go home is getting harder for me to do. I want you to consider the fact that I love you, and I'm committed to you alone. I guess I want to know where this relationship is going." He smiled. "I know it's usually the woman who asks about commitment, but I need to know. I have to get back to the station, but I'll be back at five-thirty. You and I are going on a date, and we are going to talk. I don't want to waste any more time that I could be spending with you."

****

Matt's watch said five-thirty when he knocked on the door and walked in. She was sitting in his favorite chair. She stood and moved gracefully toward him.

"Do you like my new dress? Reba bought it for me." She twirled in front of him.

He nodded; his mouth suddenly dry. There was no way he could describe the dress if his life depended on it. "Beautiful." He pulled her close to his chest and wrapped his arms around her. His chin rested on her head. "Stunning." His words caught in his throat. He held her tightly and inhaled her scent.

"Are you all right?" Her voice softened.

He nodded. "I needed to hold you for a minute. I've been around scum all day. You're like a breath of clean, fresh air." He moved away from her. "Do you have a coat? The air is still a little chilly at night."

"Where are we going?" She slipped her arm in the coat he was holding.

"My surprise." He opened the door for her. "I have a few of them for you tonight."

They had a lovely dinner at a new restaurant outside of Blue Cove. He couldn't take his eyes off her. Matt didn't know how he got through the meal or what he ate. She was nervous, he could see it, but he couldn't seem to help himself—he was too. Everything was riding on this night.

The drive back to Blue Cove was quiet.

"Are you sure you're okay?"

He smiled. "I'm great." He parked the car at the Marina. They walked to a bench where they could watch the boats rocking gently in the water and talk.

"Are you warm enough?" He pulled her into his side.

"Yes, it's a beautiful night." She sounded breathless.

"Jess, the thing is"—his deep voice sliced through the stillness—"I love you, and I want to marry you." Matt turned to face her. He held his hand up to keep her from responding. "I don't have a ring in my pocket, so you can relax. When I ask you to marry me, you'll be begging me to." He grinned. She was ready to get in his face. "Now you can relax."

"Begging you?" She shook her head and smiled at him.

"I mean, every man can dream, can't he?" He gave his crooked grin.

"A pipe dream is all it is if you expect me to beg you to marry me." She laughed.

"Honey, I'm good for you, and you know it. I lied when I said I didn't have a ring." He pulled out the box. "Before you get all weird on me, this is a gift. It's a promise from me that at some date of my choosing, in a place that I've selected, I will pop the question, and you will be ready to say yes. Until the moment I choose, you'll look at this little trinket and think of me. You'll want my arms around you while you sleep and desire me when you first wake up in the morning. I want you to think of how our kisses can get so hot, and how it feels so right when we're together. I sure as hell think of you this way every day and night." He opened the box and took out a beautiful sapphire ring with two small diamonds chips on each side. He slipped it on her right hand. She glanced at the ring with tears running down her cheeks, moved closer to him, touched his face, and then melted into his arms.

A word from the author…

I live in Colorado with my husband of many years. I have three grown sons and five grandchildren.

Long before I was a writer I was a reader. I always imagined different scenarios and outcomes in the books that I read. As far back as I can remember I had stories in my head. Those stories found an outlet in public speaking and teaching. Eventually they found their way to writing classes and short stories. However, it was in writing a novel that I found my home. I loved developing the characters, the scenes and interaction between the characters. Writing, like reading, is a joy to me.

http://www.ionamorrison.com

Thank you for purchasing
this publication of The Wild Rose Press, Inc.

If you enjoyed the story, we would appreciate your
letting others know by leaving a review.

For other wonderful stories,
please visit our on-line bookstore at
www.thewildrosepress.com.

For questions or more information
contact us at
info@thewildrosepress.com.

The Wild Rose Press, Inc.
www.thewildrosepress.com

Stay current with The Wild Rose Press, Inc.

Like us on Facebook

https://www.facebook.com/TheWildRosePress

And Follow us on Twitter
https://twitter.com/WildRosePress

www.ingramcontent.com/pod-product-compliance
Lightning Source LLC
Chambersburg PA
CBHW071518260626
47170CB00002B/424